UNDER ANOTHER SUN

A Novel of the Vietnam War

David S. Lewis
and
Dana C. Welch

Deer Run Press

Copyright © 2020 David S. Lewis and Dana C. Welch

All rights reserved

MMXXI-II-A

Cover Photo: © 2020 Jamie Cruz. Pictured: Short Range Ambush Platoon (SRAP) Medic, Ventura Rodriguez, 1st Battalion 50th Infantry. Cruz was also a Medic in the same unit.-

The characters and events portrayed in this book are fictitious. Any similarity to real persons, living or dead, is coincidental and not intended by the authors.

No part of this book may be reproduced, or stored in a retrieval system, or transmitted in any form or by any means, electronic, mechanical, photocopying, recording, or otherwise, without express written permission of the publisher.

ISBN 9798678627216

Library of Congress Control Number: 2018675309
Printed in the United States of America

ACKNOWLEDGEMENTS

- First, I must acknowledge the contribution of my coauthor, Dana C. Welch. Without him this novel would not exist. This story began over 45 years ago, when we set out to write the *Catch 22* of the Vietnam War. The story took an unanticipated turn, when seemingly on its own, it became more directly serious. But, after a while, it gasped, lay down in a stationery box, and slept. When I began a rewrite a year ago I could not locate Dana, so he is MIA at this time. If you know of his whereabouts, please let him know of this book, and have him get in touch with me at dslewis46@gmail.com.

+ + +

- Special thanks to Barry Hoffman, long-time editor for Gannett and Times Mirror, as well as Founding Editor of HealthDay, a daily consumer health and medical wire service. Barry is a treasured friend. We served together in Vietnam where we forged a lifelong friendship. His able eye served as Copy Editor for this book, but also contributed to both style and content. Any errors you find are mine, and mine alone. He probably re-wrote this paragraph.

- Great thanks to my friend from the General Society of Colonial Wars in Maryland, Mr. George A. Hughes, whose early intervention reminded me that *Catch 22* had already been written.

- Mr. Franklin Cox, Author of *Lullabies for Lieutenants, Memoir of a Marine Forward Observer in Vietnam, 1965—1966*, for his thoughtful review of a near-fatal manuscript of this book. The eyes of both a Vietnam Veteran, and one who was awarded the Silver Medal by the Military Writers Society of America for his outstanding work, proved invaluable to this story.

- To family members who assisted in proofing this story, and adding much constructive commentary, but mostly to my wife Patricia, who has lived with this story for almost as long as I have, and has put up with many drafts and revisions. She has earned her *Vietnam Veteran* baseball cap. But also, to my two daughters, Amy Hooper and Katharine Ogletree, son, David, and son-in-law and Navy Veteran, Wade Hooper. I turned to my brother Andrew for aviation related help. He is the best, and handiest pilot I know.

Dedications

This book is dedicated to the 58,318 individuals whose names are carved in black granite on the Vietnam Veterans Memorial in Washington, DC.

It is also dedicated to the 2,709,918 Americans who served in Vietnam This represented 9.7% of our generation.

Also, to the intrepid reporters, both written and audio, and to the still and motion cameramen, and combat artists who recorded the actions of those in the combat arms for Headquarters United States Army Vietnam—Information Office.

And, to the men of the 3d Battalion, 187th Infantry Regiment, the Iron Rakkasans, of the 101st Airborne Division (Airmobile) who gave so much in blood and valor in taking Dong Ap Bia, Hamburger Hill, in May, 1969.

FOREWARD

A tour of duty for American soldiers during the Vietnam War was usually 365 days. That is if you weren't killed or wounded. Then it was shorter. There were a lot of ways to count the time. Some guys kept a short-timer's calendar starting at 365 and ending at Zero, and marked off each day as a separate triumph. Other guys kept the numbers in their heads and ran a silent countdown. There were even experts who knew things like the number of hours in February.

These soldiers, whose average age was 20, referred to the United States —to their home—as "The World." This new reality reflected the sense that they had, somehow, been transported away in cosmic distances to another world under a blistering and foreign star. They felt an estrangement from America, from their homes, where people were going about their lives as if nothing much was going wrong, while in this other world everything seemed to be through the looking glass and wrong.

PERSONNEL

The Squad

- Sergeant Kelly – Squad Leader
- Specialist Four Monaghan, Fireteam Leader
- PFC Haynes, Rifleman
- PFC Jennett, Rifleman
- PFC Maxwell, Machine Gunner
- PFC Prescott, Rifleman and Assistant Gunner
- Specialist Four Johnson, Fireteam Leader
- PFC Jones, Rifleman
- PFC Saunders, Rifleman
- PFC Wood, Grenadier
- PFC Shilling, Grenadier
- PFC Drew, Rifleman, Radio Telephone Operator (RTO)
- PFC Bayaban, Replacement Machine Gunner

Others

- The Lieutenants—Platoon Leader (Officers rotated out of the field after six months, so his is a composite character known simply as "the Lieutenant," or "LT")

- An Ensign, the US Navy's equivalent of an Army Second Lieutenant, the lowest officer Rank

- A Naval Lieutenant, the Navy's equivalent of an Army Captain

- Staff Sergeant Edison—Platoon Sergeant

- Specialist Four James Cruz—Platoon Medic

- Specialist Four Thomas Grey, Command Information Office, Public Information Office, United States Army Vietnam Headquarters (USARV-IO)

- Sergeant First Class William Smithson, NCOIC of the Command Information section, Public Information Office, United States Army Vietnam Headquarters (USARV-IO)

- Specialist Five Jim Briggs, Editor, Command Information Office, Public Information Office, United States Army Vietnam Headquarters (USARV-IO)

- My-Duyen and Linh, Girls in the Blue Swan Hotel, Saigon

- Staff Sergeant MacEvy, Military Intelligence, Military Assistance Command Vietnam (MACV)

- Sergeant Tran, Army Republic of Vietnam, Intelligence (ARVN)

- Master Sergeant Kolisch, MACV—Advisor to Vietnamese Popular Forces

- Nguyen Thi Hoa, Hotel Girl, Hue City

- Specialist Four Jeffers, Air Traffic Controller, LZ Jane

- Specialist Four Marlin, Air Traffic Controller, LZ Jane

- Specialist Four Pearson, Air Traffic Controller, LZ Jane

- Lieutenant James 101st Airborne Division, Public Information Office

- Specialist Five Cole 101st Airborne Division, Public Information Office

CONTENTS

Title Page	
Copyright	
Acknowledgements	
Dedication	
Personnel	
The Dike	1
Republic of Vietnam	20
The Road to Hue	28
Ambush	53
Nguyen Ti Hoa	68
Firebase Normandy	75
Firebase Blaze	89
Hearts and Minds	101
Interlude	116
An Operation	143
The Citadel	150
Camp Eagle—Intersection	167
The Squad—Re-Fit	202
The A Shau Valley	213
Funeral	230
Firebase Berchtesgaden	236

Day in the Life	250
The Mountain of the Crouching Beast	271
And So it Goes	294
Epilog	299
Author's Note	303

THE DIKE

Grey—64 and a Wakeup

A gray US Navy Sikorsky UH-34 helicopter hovered over a helipad amidship on the USS Benewah. The Benewah was a giant olive-green barracks ship that served as the flagship for the Commander Task Force (CTF) 117, the Mobile Riverine Force operating in the Mekong Delta. It was moored in sweltering heat near My Tho—the 9th Infantry Division's base camp of Dong Tam. The ungainly looking helicopter gently rocked back and forth as it set down on the deck like a giant dragonfly.

As the helicopter engine began to cycle down, the crew chief opened the large sliding door and kicked out several large, red mailbags. Closely following the mail, a soldier climbed down from the chopper. He was just over six feet tall with sun-bleached brown hair. He wore faded jungle fatigues, worn boots, a rucksack on his back with a steel helmet attached to it by its chinstrap. Nearly covering his eyes was an olive-green baseball cap pulled low and a pair of Ray-Ban sunglasses. He carried a black M-16 rifle over his shoulder, two bandoleers of ammunition for it, a medic's pouch that housed his Leica cameras and film.

And, he carried an attitude.

He stood briefly wondering where to go next. A short Ensign appeared, climbing onto the elevated landing pad from below. He motioned to the soldier, to follow him. Once below the helipad, and away from the aircraft noise, he asked, "Are you the Public Information guy?"

"Yep," replied the soldier, Thomas N. Grey, a reporter for the command information section of the Public Information Office (PIO) at Headquarters, U.S. Army, Vietnam.

"Well?" the officer asked, facing the young reporter. He was wearing starched fatigues and spit shined jungle boots. His sleeves were rolled to precise levels on his upper arms.

"Well, what?" Grey said after a pause, shifting the weight of his rucksack on his back. "Sir."

"Well, aren't you going to salute?" smirked the Ensign.

"Sorry, sir," Grey said, snapping a West Point-grade salute. "I didn't think saluting was a Navy thing," Grey said, lying.

"Well, it is," the officer said, returning Grey's salute in a desultory, lazy fashion he thought made him seem an 'old salt.' "Follow me," the officer instructed brusquely. And Grey did.

They descended down several decks, until finally reaching a paint-chipped gray hatch. The officer opened it, and Grey was nearly overwhelmed by the stench of hundreds of unwashed human bodies.

"Here ya go," the Ensign said, gesturing for Grey to step over the sill into the large troop bay. "You can find an empty bunk in there."

"Where would you put Walter Cronkite if he were here?" Grey asked, not moving to enter the large troop bay.

"I dunno," replied the officer, looking puzzled, "Why do you ask?"

"Because that's where you are going to put me," Grey asserted, shifting under the weight of his load.

"What?" exclaimed the young Ensign, half-way between confusion and outrage.

"Yeah..., ah, Sir. I'm a certified reporter just like Cronkite, and I stay where he stays."

"Shit," the young officer said. Something like this ragged looking soldier was outside of his training or experience.

What he did know is that his Department Head, a Lieutenant, had instructed him that morning, after he had asked a question, "Don't bring me problems, *Ensign!* Bring me solutions, *Ensign!*" The Lieutenant placed special emphasis on the word 'Ensign,' signifying his contempt.

So, the Ensign led Specialist Fourth Class Grey to "junior officers' country," and found him a third-tier bunk, just under an asbestos-wrapped steam pipe. "Here," he said, turning suddenly, and leaving Grey to his devices.

"Fuckin' asshole," Grey muttered.

Thomas N. Grey arrived in Vietnam just over 10 months before he grudgingly saluted the Naval Ensign. When he first arrived in Vietnam, he was untainted by the growing anti-war movement in the United States. As a recent journalism graduate and unmarried, he was, in short order, drafted into the U.S. Army. Grey was surprised to find that the Army had a home for a journalism major.

After basic training, he was sent to the Defense Information School. When he graduated from that, he was given orders for Vietnam. Grey was excited by the orders. To Grey, the employer didn't matter as much as did the war, which he saw as an opportunity to be a war correspondent. Perhaps, he thought, he would find the same muse that Hemingway had. It did not occur to Grey that he might discover the same violent end as Ernie Pyle. But, as it was with so many, Tom Grey saw it as a great adventure.

Over the months in Vietnam, his optimism had waned, while a corrosive cynicism had grown. With each story he filed, the monotony of combat assault after combat assault with the same tedious result of apparently nothing gained, but much lost with each soldier's death, added to his malaise. "Nonsensical and tragic" were the words he used in his private notes.

As an Army Combat Correspondent, Grey spent a week or two each month chasing stories across Vietnam. His travel orders gave him the same status as a courier. That sheet of mimeographed paper gave him a priority when it came to hitching rides on almost anything that moved in the American inventory.

The dark, olive-green-colored Huey helicopter, second in a stick of five from the 9th Infantry Division's 9th Aviation Battalion, vibrated in tune with the rapid rotation of its two massive blades. Army Specialist Fourth Class Tom Grey watched while the skin on his arms rippled in the 90-knot slipstream.

The helicopters in the formation sped less than 500 feet above the shimmering yellow-green rice paddies of Vietnam's seemingly endless Delta like angry wasps.

He sat on the right-hand edge of the canvas seat with his back resting against the gray quilted fabric on the aft bulkhead. He held his M-16 rifle by the handguard loosely in his left hand, the rifle butt resting on the aluminum deck between his scuffed and worn jungle boots. Along with his rucksack, he wore under his left arm a .45 caliber Army-issue pistol in a scared brown leather shoulder holster. In his right hand he held a small silver and black 35mm Leica camera. The camera had a thin leather strap draped around his neck along with his dog tags and a bandoleer of M-16 magazines. He wore a canvas medic's bag draped across his chest that held the remainder of his camera gear: film, and extra lenses. He also carried three canteens, a bayonet, and a medium-sized Buck knife in a black scabbard.

To his right and slightly behind him sat the helicopter door gunner in his small alcove. The gunner's M-60 machine gun, hanging from a bungee cord attached to the helicopter ceiling, was pointing out and down. A belt of 7.62mm caliber linked ammunition was fed directly from an ammo can into the machine gun. The gunner swung the snout of the black gun in a circular fashion as he searched for threats. To Grey's left sat the platoon leader, a Second Lieutenant. A Vietnamese soldier with bad teeth sat next to the Lieutenant, and a Staff Sergeant, the platoon sergeant, sat on the opposite side of the bench.

On the floor, feet dangling over the sill, sat the platoon radio telephone operator, the RTO, and the medic. The RTO. held the antenna from his paint-chipped radio that he carried on his back. The flexible radio antenna was bent over his left shoulder. He gripped it along with the handguard of his M-16 rifle. On the other side of the helicopter sat two other infantrymen who were sitting in the helicopter door with their legs hanging over the side. Grey watched as the RTO, who did not let go of the whip antenna, and the other soldiers as they charged their rifles, chambering rounds, preparing for the assault. He did likewise.

Grey was an unknown quantity to the people he was with, and therefore, an unknown threat. These were experienced soldiers who had come to learn that the guy next to him often had his life in his hands.

He was traveling wth a platoon of 9th Infantry Division's Mobile Riverine force on a week-long mission through the myriad twists and turns of the Mekong River. He intended it to be his last trip to the bush before he boarded a "freedom bird" and flew back to "The World." Sixty-four days and a wakeup according to his short timer's calendar.

Several days before, the Company had boarded Tango boats, World War II—looking landing craft adapted for the patrol and assault missions peculiar to the Vietnam Delta region. Aft of the troop bay, which was directly behind the blunt bow-ramp that dropped to the beach to off-load assaulting troops, was a superstructure. It consisted of an armored wheelhouse, festooned with radio antennas and a fifteen-foot mast flying the Stars & Stripes.

On either side of the wheelhouse were cylindrical turrets housing .50 caliber machine guns and 40mm electric grenade launchers. Between the two machine gun turrets, and behind the wheelhouse was a third turret which contained a 40-millimeter cannon with a 180-degree horizontal arc-of-fire. On either side of the bow were two M-60 machine guns mounted in lightly armored positions. These positions were designed to cover the assault, much as helicopter door gunners did for airmobile assaults. These guns, like the rest of the boat, were manned by U.S. Navy enlisted personnel.

The front two-thirds of the boat housed the troop bay. It was covered by a dark green tent-like awning whose ridge ran the length of the bay.   Stenciled in white atop the canopy was the boat number, T-112-3, in yard-high numerals and a white star, the top point pointed forward. Beneath, in its shade, a platoon of infantry sat sweltering on the steel deck or leaning against the steel bar armor that ringed the boat, gazing at the tepid brown water as it swept by.

Bar armor, which resembled the steel reinforcing rods used in concrete construction, stood several inches from the primary steel armor. The rods spaced about four or five inches apart in horizontal rows. They were designed to detonate RPGs-rocket-propelled-grenades-before they could impact and penetrate the flat steel surface armor of the boat. The boat throbbed to the beat of a diesel engine, as it churned along in a line of other Tango boats. Grim looking monitors prowled each end of the flotilla.

Monitors were named after the U.S.S. Monitor that fought the Confederate ironclad Merrimack to a draw in the world's first battle between ironclad vessels. The epic struggled took place over 100 years before during the Peninsula campaign of the U.S. Civil War. Like the Monitor, its Vietnam War descendant's gunwales rode close to the water. Forward on the modern vessel was a semi-conical turret housing twin 40-millimeter cannons. Each gun was capable of firing 240 two-pound high explosive rounds per minute and probed the river like a lethal snout. Amidships was a protected 4.2-inch mortar pit, and aft was a wheelhouse and turret arrangement similar to the Tango boats. Thunderous broadsides from monitors sliced trees whose trunks measured over two feet in diameter like dry summer wheat before a scythe.

Grey lay on his back atop canvas, his shirt next to him. He was sweating in the tropical sun. The three-knot breeze, if you could call it that, did little to mitigate the 105°, 90% humidity as it passed like hot soup over the boat. The air smelled of stale water, rotting vegetation, heavy diesel fuel, oily engine exhaust, and gun oil. It was 0835 hours. He held a copy of James Michener's *Hawaii* at arm's length, the pages shading his lean face, and his eyes squinted against the bright glare of Vietnam's Sun. Most of the infantrymen below him envied Grey's independence and freedom to place a tan above danger. They secretly admired him, too, because he did not have to be there with them in their crucible. But he was.

Tom Grey was ten months and counting down his one-year tour of duty in Vietnam. Like most G.I.'s in Vietnam, Grey maintained a short-timer's calendar. Beginning with "365, and ending with "One." He religiously X'd out each day, hoping to reach less than one, and a ride home to The World. He kept the calendar in his wallet, behind his military I.D. and Army press credentials. It was a folded file card stained red with Vietnam dirt. This small piece of paper meant more to him than anything else he had with him in Vietnam.

The platoon's leader, a Lieutenant, variously known to his men as "L.T." or "Three-Six," his radio call sign, was also envious. About the same age as Grey at 24, he wondered if Officer Candidate School had been the smart choice. Like Grey, he was a recent college graduate. Unlike Grey, he had been wounded once, shot in the chest, collapsing his right lung. Unlike Grey, he spent his time, when not in the hospital, pushing his troops through the mud and muck on the mighty Mekong. But like Grey, he often thought of his rotation. Soon he would rotate from the field to a position in the rear, probably as a company executive officer and R.D.C., Rear Detachment Commander, or as some staff lieutenant at Battalion or Brigade. Perhaps he would get a good slot as an S-1 personnel officer. "Laundry and

Morale" officer was okay with him. In six months, twenty-six days, he would DEROS—Date eligible for return from overseas—home.

Sighing, the Lieutenant busied himself with his plastic-covered map, trying to anticipate the Company's assault on a small village. The Tango boats, sheltered by the Monitors, would sail in-line until they were nearly abreast of the collection of huts and small buildings, but just upstream from it. The lead Monitor would stand off the village, its guns and mortars cleared for action.

When supporting battery of 105mm howitzers on barges located on a canal a few miles away, sent a few registration rounds near the village, the four Tango boats would turn abruptly to starboard and ram the "beach," dropping their ramps onto the mud banks and dismounting their troops. The trailing Monitor would patrol the Tangos' line, providing reinforcing covering fire if needed. The fifth Tango boat, with a light steel helipad mounted over the bay, would stand by, just upstream from the others to handle casualties.

"Three-Six" was scheduled to anchor the Company's line on the left. They were in the lead boat and would come ashore nearest the village. The Lieutenant would string his three squads along the bank, inland about thirty meters. If the beach was contested by the Viet Cong, they would have to fight it out until the other two platoons added their firepower. Once established, the platoon would link up with the Company commander's command group to the right. His command post consisted of his platoon sergeant, the medic, and his radio operator. It was the only reserve force and would take a position just behind his center squad.

His platoon would remain relatively fixed on the left flank, and the other two platoons would sweep through the village from the hinge of his right-hand squad. Where Grey planned to fit into this was a mystery to the Lieutenant, and he didn't much care. He figured Grey was Grey's problem.

Grey did not do much to endear himself to the Lieutenant or any other officer in the Company for that matter. To begin with, Grey's uniform was faded and worn and bore only the barest concession to rank and insignia regulations. He appeared unkempt, even for a hardened "Boonie rat." Second, there was the Cronkite matter when he declined to stay with the enlisted men in the over-crowded cargo hold of the U.S.S. Benewah He implied he had some extra-legal status authorizing him to bunk in nicer quarters. Remote, and even rude, Grey made it clear to the Lieutenant that he was here for the week, and that he was just marking time until he DEROSed.

Despite the worn uniform, the Lieutenant thought Grey was a REMF - a rear echelon mother fucker, and wondered what he'd done wrong for the C.O. to assign him this asshole reporter.

What Grey really was was a seasoned combat reporter. He had covered the war from the 1st Cavalry and the 101st Airborne divisions in I Corps in the north to II Corps in the Central Highlands with the 4th Infantry Division and the Combat Engineers.

In III Corps, he had humped the Parrot's Beak with the 25th Infantry Division, patrolled near Saigon with 82 Airborne Division, and scrambled through firefights in the Iron Triangle and along Thunder Road with the Big Red One, the 1st Infantry Division.

He had joined in special operations with an A-Team from the 5th Special Forces. He earned his Vietnamese Basic Airborne badge by jumping from an aging VNAF, South Vietnamese Air Force, de Havilland Canada DHC-4 transport while half sober.

Grey was a veteran of the A Shau Valley and had spent nights on Monkey Mountain reclining on a lawn chair in front of the AFVN, Armed Forces Radio and TV, station, drinking Scotch Whisky. Almost nightly, the radio station staff spent the evening counting 122-millimeter rockets as they streaked overhead in the dark, the bright orange exhaust marking their arc to Da Nang, and a flash of light when they hit. Saigon, Hue and Nha Trang; these places, and more, had been on his itinerary at one time or another. Grey didn't think a mattress six inches from a steam pipe on a third-tier bunk in officers' country was too much to ask, along with some peace and quiet.

He knew this was his last trip to the field. There were plenty of new guys to take up the slack for his office. Briggs, his editor, assured him of a nice, quiet berth putting together the *I.O. World Report,* a morning newsletter condensing Associated Press Wire Service reports that came in from the "World." Stacks of these little newspapers were delivered to each mess hall at Long Binh Post before breakfast and substituted for *The Times, The Post, The Inquirer,* or the back of a cereal box.

According to Briggs, this trip to the 9th infantry should be a piece of cake. He was scheduled to participate in a population control exercise designed to weed Viet Cong from the rose garden population of pro-government citizens in the Delta. During the next few weeks, elements of the 9th's 2d Brigade would be encircling and sweeping villages near the Delta coast, checking I.D.s, and generally scoping out the neighborhood. It promised to be hot, tiring, mosquito-infested, and little more. Perfect for his mission.

As it turned out, the assault on the village that morning was just as Briggs had advertised. The Americans could smell the village before they saw it. A haze of wood and dung smoke previewed the collection of huts and small stucco buildings, smelling of unwashed humanity, pigs, water buffalo and chickens, rotting vegetation, and drying and decaying fish. Grey dropped down into the troop bay as the diesel engine revved up before turning into the river bank. He fastened his brown leather shoulder holster and .45 pistol around his chest, shrugged into his rucksack, looped his camera equipment and a bandoleer of ammunition over his head and across his chest, settled his steel pot on his head, and picked up and charged his black M-16 rifle just before the boat made contact with the mud and dropped its bow.

Just in case, Grey was the last soldier off the boat.

The Company cordoned off the village without incident, and with the help of an ARVN, Army of the Republic of Vietnam, military police platoon, they sifted the locals, separating them into three groups.

Those with proper Government identification cards, who were presumed to be "good guys," were sent to the center of the village where a Government spokesman exhorted them. At the same time, their I.D.s were laboriously checked against tax rolls by a district administrator. Those with expired or otherwise deficient identification were interrogated and either issued new papers, which were checked against the tax rolls, or sent to the third group. The third and smallest group sat, stood, or squatted beneath a small grove of palm trees outside the village. They were tied at the wrists and had dark green fabric tape wrapped around their elbows. Blindfolds of a variety of colored materials, gleaned from the villagers, were wrapped across their eyes. In one case, a dark blue cloth bag, like a small laundry bag, completely encased a man's head. They had buff-colored tags, like luggage tags, tied around their necks.

The prisoners, suspected Viet Cong as they were called, were guarded by several bored-looking Vietnamese soldiers. The latter slouched about smoking Salem cigarettes and listening to a cacophony of Asian music on an old brown plastic radio connected to a car battery, which they had liberated from the village. The soldiers, members of the Regional or local Popular Forces, "ruff-puffs," the Americans called them, were outfitted with a motley mix of World War II vintage equipment. The M-1 rifles or BARs appeared much too large and cumbersome for the slight-statured Vietnamese. Their uniforms, also, were a casual mix of castoff military and civilian attire. Scattered about were several olive drab jeeps, two two-and-half-ton trucks, and a blue and cream-colored dented Renault taxi of uncertain utility. The taxi driver was asleep behind the wheel.

Grey wandered about, observing the morning's activities. He didn't even take a photograph, having recorded scenes like these in the past several days. After a while, he sat on a stump near the Lieutenant. He was opening C-ration peaches when the platoon RTO took a signal from the Company CO.

"Charlie Six," he said, passing the handset to the Lieutenant, Grey heard, "Six, Three-Six here... That's a roger, Charlie Six. I read you five by."

The Lieutenant pulled his map from his right leg cargo pocket and unfolded it. He marked a position about a klick outside the village with a red grease pencil and unfolded the map to get a larger picture. Sweat dripped from his nose as he ran his finger along an imaginary path on the map.

"Roger, Six, I copy.. We'll mount five for Eagle Flight, and meet you back at the Benewah for supper, over." The Lieutenant smiled at something he heard over the radio handset and said, "Roger that, Six. See ya. Three-Six out."

The Lieutenant thought that his CO was a posturing shit. He

could see him about 200 feet away during the radio exchange crouched over as if he was under fire. The Lieutenant tossed the handset back to his RTO. and climbed to his feet, saying to his platoon sergeant, "Well, Ed, the easy shit is over."

"Yeah?" the Staff Sergeant grunted.

"Yeah. We gotta mount up on some slicks and Eagle Flight the area looking for strays," the Lieutenant said. "Let's get mounted up and move up the trail to a pickup point. In minutes the platoon had formed its three squads, each with eleven men, into two loose lines on either side of the road that led out of town. They were led by a point element—a rifleman and an M-79 grenadier followed by the CP. The rest of the platoon followed, strung out along the road.

In a fantastic piece of Army scheduling, or just dumb luck, Grey thought, the five helicopters with two accompanying Cobra gunships swept over the appointed position as the platoon arrived. The platoon sergeant formed the men into five six-man "sticks" for the flight, each about fifty yards apart, three on each side of the road.

These loads, consisting of 28 men, were informally calculated by the platoon sergeant based on aircraft weight and density-altitude (itself figured from a ratio of air temperature and altitude). This does not mean that the sergeant used something to make these calculations. He instead relied on experience.

Grey fell into place with the Platoon CP, which consisted of the Lieutenant, the Platoon Sergeant, the RTO, the medic, the Vietnamese soldier, two infantrymen leftover from the load count for the other ships,

The UH-1D Huey helicopters settled down, dust and grit swirling beneath their blades. The men, ducking through the prop wash grit, quickly mounted up.

The soldiers were traveling light, without rucksacks, just suspenders and utility belts with canteens, bayonets, machetes, ponchos, first aid kits, entrenching tools, assorted Bowie knives and the like from home, grenades—both smoke and antipersonnel, bandoleers of M-16 ammunition and several with bandoleers of linked M-60 machine gun ammo. A few men had cans of C-Rations stuffed into long green socks, tied to their belts, in case they got hungry.

Grey knew that an Eagle Flight was a tactic with platoon or company-sized units flying and landing at seemingly random places. The idea was to try to surprise enemy formations, fix them in place, and then call for reinforcements. In Grey's experience, *ad hoc* Eagle Flights like this one did not often make contact with Viet Cong or North Vietnamese Army units. For that reason, Grey went along.

The Lieutenant had picked up the Vietnamese soldier somewhere, presumably to sort out the good guys from the bad. He was small, furtive in his movements, and had bad teeth. He carried an old U.S. M-1 carbine and had a two-magazine canvas ammunition pouch on his belt and a single canteen. Grey thought he was probably some *Chieu Hoi* bastard—a Viet Cong who had turned himself in to the government under their "open arms" policy. He seemed shifty to Grey, who resolved to keep an eye on him.

The helicopter banked sharply, following the one before it in a tight sweeping turn toward a tree line. The first Huey flared, nose rising slightly as it came to a close hover about two feet off the ground near a tall dike wall. Grey watched as its occupants clumsily exited the aircraft. "Not at all like the Cav," he thought, remember the 1st Cavalry Division's Sky Troopers. They could exit a helicopter and assume a defensive position in well-coordinated seconds. He gripped his M-16 rifle tighter and shifted the medic canvas bag he used to carry his camera gear further back by his left side.

As the helicopter flared, the vibrations increased to a physical chopping and shuddering. Grey hefted his rifle and turned on the canvas bench to comment to the Lieutenant on the proximity of the tree line, which was no more than 60 meters off to their right. Suddenly, the Lieutenant raised his righthand throat-high like John Kennedy in the Zapruder film. His head snapped back in a crimson spray against the bulkhead, and his helmet slipped down over his face as his body went slack.

Grey, like a snake, whipped to the right and flung himself from the helicopter, falling the four feet to the soft, sandy earth amid a shower of hot brass cartridges from the door gunner's M-60. He felt a weight fall across his legs as he attempted to scramble forward. In a blast of wind and sand and a roar of the turbine engine, he felt the helicopter pull pitch and race out of the Landing Zone.

Turning, he kicked himself free from the dead medic, as the RTO scrambled up next to him. Grey reached down and stripped the medic bag from the dead man's shoulder and, dragging it, crawled toward the shelter of the dike wall. Gasping, sweat pouring into his eyes, he reached the wall and leaned back against it, facing back toward the L.Z.

Grey could see the dead medic and another body, the platoon sergeant, as it turned out. Two infantrymen low crawling toward him through the dust, eyes wide and terrified-frantic. Grey couldn't find the ARVN soldier, dead or alive, and he'd bet he never got off the helicopter. "He's smarter than I thought," Grey muttered.

To his right, the lead Huey sat, broken and idle, where it had touched down. The large blades hung down in the slowing rotation. Grey could see the right-side door gunner hanging in his harness and could just make out the slouch of the pilot's helmet over the back of his armored seat. All eight infantrymen from that ship had reached the wall, and the co-pilot and the other door gunner—the crew chief—crouched by the front strut. Grey knew the gunner had to open the door for his co-pilot. Side armor, retrofitted after the Huey was built, blocked the pilot's access to the door handle.

To his left, the third helicopter in the stick was just lifting off, leaving a litter of dead G.I.s like abandoned eggs. Of the eight infantrymen who rode in, only two were crawling toward the dike. The fourth ship flared at about thirty feet, arresting its descent, and pulled rapidly up and to the left, away from the Landing Zone. The fifth didn't even make a pretense of landing and followed the fourth out in a lazy arc. "Chickenshit," Grey thought. He did a quick assessment: Twelve of the twenty-eight men in the platoon were clustered along the dike wall. Grey made thirteen. A pilot and door gunner were dead or wounded in their ship. The other door gunner and the co-pilot were exposed to enemy fire as they crouched beneath the disabled helicopter. The door gunner was the only American returning fire.

Rounds ripped and snapped overhead, and puffs of dust were kicked up near the gunner and the pilot. The pilot lay prone frantically trying to chamber a round in his corroded and rusted AR-15. He could barely pull the cocking arm back before he was shot through the helmet and head and died.

Grey watched as the gunner, under covering fire from the two Cobra gunships spraying lead into the tree line, scrambled toward the rear of the helicopter. Reaching up, exposing his belly and chest, as he pulled two cans of M-60 ammunition out. Then the gunner crawled under the tail of the helicopter, dragging the 23-pound gun and the two cans of ammo. He rose to one knee, firing the weapon one-handed, and suddenly began a dash for the dike. Quickly, several of the infantrymen rose up along the dike and tried to give him covering fire. It didn't work.

Grey could hear, more than see, machinegun fire lancing up from the trees toward the darting Cobras, driving them off. Grey looked at the RTO., who stared at him with eyes so wide Grey could see whites all around the irises. "Don't you think you better call this the fuck in?" Grey yelled. The RTO fumbled with his CEOI, communications, and electronics operating instructions, which contained his call signs and codes.

"Gimme that," Grey yelled, snatching the handset from the startled RTO. For the first time in his Army life, Grey used a radio, "Anyone on this net, we're in deep shit here!" he yelled. "We got dead all over the place, including the Three Six!"

The RTO tapped Grey on the arm and snatched back the handset. "Charlie Six! Charlie Six! This is Three-Six Alpha. Got men down, got a chopper down, got KIA.s, got WIAs, over."

Grey watched the RTO. as he listened to the reply. "Roger, Six. Don't know who's in charge here. Looks like the Sarge is KIA. too." The RTO paused, taking in a shuddering breath. Grey could see a small stream of tears emerge from the inside corners of the RTO.'s reddened eyes and begin winding through the dust on his face toward his quivering chin.

Grey could hear the slower firing M-60 join in with the more rapid burps of the M-16s as the noise-level amped up. The two Huey Cobra gunships clattered overhead, releasing 2.5-inch rockets and firing miniguns that sounded like a dentist's drill at Viet Cong positions inside the tree line.

"Jesus," he thought, stripping off his camera bag and camera, and fingering the brown leather shoulder holster for reassurance with one hand, and wiping sweat from his eyes with the other. "It's gonna be a long day," he said to himself.

REPUBLIC OF VIETNAM

Grey—50 and a Wakeup

Tom Grey sat with his feet up on his desk in the Information Office for the Headquarters United States Army Republic of Vietnam at Long Binh Post. Long Binh was a sprawling U.S. Army logistics and headquarters facility located about 20 klicks northeast of Saigon. Tom Grey it called home. He squinted at a photograph of Richard M. Nixon in a two-week-old edition of the *New York Times*.

"Shit," he said, swinging his booted feet down onto the green and white checked floor tile common to most U.S. military installations. He tossed the paper with its permanently rolled shape onto his typewriter. He checked his battered stainless-steel Seiko watch: 7:15 PM.

His lean form had had the baby fat burned off by Vietnam. His sandy brown hair was worn slightly longer than regulation. Grey rolled his chair back, stood while reaching into the top right-hand desk drawer for his olive-green baseball cap and a couple of letters from back in The World. When he first arrived in Vietnam and experienced his first fire-fight, a small thing that resulted in no casualties on either side, he had written his parents about it. His father had written back saying that Grey should not write such things again. So, in the infrequent times he wrote home, Grey stuck to the weather and how lovely Vietnam was.

"Where'n hell you think you're goin"?" snapped Master Sergeant William Smithson, NCOIC, Non-Commissioned Officer in Charge, of the Command Information section without lifting his gaze from the paperback novel he was reading.

"I've been in the field for two weeks," Grey said wearily while picking up his rucksack, helmet, and weapons.

Sergeant Smithson, without looking, up sighed slightly, pushing his black-framed glasses higher onto the bridge of his nose with his right index finger. "Take the jeep."

"Thanks, Sarge," Grey said, surprised at the offer. Sergeant Smithson was not known for his thoughtfulness. Stooping, Grey collected his gear and headed out to the jeep.

Grey had just returned from the assignment with the 9th Infantry Division in the Delta and had stopped by the office to drop off film for processing. He would write up his story tomorrow.

Grey started the unit jeep acquired from some Air Force MPs in exchange for a couple of boxes of Scotch Brand recording tape and Kodak Tri-X 35mm film. The MPs had even painted their unit numbers on the bumper. They hadn't asked the MPs where they got the jeep.

He drove through the twilight, down the curving road that led from Headquarters to his company area.

He drove past the "Holiday Inn East." Holiday Inn East was the barbwire and bunkered compound that housed general officers. It resembled a set of cabanas at some ritzy Hawaiian resort hotel, complete with strategically placed palm trees. Grey hoped he wouldn't get shot by one of the security guards. He turned on the headlights, hoping the guards wouldn't think a dink sapper would be driving to work.

Grey parked the jeep in front of his barracks, unloaded his rucksack and helmet. He strung the 45 pistol, and shoulder holster, the canvas medic camera bag, and his M-16 rifle with two bandoleers of ammunition over one shoulder. Kicking open the screen door, he carried his load down the center hall, passing several sleeping members of his unit.

About midway down on the left, he stopped, tossing the rucksack and steel pot onto his bunk. He stuffed the weapons and cameras in his locker, padlocking it before starting out the barracks' back door. "Definitely not a regulation disposition of firearms," he thought to himself stepping onto the wooden sidewalk that ran the length of barracks row.

Walking past the tin-roofed mess hall, Grey headed straight for the NCO Club next door. Once inside, Grey squinted through the smoke. Spotting his editor, he said to himself, "Ah, Mr. Briggs..."

Specialist Five Jim Briggs saw Grey at the same time and, while laconically waving a can of Budweiser, yelled over the hum of the post-dinner crowd, "Over here, Tom!" Grey paused, pulling off his battered and sweat-stained baseball cap. He snapped it against his right thigh a couple of times. Purposefully he threaded his way through the dozens of round Formica topped tables until he stood, a thin, slightly stooped six feet, over Briggs. "Sit down, old boy. Sit down." Briggs said with an expansive fake British accent. He smiled broadly, a little drunkenly. His smooth face glowed pink from, and his receding blond hair stirred in the gentle ceiling fan breeze. Looking up at Grey, Briggs' glasses reflected the overhead florescent lights, twin curves of white blanking his eyes.

Grey jerked a chair from beside Briggs, and with a twist of his wrist, he turned it, slammed it down and quickly straddled it. He stared long and hard a Briggs. Abruptly he pulled Briggs' half-empty beer can to him and drained it. Briggs was startled by the fierceness of his actions.

Wiping his mouth, Grey muttered, "You bastard. You said the story with the 9th Infantry would be the last. You said it would be a piece of cake..."

"Well?"

"Well, what's this shit about another assignment? The Major says he wants me to go do a story on some German Red Cross ship off Hue."

"You stink." Briggs interrupted.

Grey paused a moment before replying. "Well, there's no shower in the fucking swamp, asshole!" Grey said, leaning on the round table.

"Haven't gotten cleaned up yet?" Briggs blandly asked.

"No, I haven't cleaned up yet," Grey said with a mincing high-pitched voice. "I wanted to see you first, and thank you for almost getting my ass shot off down in the Delta."

"Honestly, Tom, I had no idea the shit would hit the fan on that operation," Briggs said, palms outspread. "Hanoi hasn't cleared me on their plans."

Briggs waved at a waitress. Smiling, he held up two fingers in a "V" sign indicating victory, peace, or two beers, depending on the circumstances. "Seriously, Tom, I wouldn't have suggested the assignment if I thought there was any chance of your getting hurt. I looked for a low-risk story for you. You know that."

"Yeah..., I guess I do." Tom, the fire suddenly out, slumped over the table, resting his forehead on his crossed forearms.

"Was it bad?" Briggs asked, his voice low, concern evident.

"Yeah," Tom said, his eyes glistening in the light. "It was the worse shit I've seen," he continued in a whisper.

"The company I hooked up with, one from the Mobile Riverine Force, hit a cold beach from Tango boats near the coast." Grey began in a monotone. "We secured an already secure area and sat around for a while. Then the platoon I was with was assigned to an Eagle Flight." He paused, taking one of the beers from the pudgy Vietnamese waitress wearing too-short shorts. He noted that, as usual, she wore too much makeup.

"We went up and down in the helicopters a few times looking for Charlie. Nothing but cold LZs—as usual..." Grey stopped talking, his eyes seemed to glaze, as he turned inward to his memories.

"And?" Briggs prodded softly.

"And then," Grey said, "We put down on the perimeter of a reinforced VC battalion... God, it was awful. What was left of a fucking under-strength platoon sitting ass-to-ass with a fucking gook battalion! We were only fifty, sixty meters, maybe less, off their perimeter. Those of us who had survived the landing were hiding behind a four or five-foot-high dike wall."

Grey reached for his beer, his right trembling slightly; his nails were cracked and dirty and yellowed from nicotine. "We lost almost half the platoon I was with on the LZ..., and a helicopter and crew. RPGs and a lot of automatic weapons fire.

"All us lucky fuckers hid behind that goddamned wall while the tide came in, backing up the river and flooding the paddy. Sucking up our cover inch-by-inch. About dawn, we had only a foot or so left.

"During the night, they probed a few times and tried to get us with mortars, that didn't work so well—for them that is. We managed to hold them off, although I don't think they tried very hard. I supposed they figured that time was on their side and that they'd be able to take us out one by one—a no-risk shooting gallery affair.

"By nine, we were out of water, almost. And ammo was low. We couldn't even evac the wounded. There were these bloated bodies of our people floating out in that paddy, and we couldn't reach them...

"My camera gear was soaked, so I took over for the dead medic. No morphine. Can you believe it?" Grey's narrative took on a rambling quality. "Just a jar of Darvon. Have you ever tried to help a guy with a sucking chest wound with just a jar of Darvon?

"About all I could think of to do with it was to bash their heads in with it. Put 'em out of their misery. "Christ, I almost did it! I almost did..." Grey suddenly leaned back and threw his beer with savage force against the plywood wall. It smacked dully, fell to the floor—foaming.

Grey began to cry. He made no sound, but as he stared at Briggs, the tears streamed down his cheeks, making bright rivulets reflecting the ceiling lights.

An NCO Club bouncer came quickly to their table. He took one look at Grey, passed on, and picked up the thrown beer can. Then he headed back to his place by the bar, his face blank. He'd seen it all before.

"Shit, man, I can't go back out there!" Grey said, his hand making a sweeping gesture. Appeal edged Grey's voice and eyes.

"You can't avoid it, Tom." Briggs said softly.

"Why the fuck not?" Grey snapped.

"Because you got over a month left." Briggs raised his hand, palm forward. "That's at least one more assignment. I know you've done more than your share. That's why we cooked up this German Red Cross ship story." Briggs said, taking anothe pull on his beer.

"What the fuck do you guys want out of me?" Grey demanded, "I've been humping my ass off all over this war for you bastards for nearly a year. Christ! What do I have to do?"

"It's your fault," Briggs said, his voice rising with sudden frustration and anger. "Right from the start, you made a reputation as a guy who loved to go to the field. You wanted to see what was happening, and now you're crying because you found out!"

Briggs motioned to the waitress, ordering another round. He continued, his voice softer, "I, on the other hand, kept away from the real war. In six and a half months, I've only been off Long Binh Post twice. The time we went to Bien Hoa for a little boom-boom, and once when I covered the opening of a new bridge a few klicks south of Saigon. That day I left at ten in the morning and was back by happy hour.

"Tom, nobody expects me to go anywhere. When they say,

'Who can we send to cover such and such an operation? Why, Grey of course, he loves that shit!' So, Tom, off you go." Briggs looked at Grey over the top of his eyeglass rims. "Besides, I'm the editor. I don't have to go." He said simply.

Leaning back in his chair, Briggs sighed, taking some military pay script, money, from his pocket to pay for the beer. "Tom," he continued, his voice brisker, "If you play this right, this story could be a three-week vacation in Hue for you."

"Yeah, well, you could be right. I know some people at MACV up there." Tom said, taking up the fresh beer. He began to feel a little better thinking of his friend at the Military Assistance Command, Vietnam in Hue City, and of Hoa and how good she could make him feel.

THE ROAD TO HUE

Grey—45 and a Wakeup

Tom Grey stood, hung-over and irritable, near Bien Hoa airport's passenger terminal watching a squadron of Vietnamese Air Force A-1D Skyraiders bank sharply in the crystal blue sky and drop to the runway. Experience had taught Tom to regard the aging prop-driven Skyraiders with respect. For close-in ground support work, the A1-D was hard to beat. They could loiter on-station for quite some time, and when things were ripe, they could pop their dive brakes, hang in the air, and put its ordinance where it was needed most. The jets usually just spread the stuff around and hoped for the best.

"Gotta light?"

Grey turned and peered out from under the narrow brim of his bush hat. The intruder was one of a platoon of replacements headed for the 101st Airborne base camp up north. Grey studied the G.I.'s new green jungle fatigues and his shiny pink sunburned face. The new guy, commonly called a "fucking new guy," or FNG, held a cigarette in his right hand. He shouted again over the engines of the C-130 transport warming up 30 yards away, "Gotta light?"

"You can't smoke here, dumbshit!" Grey answered sharply.

The young man nodded his head and turned away. The replacements sat baking in the Vietnamese sun between Tom and the tin cattle shed of the passenger station. They had rucksacks, rifles, helmets, and heavy duffle bags, everything they owned.

Tom felt a tinge of pity for them but quickly buried the feeling. "Fuck 'em," he thought, "They've got mothers to cry for 'em."

The C-130 revved its engines and sent prop wash gusting across the concrete, spraying Grey and the replacement troops with grit and jet fuel exhaust. The FNGs ducked and averted their faces. Grey lowered his chin and squinted, ignoring the discomfort.

The loadmaster, standing on the lowering cargo ramp, motioned the men to the plane.

Grey slung his half-full rucksack, camera bag, and rifle over one shoulder and headed for the aircraft.

Beside him walked a plump black with E-7 sergeant stripes. The legendary white eagle's head on a black shield patch of the 101st Airborne Division was sewed high up by the left shoulder on his shiny new fatigues. He walked with a handful of mimeographed travel orders attached to a dark brown clipboard. The loadmaster, in deference to Grey's evident old-China-hand status, took his papers first. He studied them for a moment and then shouted above the roar, "USARV-IO?"

Grey grinned and nodded his head, "You got it."

The airman shrugged his shoulders and motioned Grey up the

ramp. Tom had the whole interior of the aircraft to himself. He chose the far-left corner of the cargo area, a niche below a small window he would share with an assortment of steel and aluminum tubes. Carefully he lowered his ruck into the conclave of aircraft hydraulics. Behind him Grey heard the loadmaster return his attention to the 101st replacements waiting before him. "Okay, Screamin' Eagle," he shouted, "What you got?"

Grey lowered his weight slowly onto the rucksack. Most of the things in the backpack were hard and angular. Included were two boxes of shells for his .45 pistol, a quart of Early Times whiskey wrapped in a towel, two paperback novels, three C-Ration meals, twenty rolls of film, spiral-bound stenographers' notebooks, pens, and a cherry wood pipe he had bought in Singapore when on R&R. Only his field jacket, an ounce of marijuana, an extra pair of fatigues, and socks made the ruck serviceable as a seat. Tom unslung the three bandoleers of M-16 ammunition from across his chest and cradled the automatic rifle in his lap, shutting his eyes behind his gold-framed aviator sunglasses.

The herd of FNGs began filing onto the plane. They sat on the floor in a jumble of equipment and bodies. The loadmaster did what he could to balance the load, and then he put on a pair of headphones with a mike and hit the "talk" switch. The pilot advanced the throttles cranking up the four big Allison turboprops, and the aircraft began taxiing. Actuators whined shrilly as the cargo ramp closed, and cool, moist air gushed into the cargo hold from the air conditioning system. The ramp snicked shut, muffling the engine noise. Conversation was limited, and what there was among the cherries was whispered.

Three of the plastic canteens Grey carried dangled from his ruck, attached to the frame with aluminum O-rings. A fourth, with a metal canteen cup, was encased in a damp canvas pouch on his pistol belt. He removed this last one and carefully unscrewed the green plastic cap. Grey took a long, slow drink and felt the whisky burn his raw and empty stomach.

Tom put the canteen away and settled against his equipment. The C-130 did a slow pivot and headed down the runway, gained speed, bounced a few times, and then lurched into the air, rising sharply above Vietnam to avoid ground fire. The steep ascent bothered everybody but the Air Force loadmaster and Tom Grey. Grey closed his eyes and let his body adjust. Around him, the aircraft shuddered as it fought for altitude. The whiskey made him sleepy.

Two hours into the flight, they hit turbulence. It shook the men roughly against their equipment and the metal deck. Grey woke to find his M-16 gouging his side. He stood up, stretched, turned, and peered through the small Plexiglas window. The brown and green carpet of the Vietnamese jungle moved slowly 12,000 feet below.

One of the replacements got to his feet beside Grey and lit a Marlboro. "Mind if I share your window?" He asked. Tom moved aside, and the young soldier craned his neck to stare through the small oval. "This is the first time I've seen it."

"Is that right?" Tom replied.

"Well, I saw a little bit when we landed from the States, but not much." The soldier turned away from the window, saying, "I couldn't believe the heat. Getting off the plane was like getting into a closed car in the summer."

Grey nodded and sat down. The soldier sat down beside him.

"I guess you get used to it, though." the soldier said. "It doesn't bother me near as much now as it did a week ago. You get acclimated. Your blood gets thinner.; that's what they say."

"That so?" Cautiously Grey worked his canteen loose and took another drink.

"You're a combat correspondent?"

Grey nodded. He wore a small black patch on his right shoulder sewn above his black and olive green shield-and-sword USARV patch that said, "OFFICIAL U.S. ARMY COMBAT CORRESPONDENT." in gold letters. "Doesn't mean much," he replied.

"Is that why you're going to Camp Eagle?" The soldier asked.

"I'm not going to Camp Eagle."

"I am."

Tom sighed, leaned back, and closed his eyes.

"Yeah," the replacement said, "I'm going to the fucking 101st Airborne Division, and I'm not even airborne. They changed the rules."

"*Sin Loi,*" Tom said. "Sorry 'bout that."

The loadmaster reappeared and had the men square up a little for the landing. Grey gathered his equipment together and put out his cigarette.

"Is there a lot of it up here?" The FNG asked Grey.

"A lot of what?"

"Combat." There was an edge to the young man's voice

"I don't know," Tom said. "I'm sorta retired now. Mostly I write about little old ladies and orphans."

"Orphans?"

"Yep," Grey was smiling. "Civic action, hearts and minds..., political stuff."

"Oh." The replacement said, apparently disappointed that he wasn't going to get a war story.

The plane did a sharp banking turn on its final approach to the Hue/Phu Bai airport. Grey stretched and took another shot from his canteen. The pilot put the C-130 down on the short, rough runway with a jolt. While the plane taxied, Tom slipped his arms through the canvas straps of his rucksack, slung the bandoleers of ammunition over his head, and slung his rifle over his shoulder. Picking up his canvas camera bag and helmet, he began to shuffle toward the rear as the cargo ramp and the engines cycled down.

A staff sergeant with the 101st Airborne patch on his shoulder strode aggressively to the waiting plane from the dirty plywood shed that served as the passenger terminal at Phu Bai. He took the mimeographed sheets from the black E-7 and clamped them onto his clipboard.

"All right, you guys, let's move it! Bag and baggage!" He shouted like a drill sergeant. The platoon of replacements scuttled out of the aircraft, hurriedly collecting their gear as they went. They formed up in four ranks on the right side of the plane.

Grey stepped down, nodded to the loadmaster, and walked toward the terminal.

"Hey, you!" Screamed the 101st sergeant, "Where the hell do you think you're going?"

Grey ignored the question. He hadn't gotten more than six feet when he was spun around by the florid faced NCO who gripped his collar with one hand, the clipboard raised in a threatening way in the other.

Tom's hand reached for the .45 automatic pistol in his shoulder holster in a flash of anger and pure reaction.

"Hey, buddy..., ah, sorry...," The sergeant said, glancing at Tom's hand on the butt of the pistol. "I didn't.... I thought you were one of mine."

"Well, I'm not," Grey said softly, "So get your goddamned hands off me."

"Sure, sure. I'm sorry. Really." the NCO raised his hand, palm forward and open. The papers attached to the clipboard in his right hand fluttered.

Grey turned and continued toward the terminal. As his anger subsided, he allowed himself to feel pleased that his reaction had intimidated the man. Smiling, Grey hunched the ruck higher on his back and slipped into the half-crouched stride that was the trademark of the American jungle fighter. "Fucking lifer probably sleeps in a bunker," he thought, smiling at the irony of his thought.

Inside the building, a few Vietnamese servicemen and civilians sat on the few benches or squatted on the gray cement floor. Grey passed a woman nursing a baby. Once he would have gawked, but now he barely noticed. Behind her were two dog handlers with their muzzled German shepherds. The dogs seemed more relaxed than their masters, who looked a little wild-eyed and twitchy. Three 1st Cavalry Division infantrymen lounged on a bench along the left wall. A cluster of 101st Troopers sat on the floor, smoking cigarettes and reading comic books.

Over the heads of the small crowd, Grey spotted MacEvy. Mac, a burly six feet two, with large forearms and a receding blond hairline, leaned against a wall by the back door talking to a Vietnamese sergeant. His light, wispy hair fluttered in the slight breeze. The light flickered through the slowly spinning blades of the ceiling fan. "Hey, Mac," shouted Tom, waving his M-16 in the air for emphasis. Mac glanced up and quickly spotted him. Nodding he said a few more words to the Vietnamese soldier and ended the conversation as Tom walked up.

The two Americans cautiously shook hands, trying to assess the effect intervening months had had on the other. "How you been, old buddy?" Asked MacEvy, eying Grey carefully.

"Still alive, How about you?" Grey answered with reserve.

"Fine," Mac said as he turned and led the way from the terminal by the back door. "Haven't been shot at seriously since that little confrontation down at Cu Chi."

"Yeah," Grey said, relaxing. "Well, that was a long time ago."

MacEvy's jeep was parked across the alley under a crude "No Parking" sign. Grey slipped out of his ruck and stacked it in the back seat. He put his camera bag on the floor. He slapped a magazine in his M-16 rifle and expertly chambered a round before climbing into the brown canvas passenger seat.

MacEvy grinned as he got behind the wheel. "It'll be nice to have a little more firepower along," he said, indicating the thirty-eight pistol that hung on his hip. "You're more cautious than you used to be."

"A little older, a little wiser," answered Grey as Mac started the engine and got the jeep moving. As they drove to the gate, Grey saw the cherries he had traveled with being loaded onto the back of a two-and-a-half-ton truck. The new men, surrounded by the lush, jungle-like tropical vegetation that had once been the French colonial airport's well-manicured grounds, appeared pensive like boys lined up for the first day of school.

MacEvy turned off the dirt road onto the two-lane blacktop of Highway 1A. The highway traveled the length of South Vietnam from Saigon to Quang Tri, a province capital almost 100 klicks north of Hue. The jeep passed between the U.S. Marine compound and XXIV Corps, the headquarters for allied operations in this northernmost military zone. Beyond the military installations, a shantytown Vietnamese village lined the road.

"Phu Bai's nice," Tom said as the jeep rolled through the gathering twilight.

"Sure," MacEvy gave a laconic reply.

"So, how are things in the Citadel of Hue?" Grey asked.

"Fine," answered MacEvy.

There was little traffic on the highway, and he goosed the jeep to forty. Grey settled back into his seat. The evening was alive with shadows. Along the road were ten-year-old kids selling dope. He wondered if he should ask MacEvy to stop.

On the edge of the shantytown was a combination Buddhist temple and orphanage. It was made of pink stucco, and the lot it sat on had been worn as hard as a concrete playground by countless small brown feet. In the twilight, the children, wearing only cotton shorts, sat quietly around the building. There were a lot of them. Behind the temple lay the sandpits and the road to Camp Eagle. It was a fringe of planet Earth where you could buy dope, get laid, or arrange an assassination without ever talking to anyone over fifteen.

The jeep moved north, out through flanking rice fields. It had rained, and the Vietnamese farmers were up to their knees in water. They worked slowly and deliberately and seemed oblivious to the traffic on the road. There were only old men in the fields now. At other times Tom had seen the paddies filled with old people, women, kids, and water buffalo. Harvest time then, he supposed. "Mind if I smoke?"

"Still a junky?" said MacEvy with resignation.

"Yep, still a junky."

It was nearly dark now, and neither man was entirely comfortable. Grey reached over the seat and dug his pipe and the bag of marijuana from his rucksack. He remembered a small stone Catholic Church that sat back from this road on a tiny square island surrounded by flooded rice paddies. He looked for it now as he lit the bowl with his scratched and dinted Zippo lighter, but, in the gloom, he missed it.

"What are you doing this far north?" MacEvy asked, his eyes glittered as he glanced at Grey.

"Hiding out till the war's over."

"You mean it isn't?" MacEvy said, glancing at Grey. Grey pulled a long drag from his pipe.

"Not quite. Almost, but not quite," said Grey, holding the smoke deep in his lungs.

"How long?"

"45 and a wake-up."

"Short," MacEvy commented.

"Yes indeed," Tom replied, exhaling noisily.

"So, what are you doing up here..., officially?"

Grey put out the pipe and took a deep breath. "Hearts and minds," he said.

"What?"

"Hearts and minds. Now that you guys have won the war, it's time for us to turn to other matters. Rebuilding Vietnam. Putting the people back together."

"Propaganda?" MacEvy asked, turning his head quickly to glance at Grey.

"Yes, propaganda."

"Too bad," said MacEvy.

"Not really. We're going to turn it into a *cause celebré*. Bring in social workers from the States, them and the Peace Corps. They're going to sweep in here with roads and hospitals, schools, the whole Great Society set up. Really going to give the Vietnamese a break," Grey said with mock enthusiasm.

It was dark when they arrived in Hue. Small dark clusters of tiny houses lined the highway. Pale yellow candlelight seeped through cracks in the plywood and tin. Quiet groups of people talked and laughed along the streets. MacEvy turned the jeep right onto a side street, passed through some barricades, and parked in front of the old hotel that served as the MACV Compound. The building, ringed by a brick wall, surmounted with concertina wire and pocked with bullet scars, ringed the three-story cement and brick building.

Grey unloaded his rifle, then pulled his gear out of the jeep and followed MacEvy inside.

"Got the munchies?" asked Mac.

"Sure."

"We'll leave your shit in my hootch." MacEvy crossed a small open space, Grey followed in his wake. Without going into Mac's room, they tossed Tom's gear inside and made their way to the mess hall. He kept his rifle and his .45.

The building was old. Its ceilings were high and studded with large horizontal fans with lighted globes attached directly beneath them. The plaster walls were cracked in places, exposing red brick and pale white mortar. They made their way to the mess hall. They were about the last ones in for dinner and had the place mainly to themselves.

As they moved down the line, a Vietnamese cook served them what passed for Salisbury steak in a brown gelatinous gravy. Other Vietnamese moved around the room, cleaning up after the Americans. Grey wondered how many of them were Viet Cong. Toward the end of the room, two soldiers set up a projector to show the evening movie.

The two men ate in silence. After a while, Mac said, "You know,

Tom, we thought you were coming up here for something else. Something bigger than this hearts and minds crap."

"What?"

MacEvy glanced around, leaned forward and said, softly, "An operation."

"I don't want to hear it, Mac. As far as I'm concerned, the war is over. No more ops for me..."

"The 101st is going into the A Shau valley." MacEvy continued in a quiet voice.

"So, what." Then Grey hesitated. "Why?" he asked. "The 1st Cav just came out of there, didn't they?"

"Yeah, but this is different." Mac slid his chair away from the table and stood up. "We got a new angle."

Grey got to his feet, and together they left the cafeteria. Tom drew a cot, mosquito netting, and a clean poncho liner from supply and set them up in Mac's room.

"Want a drink?" MacEvy asked.

"Sure do."

Mac took a bottle of J&B Scotch from within the makeshift bar. The room was excellent; a small refrigerator, stereo, fan. The only reason Mac didn't have a television was that the most northern of the Armed Forces TV stations was on Monkey Mountain near Da Nang. The mountains that intervened between the two cities blocked its signal.

"You guys in the Military Assistance Command live pretty

well," Tom said as he sat in a worn and faded armchair. The cushion made a sighing sound as air compressed through the tiny holes in the brass brads on the sides.

"Too well," said MacEvy as he handed Grey a drink. "We always have company."

"I suppose," said Tom with a smile. Then he changed the subject. "Is Hoa still around?"

"Hoa..., ah, yes." Mac grinned. "Your lady. She used to ask about you a lot, but I think she's given up. She's working down the street." Mac eyed Grey as he sipped his drink. "If you like, we'll go there a little later."

"Why not now?"

"Because now I'm going to fill you in on this operation," Mac said, pulling a map case from his top bureau drawer.

Grey surrendered, "Okay," he said, slouching deeper into the armchair.

MacEvy spread the map out on the old, scarred wooden card table, nudging aside the bottle and a canteen of water. "When the Cav went in, they conducted a standard Reconnaissance-In-Force, a RIF, toward the Laotian border. We figured that a brigade of the North Vietnamese 12th Division was in there, and we figured, too, that they would pull out rather than fight. That being their strategy ever since they got chewed up by the Marines at Khe Sanh. They lost a ton of guys up there. Along the border, we inserted a couple of dozen LRRP teams," Mac paused. "Those are Long Range Reconnaissance Patrols."

"I know...," Tom interrupted impatiently, waving his hand.

"Yeah, well, as I said, we thought that the NVA would pull out, and when they did, they'd run smack into the LRRPs who would act as artillery forward observers. Then we could bring some H.E. from the batteries at firebases Eagle's Nest, Georgia, Berchtesgaden, and Blaze, which we're reactivating, by the way." MacEvy pointed out the three firebases on the top of the Eastern mountains of the northern A Shau Valley, "Here, here and here," he said as he tapped the plastic cover with a blunt finger.

MacEvy poured more Scotch into both the glasses and mixed in some water from the canteen. "Only nothing happened. The Cav got ambushed a couple of times, and the LRRPs shot a few gooks, but nothing like we expected. We got some pretty good infrared pictures, and the Cav got a bunch of intel when they caught part of the NVA by surprise. They left food on the table and, in some cases, engines running in trucks. By the time we figured out what was going on, the weather went to hell, and we had to pull out."

Grey understood the reason for the pullout. Allied troops in the A Shau Valley, which split a mountain range that ran along the Vietnam-Laotian border, had to be resupplied by air. If the weather deteriorated, the combat situation could change drastically. Still, he did not see what Mac was getting at.

"Apparently," continued MacEvy, "our friends from the north have been very busy with their little shovels again. When our troops showed up, they just crawled back in their new holes and waited us out.

"There's a chunk of rock overlooking the Valley near this trailhead. See, right here facing the Lao border." Mac hunched over the map, pointing with his glass. "The damn thing must be hollow. All sorts of people went in there. It's called Dong Ap Bia." We think the NVA's 29th Regiment is holed up on that mountain

It made sense, Tom reflected, his forehead furrowing. A spur of the Ho Chi Minh trail ran down the center of the A Shau. In 1966 and early '67, Americans and North Vietnamese had fought some pretty sharp contests, with the NVA virtually throwing the Marines and the Green Berets out of the place. The result was the NVA had pretty much a free rein in the Valley. It acted as a staging area for the attacks against Hue during the Tet Offensive the year before and might do so again.

Mac said that traffic in the Valley was pretty much back to normal within hours after the 1st Air Cavalry was extracted.

"So, now the 101st is going in to kick some ass," Grey stated, rather than asked.

"Hopefully," Mac said, smiling. "Part of the ARVN 1st Division will set up as a blocking force to the south of the mountain between these two approaches. The 101st will do pretty much what the Cav did until we figure the NVA are settled down to wait and then go dig them out.

"This is a pretty big deal. We're sending in around ten infantry battalions, including a Marine Regiment, the 9th, to block exits into Laos from the north. Also, a couple of ARVN regiments, one to join with two 101st battalions to RIF from South to North to drive what NVA/VC is in the Valley, and one battalion to assault and take Ap Bia Mountain along with the 101st. The helicopter lift alone will take over 60 birds. It's a big deal.

"Tom, this is likely to be the largest air assault in the war so far. Maybe this will be the Vietnam War's D-Day."

"Why not use artillery and airstrikes?" Tom asked.

"We're gonna," said Mac enthusiastically. "We'll be putting a lot of cannon-cockers to work on the LZs—about ten artillery batteries on several firebases in support. We've got what constitutes a carte blanch on air support, including B-52s. But you know as well as I do that sooner or later, some poor bastard with a rifle and a bayonet will have to go in and mop it up."

"It looks like it could get rough," Grey observed, swirling the remaining ice in his glass.

"Yeah, it could," Mac replied, looking away.

"I've got a pretty good friend in the 101st—a guy I sort of met on R&R. He'll probably be one of those poor bastards."

"We were hoping you'd be going in," MacEvy said, looking sideways back at Grey.

Grey laughed, "Are you out of your *fucking mind!*"

Mac refilled the glasses again.

"This could be a huge story," he said, "And the civilian press won't know anything until it's over. My old buddy Tom's not going to pass up a scoop, is he?"

"I grew out of chasing fire trucks."

"You might not have much choice." MacEvy countered.

"Bullshit!" Grey didn't like the direction of the conversation. "My office sent me up here for stories to back up the 'Hearts and Minds' program," he snarled. "Whether you assholes like it or not, there is another aspect to this war, and many people are beginning to realize just how important it is."

"Getting chicken?" Asked MacEvy with a lupine grin, his hands spread on his large thighs.

Grey gave him the finger.

"I've been all over this damn country. I've got about 45 days and a wake-up, and I'll be go-to-hell if I'm going to give up this sweet assignment on the Red Cross boat so I can have another crack at the A Shau Valley!"

Mac grinned again. "Calm down, hotshot," he said soothingly. "Let's go see Hoa."

◆ ◆ ◆

The whorehouse was an old stucco French hotel near the river. Mac parked the jeep in the back, and the two GIs ducked inside.

Grey walked around a small sandbagged bunker in the center of the lobby to the old mahogany registration desk. He asked the madam at the counter for Hoa, and one of the girls went to get her, glaring at Tom as she passed.

MacEvy, meanwhile, had rounded the bunker on the other side and headed for the hotel bar.

Hoa came down the stairs. She was five feet tall and slender. Her black hair was cut short in a pixie cut, and she wore an old red sweater off her right shoulder, and black slacks with red high heels. She was surprised to see him and did not speak for a moment, pausing on the bottom step, her hand gripped the railing. Then she asked, "Why you come to Hue, Tom?"

"To see you," he replied, standing away from the desk.

"Okay," her voice was hard and bitter. "Wan a beer, G.I.?"

"Upstairs."

She did not take him upstairs.

Instead, she got two cans of Budweiser from the bar and led him to a small bedroom off the lobby. "I thought you had gone back to America," she said sadly as she closed the latticed wooden door.

"Not yet."

"But you go." It wasn't a question.

"Yes."

"Soon?" she asked softly,

"Yes," replied Tom quietly. Then he put his arms around her and kissed her full, soft lips. She wore a jasmine-scented perfume. After a moment, she moved away from him and sat down on the old metal bed, which sagged and squeaked under her weight. Grey sat down beside her while she searched in the nightstand for a can opener.

Tom lit a cigarette and tried to think of something to say. "You mad?" he asked finally.

"No. Is not your fault." She found the opener, and Grey popped the two lukewarm beer cans.

"You know, is hard," Hoa said. "First you go, I think to you come back. I think a lot of dream." Her voice was pitched high like a child's but was soft in tone. When she spoke, she did not look at him. "But then I know you are G.I. and I am prostitute and so can be nothing. Is like that." She sighed and sipped at her beer.

"I love you," Tom said.

"Doan say." she turned away from him.

"I'm sorry," he said.

Hoa turned and looked up at him. "Is okay." She shrugged her shoulders. "What can do?"

At first, they did not realize what the incoming rockets were. They sounded like thunder. Then the girl bolted from the bed. Tom grabbed her wrist. "Stay here," he shouted, "It's safer!" But Hoa was scared and pulled him toward the door. Reluctantly Tom snatched his beer and allowed her to drag him from the room, flapping from her arm like the tail of a kite.

Hoa guided Tom through the now darkened lobby to the small green sandbagged bunker. She led Tom into the shelter, and they found an open space in a corner and huddled down with the madam, several of the girls, and their patrons.

The rockets were not very close, but there was a knot in Grey's stomach, and he could sense the fear in the girl's body. He held her so tight he could feel her heart beating, and their emotions seemed to melt together. She desperately clung to him, and the two of them began to occupy a separate, private world.

"Grey," shouted MacEvy. "You in here?"

The spell broke. Tom propped himself up on one elbow and answered, "Yeah."

"Well, come on, let's go!"

Hoa hugged him briefly and whispered, "I'm glad you come back, Tom."

"Me too," he whispered. Aloud he yelled, "Fuck you, MacEvy."

"Damn it, come on! There'll be an alert, and they'll be looking for us."

"Man, its raining fucking rockets out there." Tom held Hoa loosely in his arms and kissed her cheek and neck. "Those aren't close."

They're shooting at the Cathedral." MacEvy stated.

"They could miss," Tom observed.

There was silence in the bunker, then, "Come on, man!"

"How long you stay?" Hoa asked, draping her right arm through Grey's left.

"Grey, I mean it. Come on." Mac sounded angry.

"It's stupid to go out there now," Grey said. "Wait for a lull."

"Damn your ass... Come on, or I'm leaving you." Mac said with finality.

"Six weeks," He paused. "Probably less," he whispered to Hoa. Then he kissed her good-bye and began crawling on his hands and knees toward the small door. "Fucking war," he muttered.

Mac was waiting outside the bunker with their weapons. The two GIs ran across the lobby and out into the alley. To the west, they could see the impact flashes of the 122-millimeter rockets. Mac started the jeep and barreled down the alley. Every dog left in Hue seemed to be barking. Grey chambered a round in his M-16 and switched the rifle to semi-automatic. The jeep swerved around a corner, and he nearly fell out. "This is insane," he shouted. "Our own people will shoot us."

"Just stay cool, man. You ain't in Saigon tonight."

They came to a barricade, and Mac had a brief conversation in shouted Vietnamese with two *Quan Canh*, the black and silver helmeted Q.C., the Vietnamese equivalent of M.P.s. Then he gunned the jeep again and accelerated into the darkness. MacEvy seemed relieved. "There hasn't been a full alert," he said.

The explosions stopped as the jeep approached the MACV compound. The gate was heavily guarded now, and MacEvy had to give a password. Inside the building, a tall, lean captain intercepted them on the way to Mac's room.

"Where the hell were you, MacEvy?" he snapped peevishly.

"Ah..., Grey. Grey here, sir. Grey just got in today, and I was showing him the perimeter. What was it, sir? Harassment?" MacEvy asked, simultaneously soaping and bluffing the officer with the ease of a career NCO.

The captain hesitated. "The Old Man doesn't think so," he said. "The Old Man figures with all those troops over on the Laotian border; they may just be getting their shit set up."

"What do you mean, sir?" asked Grey.

"Did we get hurt?" Asked MacEvy.

"They blew the crap out of *Lycée Quoc Hoc*, ya know, the high school," the captain replied. "Messed up a half a dozen civilians over that way, by the Citadel." He gestured vaguely with one hand.

"What do you mean about getting their shit set up?" asked Grey again.

"They set up rocket launchers and mortar tubes and then fire a few rounds," explained MacEvy. "Tomorrow they'll see how close they were, correct their aim, and let us have it again in a few days. When they hit here during Tet, they had damn near perfect fire support.

"They just leave the stuff set up; in the bush until they're ready to attack."

"Swell," Grey said.

"You up here from the Public Information Office?" asked the captain, looking more closely at Grey.

"Yes sir, PIO," Grey confirmed.

"You up here for the valley operation?" the captain asked.

"No.., not really, sir." Tom said, knowing what he was about to say would sound lame. "There are a couple of outstanding human-interest stories up here and, since we've got a push on with this Hearts and Minds thing, I thought I would..."

"Probably didn't even know about the A Shau operation," the captain interrupted, looking to MacEvy for confirmation.

"Well, to tell the truth, sir..."

"You've got that luck, Grey," the captain interrupted again.

"We're not too interested in combat right now, sir." Grey plowed on.

"That reporter's luck." the captain continued, speaking over Grey. "Being in the right place at the right time." The captain shook his head sagaciously. "I'm going to have a talk with the Old Man and get you *absolute* clearance on this whole operation," he said, looking down and hacking his had in a karate chop motion on the word 'absolute.

"Actually, sir, my office is a lot more interested in the story about the kids and the hospital ship."

"Plenty of time for that before the operation. Plenty of time," the captain said with enthusiasm as he moved off down the hall.

"Bet he doesn't go," Grey said, watching the captain take the stairs two at a time.

"He doesn't go anywhere." MacEvy confirmed. MacEvy thought it was just and humorous that Grey was headed for the woods. It proved the working of some cosmic force, the Universe stabilizing. *"Over hill, over dale, as we hit the dusty trail..."* he sang.

"I ain't going." Tom insisted.

"...as the caissons go rolling along."

"Go ahead and laugh, you son-of-a-bitch," Grey snarled. "I bet I get out of it."

"How?" demanded MacEvy.

"I'll think of something," Grey said, sounding miserable.

"What about your sense of duty, your comrades in arms, the public's right to know?"

"I can lie just as easily from here as I can from the jungle.

"It's just not the same," Mac Said. "You'll get the heroes all mixed up.

"Hearts and Minds, MacEvy, that's what this war is all about. Rebuilding the savaged land, giving the Vietnamese a leg up into the twentieth century."

AMBUSH

The Squad—A Game of Chess

The side of the mountain was about twenty degrees short of perpendicular. PFC Mike Haynes struggled against it in a state of agony that he had first learned to endure during high school track practice. "Make it hurt! Make it hurt!" the coach had screamed. "If it doesn't hurt, it doesn't help!"

"It hurts," thought Haynes with a perverse feeling of accomplishment. His vision was blurred with sweat, his lungs ached, and his legs were starting to feel rubbery. Only the knowledge that he could take as much as the others kept him going. When the word finally came to break, he collapsed against the trail and gasped for breath. It was several moments before he fished a canteen from his web gear and took a long, loving drink of the tepid water.

"How much farther?"

Haynes turned his attention to Maxwell, the machine gunner who lay like a heap of equipment and flesh that lay five feet below him on the trail. "Another hour, maybe," he said. "Kelly wants to set up early."

"Fuck Kelly," the heap said. "He's a lifer."

The jungle was silent except for the incessant buzz of insects. Haynes adjusted his rucksack against the slope of the mountain and tried to make the best of the break. He was thinking of lighting a cigarette when the word came to "saddle up!"

They had been moving hard since dawn when the three platoons of the company split apart. Small groups of NVA were known to be in the area. By breaking up, the Americans hoped to make contact with the enemy, fix them in place, and then call for artillery to finish them off.

The pace of the march was slower now. The platoon stopped more often, and periodically the gentle openhanded signal for silence was passed down the column. They were getting close to something. Haynes' thumb toyed nervously with the selector switch on his M-16 rifle.

As they approached the crest of the ridge, the slope of the mountain began to taper off. Then, suddenly, they broke out of the dense jungle and onto a high-speed trail. Haynes slipped quickly into the sidewalk-wide tunnel through the trees. He flicked his weapon onto semi-automatic and faced down what seemed a highway compared to the torturous footpath they had been following. He did not move until the man behind him stepped onto the trail and turned his weapon down the path.

Kelly was waiting for them at the top of the mountain. He was a wiry five foot eight, with sandy hair cut short. The young sergeant gathered the squad around him within the hastily established perimeter. Drawing a crude map in the dust with his finger, he sketched two narrow Ys sharing a common, sinuous stem.

Facing him to his left was one fireteam consisting of Sp.4 Monaghan, team leader, PFC Haynes, rifleman, PFC Maxwell, machine gunner, and PFC Prescott, rifleman, and assistant machine gunner. The other team consisted of Sp.4 Johnson, team leader; PFC Jones, rifleman; PFC Saunders, rifleman; PFC Wood, Grenadier; and PFC Drew, rifleman.

"We know the gooks are around here, and we know they're moving at night," Kelly said. "We've got two trail intersections here within fifty meters.

"The Third squad is going to watch the other end, The first squad covers the flanks and rear security, and we're going to set up here," he concluded, indicating a spot on the map. "As I said, the rest of the Company will be pulling flank and rear security for us, so we can concentrate on the ambush," Kelly concluded.

Kelly was new both as a member of the 101st Airborne Division (Airmobile) and as a squad leader. He had spent a year as an infantryman with the 1st Air Cavalry Division (Airmobile) and now, as a buck sergeant fresh from the NCO Academy, on his second tour in Vietnam. He was taking his first steps up the ladder of command.

Kelly paused a moment and glanced at the men around him, trying to learn something. The white troopers' faces were tanned almost bronze by the tropical sun, and the black soldiers' faces glistening with sweat. Their faces told him little. At twenty-four, he was the oldest member of the squad. He knew he had to prove himself to them before they would trust him.

"If they come," he continued finally, "their point man's going to be twenty or thirty feet out in front. I want a claymore and a trip flare twenty feet down the track. Because of this loop in the trail," he said, still pointing at the map, "The intersection is only twenty-five meters from our perimeter. By the time their point man hits our flare, quite a few of them should be past that point. I want the rest of the claymores in an arc behind the intersection, and I want them facing back toward us."

Kelly got to his feet and began pointing out positions. He assigned men and weapons quickly and efficiently. Haynes drew the center position just off the trail itself. He would share a fighting hole with Maxwell, the machine gunner, and Kelly.

The squad leader concluded with a few brief orders. "If you hear them, wait as long as you can. If they hit the flare, the machine gun position will fire the close-in claymore. That should get the pointman.

"The gooks further back will turn and run. After that first claymore goes, I want the rest of them fired as soon as possible. Our friends should run right into them. When the mines are gone, let 'em have everything we've got. I want you all to check back down the trail so you'll know where to direct your fire." he said, straightening up. "Oh, and don't forget to duck when you fire the claymores. They have an effective range of fifty meters."

"Everybody got it?" Kelly asked, looking each man in the eyes.

There were no questions.

"Okay, set up your positions and get the mines out. I want two-hour guard shifts with a man awake at every position. Work that out yourselves."

The session broke up, and Haynes moved his rucksack to the edge of the dusty trail. PFC Maxwell brought the M-60 machine gun over, along with a can of M-60 ammunition. The two men were setting up when PFC Jones and Sp.4 Johnson came by with a collection of claymores. Jones was a black soldier from Alabama. He was soft spoken, but not shy. Johnson, also black, was lean, and from the hard streets of Chicago.

The claymore mine threw out 700 steel pellets ahead of it an arc of about 60 degrees. Maxwell started digging a fighting hole, and Haynes went down the trail with Jones and Johnson to help put out the mines. They dropped one mine and a flare near the perimeter and then moved down to the intersection.

"Lot of fuckin' wire," Jones said.

"Yeah. Gonna string all this fuckin' wire tonight. Tomorrow we gonna come down and roll it all up." Johnson replied.

"Maybe," Jones said as he pulled yard lengths of wire from the spool while walking backward beside Jones, who was doing the same thing.

"What maybe. We ain't seen a gook in a month."

Haynes busied himself with the mechanics of death. There was a subtle geography involved in arranging the gray-green plastic mines to ensure the maximum killing zone. Haynes was impressed by the small package of C-4 explosive, heavyweight buckshot, and electronics that sat on four spindly wire legs you couldn't sell with an erector set.

"We do have a lot of wire here," Johnson said. "We can't lay it in the trail. One of our gooks might trip on it."

Haynes had that figured out."Let's take them all together and twist them into a cable. We can lay back about three feet into the jungle and run it to the perimeter."

"How will we know which one's which?"

"It doesn't matter," replied Haynes. "The only one that has to be separate from the rest is the close one. We haven't put it down yet. We can rig it later."

"That's a rog," Jones said, sitting down cross-legged in the middle of the trail. The dense jungle around them was silent. He began to fill his pipe from a clear plastic bag of marijuana.

"Hey, what the hell," Johnson exclaimed.

"You cover us for a minute or so, "Jones told him. "There ain't no gooks around here."

"It ain't gooks I'm worried about, it's that son-of-a-bitch Kelly."

"Tell him you're related to the President." Jones took a long drag off the pipe.

"He ain't gonna believe no Brother's related to no President." Johnson countered.

Jones exhaled slowly. "Never know about them Texans," he said with a grin his black friend did not appreciate. Haynes squatted down and took the pipe. He did not smoke often, but he felt that the day's hard humping had earned him a break. The grass tasted hot and clean.

Johnson watched nervously while the two men finished the marijuana. He was worried that Kelly would come down the trail and bust them all, him especially. He was one of the squad's two team leaders, and things were tough enough without getting on somebody's shit list.

When the smoke was finished, they bundled the wire and began to string it back towards the perimeter. The soldiers moved slowly and were careful to camouflage their handiwork. When they reached the point where Kelly wanted the trap for the pointman, they stopped, and Jones set up the trip flare. Haynes took the final claymore, which resembled a collapsed Polaroid camera that someone had bent into a gentle curve, and placed it for maximum effect.

He calculated where the man would be standing when he hit the flare and when set the mine to blow him away. It was a little like taking the guy's picture.

At the perimeter, they split up the cable and ran wires to the now established fighting holes. They had just finished connecting the firing handles when Kelly and the Lieutenant started down the trail to check the arrangements.

Haynes returned to the machine gun, and he and Maxwell finished digging in. Kelly and the lieutenant came down the trail and began checking the squad's positions. When the lieutenant was satisfied, he returned to his Command Post. Kelly started setting up his own equipment by the M-60. "You guys did a good job down there," he said.

"Thanks."

Maxwell took the first shift, so Haynes dug into his ruck and got out some C-rations. The company had been resupplied the day before, so he had a more or less complete menu. Finally, he settled on a can of greasy spaghetti and began cooking it over a couple of heat tabs. Kelly made himself a cup of coffee and lit a cigar. "This is a good spot for an ambush," he said. "With a little luck, we could get a nice body count."

"We ain't even had a warm trail for a month," Maxwell said

without looking away from the jungle.

"Don't mean shit," replied Kelly. "Chuck fights when Chuck wants to. They're moving at night, trying to get their men and equipment out of this area. They'd rather fight 'legs' anyway, it's less expensive."

Haynes believed that. He had worked hard for the airborne wings on his chest, and he was proud of them. He liked being special even if he didn't do anything different from straight leg outfits like the 1st Cav. Intel reported that the 101st had a bad reputation with the VC and NVA, and Mike figured they deserved it.

"What's the problem with Saunders?" Kelly asked.

Neither man answered.

"Dope?" Kelly asked.

"Yeah, he's a dope all right," Maxwell answered.

Kelly stared at Maxwell.

"I don't give a damn what a man does as long as he does his job," Maxwell added. "Saunders doesn't do his."

"He's a cherry," Haynes said. "He's only been here a month."

"If he doesn't shape up, he won't be here another month," Kelly stated flatly. "The hell of it is that guys who make mistakes don't just get themselves killed. I've seen it before."

The first law of the jungle was, as Haynes understood, that there were two kinds of soldiers; good ones and dead ones. Saunders wasn't good, and the other men in the squad were already on his ass. Now it looked like Kelly was planning to come down hard on him too.

"Has he got a personal problem?" asked Kelly probing.

"Yeah," Maxwell answered, "He's scared shitless."

Haynes could not help but feel some pity for Saunders. The man didn't have any friends, and he wouldn't have any as long as he continued to fuck up. Saunders was scared and unhappy. His mind wandered, and he made small, irritating mistakes. The others would ride him until he either improved or cracked.

There was an element of gleeful savagery in the situation that disturbed Haynes. It was like chickens, the strong killing off the weak. What bothered Haynes most was his own growing suspicion that it was necessary.

Kelly got up, shouldered his M-16, and left to check the squad's positions. Fifteen minutes later, he was back and asked, "You play chess, Haynes?"

"A little."

"How about a game?"

"Okay."

Kelly got a small plastic box from his ruck and removed the several large rubber bands that secured the lid. Next, he removed a carefully folded clean olive drab handkerchief from over the small plastic players pegged onto the board. He ritually placed his hands behind his back with a white pawn and a black one in each side. Haynes tapped Kelly's left shoulder: white.

Haynes thought a bit, then selected his opening move, King's pawn to King Four.

Haynes was reasonably good, if untutored, but he was no match for Kelly. By the time it was his turn to stand guard, Mike had lost two games and was in trouble in a third. As he took up his position behind the machine gun, Maxwell wryly said, "Beware of the man with his own chess set."

"That's a rog." Haynes replied, feeling relief now that the pressure was off.

He heard Kelly snapping the rubber bands back into place, securing the top to the set.

Twilight and dawn were the worst times to pull guard. The changing light made the jungle a wall of indistinct shadows that played visual tricks. The small animals and the insects were naturally more active, and their movements confused both sight and hearing.

Haynes lay with his right shoulder to the M-60 and held a claymore trigger loosely in each hand. It would be a long night.

"Back in the World, they're having supper," he thought, then he corrected himself. "At home, they're getting up, and it's yesterday morning." He started to think about his family but stopped. He had learned a long time ago that it was better to put the other World out of his mind as much as possible.

Thinking about home always left him feeling bitter and lonely, afraid that he would never see it again. It was easier for him to bear the hardships and the loneliness of this life in this Asian world if he could forget the comforts and the love of the other one. "War," as PFC Prescott, another rifleman in the squad, said, "Is like cancer. Once you got it, you ain't got any other problems."

The two hours passed, and Kelly took his turn at the M-60. It was dark now, and Maxwell was asleep on the ground behind the foxhole. Haynes crouched down below the lip of the hole spread insect repellent over his face and neck. Rumor had it that gooks could smell it, and it did not repel mosquitos.

"You play a pretty good game of chess," Kelly whispered.

"Not good enough, I guess."

"You'll get better. You just don't know the openings."

"Not very well."

"You'll get them," Kelly said in encouragement.

Haynes had an idea of how he would get them. One at a time, right down the throat.

There was a subtle but different sound in the jungle, and both men were instantly alert. Haynes' stomach knotted with fear and excitement. Nothing, but nothing existed in the world for him but the dark, threatening jungle. Then Kelly spoke in a barely audible whisper, "Monkey." Haynes continued to listen intently for a moment and then nodded his head in agreement.

"I can read this jungle like a book," Kelly breathed. "I read it with my eyes, my ears, it's like I'm subconsciously tuned in. Anything unusual, and I know it."

"I know."

"Kelly paused and nodded his head slightly. "Yeah, I guess you would. You've been here awhile yourself."

"Awhile," Haynes whispered.

"How do you like it?" Kelly asked.

"Love it."

"I'll bet." Kelly fell silent then. He had said more than he wanted to say. He had relaxed in a situation where you could never relax. Kelly knew that it was a way of life. Never let your guard down, never expose your emotions, and never let anyone see inside you. That was part of Saunders' problem. He was open, and the others saw into him, and they saw weakness.

The guard changed again, and it was Haynes' turn to try and sleep. He rolled onto his back and stared up into the trees. He had not changed his fatigues or had his boots off for a week. The ground was hard, and the insects were active. Still, Mike was comfortable and content, grateful for the chance to rest. He wrapped himself in his poncho liner. A soft *drip, drip, drip* sound of water falling on a broad-leaved evergreen over his head lulled him to sleep.

Kelly woke him a few minutes early for his turn at guard, It was after midnight, and the jungle temperature was cooling and nearly silent. Maxwell slid from behind the M-60, and Mike took his place. He was tired now, and his eyes felt gritty. To his sleepy mind it seemed a little ridiculous to lie in the weeds waiting to kill or be killed while most of the people in the world slept peacefully in clean beds.

There was a sound in the jungle.

Haynes knew instantly that it was a man. Maxwell knew it too, and both men silently readied their weapons. Maxwell touched Kelly's shoulder, waking him instantly.

The whites of Kelly's eyes glowed in the partial light.

Haynes was tense with excitement.

The enemy pointman was close enough to see, silhouetted by the moonlight seeping through the trees. He moved slowly, his AK-47 slowly sweeping the trail. His foot snagged the tripwire. There was a flash, and Haynes squeezed the claymore trigger in his right hand. The claymore's dull, flat explosion was his signal to fire the one in his left hand.

Its blast was lost in a chorus as the squad fired the rest of the mines. Down the trail, the night was split by a bright white salvo. Haynes fumbled as he pulled the stock of the M-60 to him. Off to the right, someone's 16 began to reach out for the enemy, red tracers looped into the night. The machine gun bucked against Haynes as he poured steel-jacketed lead into the jungle.

Tracers from the thundering gun scribed a solid red line in the darkness. Ricocheting rounds swirled heavenward, their glow evaporating. From their secure position, the squad members furiously pumped rounds at the area along the trail. There was no return fire.

Kelly called a "ceasefire" and got to his feet. "Come on," he ordered Haynes and Maxwell as he scrambled out of the fighting hole and started down the trail into the darkness.

"Oh shit," Haynes thought as he snapped the receiver down and re-cocked the M-60. "The sonofabitch is playing a hunch."

Haynes and Maxwell scrambled out of the hole and followed their sergeant down the trail. They reached the NVA pointman. Kelly drew his knife and knelt over the body in the darkness.

Silently he slit the man's throat.

Then he began moving in a crouch down the trail, his rifle barrel swinging in a slow arc seeking the enemy. At the trail intersection, they found four more bodies.

Kelly's knife flashed again. He signaled Maxwell to help. When Maxwell hesitated, Kelly hissed, "Cunt." He did the work himself. One of the Vietnamese thrashed briefly in the dark.

Kelly placed the three of them into a hasty position opposite the intersection, guarding the kill. Haynes was afraid now. They were alone, and he was sure the enemy knew where they were. The natural, almost unconscious way he read the jungle had evaporated, smothered by fear. He had to fight to keep control of himself. He wanted to run; to fire at shadows. His legs and hands trembled in the night.

It was half hour before they heard movement again. Haynes' guts were in a knot. Fear coursed through his body like pain, his jaw hurt from clenching, and sweat poured from him. A sound!

A small clink. The sound was in Haynes' section of the small perimeter.

Carefully, he raised the weapon's muzzle and let it track on the rustling sounds in the bush.

The enemy slowly moved closer.

"They're coming back for the dead," Haynes thought, brushing the sweat from his eyes. "For their dead and their equipment.

Haynes felt Kelly tap his shoulder, and Haynes fired a short, vicious burst. There was a flash of tracers and a cry in the dark.

An hour later, there was another movement, and again Haynes fired into the jungle. "They're throwing good money after bad," Kelly whispered, satisfied.

The last movement came a little before 4:00 AM.

Then it was quiet. At dawn, the lieutenant led a patrol down the trail from another squad to the second ambush site where Kelly, Haynes, and Maxwell hunkered amidst a shiny circle of spent brass. There were four bodies, their backs ripped out by the claymores' force, and two heavy blood trails leading away from the intersection. In addition, they found another body in the brush where Haynes had fired and another bloody trail.

Kelly, Maxwell, and Haynes started back to the platoon with a feeling of relief and accomplishment.

They stopped on the way and examined the enemy pointman. The blast caught him at the waist, and his guts were flopped out in the dust like over-cooked spaghetti. His body smelled of urine and excrement, and ants had already begun their feast. Haynes felt nothing as he studied the dead man's startled brown face.

NGUYEN TI HOA

Grey—40 and a Wakeup

H o a was asleep.

Tom sat on the edge of the bed and smoked a Marlboro. The hotel and the city were quiet. He watched the smoke curl toward the high ceiling getting lost in the gloom and thought about going for a walk. He realized that it would be extremely impractical as Hue was technically off limits to Americans other than the MACV personnel and the MPs assigned there.

"The hardships of war," he thought. The little things were beginning to bother Grey as much as the big things. The war was chipping away slowly at the idiosyncrasies of his personality. Like a sculptor working backwards, it was turning the statue into a rough block of stone. He stubbed out the cigarette in the green glass ashtray on the nightstand.

In the dark he sought his clothes and took a clear plastic packet of marijuana cigarettes from the shirt pocket. As he held it, he saw that his hands were trembling. Slowly he replaced the vinyl packet and walked to the window. With his arms firmly crossed he looked out over the city. From his window he could see the dim outlines of the *Cercle Sportif,* the old French sportsman's' club. In the silver moonlight its once elegant verandas and grounds seemed haunted. It was there that he had met Hoa.

◆ ◆ ◆

The press party had almost been a success. They had given the old colonial building a thorough cleaning. The food and drinks were plentiful and the Americans and the Vietnamese who gathered on the veranda by the river were gay and attractive. But they were too few.

The lack of furniture made the sporting club seem cavernous and the laughter echoed off beige stucco walls and footsteps on the teakwood parquet floors boomed loudly. It seemed to Grey a somewhat pathetic attempt to revive a dead era.

He walked first around the cracked and netless tennis courts on the east side of the two-story building, then around the back to the empty swimming pool. The lush bougainvilleas had grown into a tangled wall studded with magenta blossoms giving the pool area a bright, but private feel.

The girl was sitting on the edge of the pool, dangling her feet in nonexistent water. She was small, even for a Vietnamese, and she was more cute than pretty. Her long black hair made her face look almost tiny.

"*Chao Co*," he said. Then he pointed to himself, "Tom."

Regarding him cautiously, and after a short pause the girl said, "I Hoa."

Grey laughed and shrugged his shoulders. "Wah," he said.

"No," she shook her head and smiled again. "Huu-ah, like Hu-e."

It was Sunday afternoon and Tom and Hoa walked along the wide shaded boulevard next to the river. It was lined with old expensive houses and the street was full of young Vietnamese on small Honda motorcycles.

When they came to the west bridge they were going to turn back, but Tom saw an old peasant man. He took Hoa's hand and started across the bridge. The bridge was two lanes wide and had low concrete sides pock marked with bullet holes. The man was standing in the middle staring down river at the Sportsmans' Club.

There was a speedboat on the river's brown water making a sharp bending turn away from him. There were two American's in the boat in green fatigues. The lily pads near the bank undulated in the wake. Two Vietnamese women in brightly colored *ao dais* strolled along the bank. This seemed to interest the old man. His long white hair and goatee were fluttering in the slight breeze, and he wore a brocaded Chinese suit of green silk. It was frayed and worn.

"*Chao, Ong,*" Tom said, determined to impress somebody with his limited Vietnamese.

The old man turned and grinned broadly at the young people. Several of his teeth were missing and he was drunk. He bowed with exaggerated graciousness and made a relatively long speech. Behind him, on the other side of the river, Grey could see the brown stone walls and the dilapidated ceremonial gates of the Citadel, the onetime Imperial Capitol of Vietnam.

Hoa was laughing. "What'd he say," Tom asked.

"He is glad know us and he wish us..., very, very much happiness and good fortune." She paused and laughed again, "...very much."

"Who is he?" Tom asked. "What's he doing?"

Hoa spoke to the old man for quite a while. "Is farmer," she said finally," He go wedding north of Hue City."

"Alone?"

"Wife is sick," Hoa explained tentatively. "Girls marry..., boys in war."

The questions seemed to deflate the old man's mood and Tom felt guilty for intruding. He said thank you and goodbye and Hoa translated. The old man smiled and wished them well again. Tom took the girl's hand and they started back across the bridge. Then the old man said something else. The two of them turned and he repeated what he had said.

"Well?" Grey asked.

Hoa's head was bent toward him in an attitude of playful submissiveness. "He say you make me walk after you or you have trouble all life."

Tom grinned. "Tell him that our customs are different."

She did and then translated the reply. "He say is nothing wrong with his custom and is foolish to argue with good advice."

Tom bowed to the old man politely and said, "Tell him that I will give his words very serious thought."

That seemed to satisfy the old man. He too bowed and then turned back to contemplate the river.

Hoa and Tom walked across the bridge. They stopped for a moment at the end to watch some boys swimming in the tan slow-moving water. Beyond them some barefoot young girls wearing white blouses and black slacks were doing laundry on the rocks near the shore. They chattered among themselves.

Back on the boulevard the Honda and Citroen auto traffic had increased. The couple created some interest because the city was officially off limits to GIs. No one stopped to talk, however, and Tom and Hoa received only a few pointed glances.

When they got to the Sportsmans' Club Tom started inside with the intention of getting a drink.

Hoa stopped. "Can no go there," she said.

Grey turned, confused. "Why not? I met you there by the pool," he indicated with a nod of his head.

The girl's face was set in a pout. "I sneak in to be alone. I did not know anyone there." She frowned. "I not one those fine ladies inside," she explained, pointing across the street to the old French hotel that stood there. "I one those ladies."

"Oh," Tom was off balance for a moment. He had been trying very hard not to pay too much attention to the girl's small, pert breasts and the gentle flair of her hips. "Well," he said, pulling a Marlboro from his shirt pocket and snapping open his Zippo lighter, "Are you working today?"

She looked at him as he squinted through the smoke. "Hollywood," she said brightly and taking his hand.

◆ ◆ ◆

Standing now in the dark by the window Grey shivered slightly in the cool breeze blowing off the South China Sea. That had been a long time ago and Tom realized that he was a different person. His odds were beginning to bother him. Sometimes he felt like a small animal fearing that it was slowly gaining the attention of a wolf. He was afraid of dying. Had that party been today, he probably would have sat on the veranda with the rest getting quietly drunk and contemplating the river like the old man on the bridge.

He felt soft warm flesh move gently against his back. "*Troi oi!*" she said.

"Hoa put her arms around his chest and squeezed her nude body against his. "What you doing?" She asked softly.

"Thinking," he said without turning from the window.

"Come to bed, is late."

He liked to believe that she was eighteen but he doubted it. Her parents were dead and she supported four younger brothers and sisters. He knew that it was true because he had once met her twelve-year old brother, the pimp. They lived in a strange concrete catacomb-like area of Hue where the streets were only as wide as sidewalks. It could have been a miniature oriental city built for a museum display.

"Come to bed, Tom, you think too much."

He turned and rested his hands on her shoulders. From the hips up she was as fragile and delicately made as a porcelain doll. But her strong, sturdy legs and her short, broad, almost square feet were 100 percent peasant. Tom kissed her full lips.

With her hair cut short she looked alert, and her small, precise features were more easily seen.

"I like your hair short," he said.

She studied him carefully for a moment and then smiled. "Thank you very much. What you wan?"

Tom grinned and shook his head. "Nothing."

Hoa took his hand and led him across the room. The sheets were still warm from her body and the two of them, arms entwined, snuggled deep into the comfort of the bed. Hoa lay on her side with one leg over him and her head resting easily on his shoulder. She was very still for a few moments and then her body trembled slightly and he knew she was asleep. Her slow, even breathing and the gentle weight of her body against his made him acutely aware of how real and living she was.

Despite the war, he was a young man and his heart was still vulnerable. He did not believe in matches made in heaven, his was a generation of cynics, but he could not deny his emotions. Lying there in the hotel with the girl in his arms he felt lost.

FIREBASE NORMANDY

The Squad—Combat Assault

It was still dark on Firebase Normandy. Haynes and Maxwell sat on the roof of a bunker while the sky turned gradually coral pink in the east. Haynes lit a cigarette. "Gonna be a nice day," he said.

Maxwell shivered in the cold, predawn air and rubbed his hands together for warmth. "Every day's a nice day," he said. "Every day's a real good time." He climbed down from the bunker and began digging through his rucksack. "Want some coffee?"

"Haynes nodded, "What'd your old lady have to say?" There had been mail-call the evening before.

Maxwell paused for a moment, "Nothing," he said.

Then his hands were busy again looking for the instant coffee packages.

"Does she still love you?" asked Haynes.

"Guess so," Maxwell said without enthusiasm.

The light was increasing. Haynes could see the mountains surrounding them, long thin ridges running north and south like a pod of giant whales whose humps protruded from the valley's misty sea.

Firebase Normandy was built on one of the highest of the mountains in the area. The Army Engineers had scraped it clean of vegetation and blown holes in the gray rock for the many bunkers. It was a small wilderness fort now with a battery of 155mm howitzers, two batteries of 105mm howitzers, and several 81mm mortar pits for local defense.

There was also a medical facility, a helicopter landing pad, and a gaggle of electronic communications equipment. It looked to Haynes like a dusty brown battleship frozen in a green and rocky ocean from the air.

Like a battleship, it had a crew. The men on Firebase Normandy worked seven days a week, twelve to eighteen-hour shifts. The men of the firebase supplied 24-hour artillery support to brigade units scattered throughout the Area of Operations. Whenever the brigade moved to a new AO, the support troops had to move to a new firebase. Consequently, in addition to their usual duties, they were always engaged in either putting the camp together or taking it apart.

Prescott, the third man sharing the bunker roof, sat up slowly and rubbed his face. "Good morning, Scotty," Haynes said cheerfully.

Prescott ignored him and looked for a cigarette.

The smooth green sandbags of the Tactical Operations Center, TOC, were cold and damp with morning dew. Generator noise ran in the background, their exhaust mixing with the morning mist. Maxwell finished making the coffee. Haynes poured about a third of the canteen cup into his own and added powdered cream and sugar. "Sure are pretty mountains, aren't they?"

"No," Prescott muttered.

"These ain't mountains," Maxwell said, "They're just big hills."

"Hills!" Prescott was visibly agitated. "You're fuckin' nuts, Maxwell. These mothers are straight up."

"Still ain't mountains," insisted Maxwell. "Mountains are like the Rockies."

"With snow on top?" Prescott sneered.

"Yep."

Haynes began rummaging through the ragtag stiff cardboard case of C-rations that the three soldiers had been living out of for the past few days. It was pretty well depleted.

"What's in there?" Maxwell asked.

"Ham 'n eggs."

"What else?"

"Nothing, just three boxes of ham 'n eggs," Haynes answered, holding up two tan C-Ration meal boxes.

"Shit."

"Give them to Kelly," suggested Prescott, "He likes them."

"You're kidding," Haynes remarked.

"No," Maxwell replied. "Kelly is one hard dude."

The firebase was waking up. Helmetless men appeared and began their day's work—business as usual. Kelly came up the path from the perimeter. "You guys ready to roll?"

"No C's," Maxwell said, pointing at the trash-filled cardboard box.

"We'll draw C's in about half an hour." Kelly was very efficient. "Other than that, are you ready to go?"

"Just a shave 'n a haircut," offered Prescott.

"You got plenty of water?" Kelly asked, ignoring Scotty.

"Six canteens apiece," answered Maxwell.

"You'll be glad you got 'em." Kelly looked around the immediate area and frowned. "Police this place up. I'll send you C's later. This bunker is the assembly point, so stick around." He turned and walked back down the path.

"Not even a 'good morning,'" Haynes commented.

"Lifer," said Prescott. "He's trying to make platoon sergeant."

Maxwell was opening a can of ham and eggs using his small P-38 can opener. "He's gonna get it too. Sergeant Edison is short, and the Lieutenant must have hickies on his ass the way Kelly's been acting."

An artillery barrage began, but the men were far enough away from the big guns to speak above the blasts. "Wonder what poor bastard is on the receiving end of that," said Prescott.

"Just be glad it ain't you," Maxwell said, fumbling with a couple of heat tabs.

Haynes sat up and watched the artillery crews. Despite the cool of the morning, the artillerymen already had their shirts off. They worked hard to keep the pieces firing, slamming home large brass encased high explosive rounds, firing, tossing aside the spent casing and ramming in another.

"I hate this war," Maxwell said as he watched the rhythmic movement of the gunners.

"Fancy that," Haynes said as a jeep and trailer pulled up. Haynes got up and went to the trailer. He tossed three C-Ration cases to the ground next to the bunker wall.

The men broke open the boxes using the flash a suppressor on Prescott's M-16 to twist the baling-wire until it snapped.

Haynes carefully sorted the cans into categories: fruit; meals he liked, beef slices and gravy, spaghetti, and boned chicken; meals he didn't like, ham and eggs, beans and franks. In another pile, he deposited such things as pound cake, crackers and cookies. Haynes then took several brown waxed paper utility packs, tore them open, and dumped their contents on the ground. He separated the packets of instant coffee, powdered cream, sugar, salt and pepper, powdered hot chocolate mix, cigarettes, matches, and toilet paper. Then he took several plastic sandwich bags from his rucksack and carefully wrapped and sealed the objects for use later. When he had finished, he went over the bulky sixty pounds of his green nylon and aluminum rucksack and tightened the dozens of cords and straps.

Jones lumbered up the trail and dumped his ruck and his M-16 in a heap.

"Let's go get high," he said to Prescott.

"Kelly will be around."

"Not for a while. We don't go in for a couple of hours yet."

Prescott got to his feet, and Haynes did the same, despite a probing glance from Maxwell.

The three men began working their way casually down toward the jungle that bordered the firebase. Jones stepped over the steep edge into the woods and sat cross-legged in the weeds. The potheads who regularly used this spot had beaten down the foliage. Three joints were lighted, and the men sat in silence, enjoying the smoke.

Haynes' perception changed. The jungle was suddenly greener, and the sky a sharper blue. He was fascinated by the complexity of the jungle floor around him. He spent a few moments studying the intricate insect civilization he was sitting on.

◆ ◆ ◆

When they returned to the bunker, several more members of the squad had shown up. Nearby some bare-chested men were filling sandbags. Haynes smiled at them. He felt a little silly. It was not until he sat down next to his equipment that he realized he had smoked too much. A wave of paranoia swept over him.

He began to perspire, and his stomach felt funny. He lay down on the bunker roof and covered his head with his arms. "Wait it out," he told himself. "Just lay here and trip."

A few feet away, Saunders and Wood, another of the squad's riflemen, were talking. They had a portable radio, and Haynes let his mind drift with the rock'n'roll. *This is the dawning of the Age of Aquarius, Age of Aquarius...* In his head, a cartoon-like dream was unfolding. It seemed as if he was in the basket of a hot air balloon drifting, drifting.

The fear passed, and he slipped quickly into the nether world of his mind. After a few moments, he stirred, brought back by the conversation around him.

"You know what bothers me?" asked Saunders. His voice sounded distant to Haynes.

"No," replied Wood, scratching at a small jungle rot patch on his left temple, not really interested.

"The killing."

Wood laughed. "You ain't done a whole lot of it, fucker."

"I know, but it's not because I haven't been trying."

The two did not speak again for what seemed a long time to Haynes. Then Saunders said, "I'm really starting to hate them."

"Who?" Wood asked, half interested in the conversation.

"The gooks."

"Everybody hates them."

"The other night, when we killed that bunch out in the mountains, it really made me feel good. I really envied Haynes for getting that body count."

"So."

"It's not right," Saunders said, pushing his black-framed Army-issue glasses up his nose with his right index finger. "It's something we have to do, but it shouldn't feel so good."

"Grow up." Wood said, turning away and spitting into the dust.

Haynes was slowly coming down. The heat was starting to bother him, and the pictures in his head had stopped. He sat up and lit a cigarette. Jones and Prescott sat cross-legged like twin black and white Buddhas, staring out into the jungle.

"Zonked," Haynes thought, smiling.

Maxwell was dozing a few feet away in the shade of the bunker. His head rested against his rucksack; his baseball cap covered his eyes. The M-60 lay across the top of the rucksack frame, clear of the ground. It gleamed a dull gunmetal blue, and silver where it was worn. The receiver was wrapped in an olive drab towel to keep the dust out.

"Man," Jones said, "I'm in *no* mood for a combat assault."

"Well, you'd better get in the mood, bro," Johnson said as he walked up carrying an olive-green wooden box. Kelly arrived right behind him and ordered the squad to get their shit together.

Haynes got to his feet and buckled on his pistol belt. He carried two canteens, a first-aid package, a couple of lemon-shaped hand grenades, his bayonet, and a six-inch Buck hunting knife he had bought in the States before shipping out for

Vietnam. He struggled into his rucksack. The weight was too familiar to be oppressive. Then he looped a few M-16 ammo bandoleers around his neck. He took four more hand grenades from the box Johnson had brought and stuffed them in his shirt's side pockets, two in each pocket. Satisfied, he picked up his rifle and slung the lightweight weapon over his right shoulder by its sling. And lastly, he picked up his helmet, holding it by his right leg. All around him, the other squad members were getting into their gear. One by one, the men began lumbering off toward the chopper pad. Each one of them a walking arsenal.

The path to the pad led along the backbone of the firebase. Kelly followed behind the soldiers like a den mother, making sure he had everybody. He herded them across the pierced steel planking, PSP, of the helicopter landing area, and had them sit grouped in fire teams beside the ammo bunker. Specialist Four Monaghan, a fire team leader, took out a toothbrush and circulated it among his men. Haynes, Maxwell, and Prescott each took a turn in the name of oral hygiene. Monaghan, once a Golden Glove Middle Weight boxer in Boston, had sandy hair, and his skin tended to burn rather than tan. Following Monaghan's lead Johnson started the other toothbrush around his own team: Jones, Saunders, Wood, and Drew.

On either side of the squad, the rest of the company stretched along the pad's edge. Most of the men were seated, but here and there soldiers stood in silent clusters. Kelly and another squad leader were a few feet in front of Haynes joking with Sergeant Edison. The sun was crawling higher in the sky, and the men were starting to sweat.

A green Chinook helicopter was circling below the firebase, its twin rotors flashing in the sunlight. A full cargo net hung below it.

The men in the company watched absently as the Chinook began gaining altitude. Suddenly the big chopper broke over the lip of the firebase, and its powerful engines set up a swirling storm of dust and sand that enveloped the soldiers. Particles of grit struck the GI's faces like sleet.

Haynes turned his head away and closed his eyes. The roar of the Chinook filled his world. He did not look again until the sound of the helicopter began to fade. When he did, he was the cargo net sitting neatly on the pad. Several shirtless men approached and began untying the net.

"Just flew in, took a shit, and flew out," Scotty said, rubbing the dust from his eyes.

"Only way to fight a war," commented Jones.

"They get their share of war," Maxwell said.

"Prescott waxed philosophical. "You know, I've been thinking about that a lot."

"About what?" Maxwell asked.

"About the best way to fight a war," Scotty answered, shifting under the weight of his rucksack. "This push-button stuff sounds pretty good. Everybody just hits the old button and then goes home and sees how they came out on the six o'clock news. Chicago is evaporated. New York is 80 percent maimed. Everybody in Phoenix dies of radiation sickness..." Prescott paused, impressed with his own idea. "None of the humpin' up and down mountains or sleeping in the mud. Quick and clean. I think it'd be a helluva improvement. Take your chances and get it over with."

Kelly appeared and gathered the squad around him. "Okay,

listen up," he said. "Our platoon's going to be the first wave, so you guy's will have to be on your toes. When you get off the birds, I want you to get away from them quick and hit the ground. Don't fire unless you know it's hot. The hunting will be a lot better if we can slip in as quietly as a stick of Huey's will make possible.

"The Hueys are going to have to turn around and fly out the way they came in, so keep your damn heads down if you don't want a face full of tail rotor. The slicks will turn to their left and circle out, each one followed by the next one. If the LZ is hot, stay where you first hit the dirt until we can get things organized. There will be an interval before the next slick comes in. "Got it?"

Kelly looked intently at each man.

The men of the squad nodded.

"Okay. They'll be here in a few minutes, so get on your feet and be ready to go."

The squad's two fire teams worked their way out onto the pad. The platoon's other two squads followed, and the men who would constitute the initial assault were assembled. Across the pad, Haynes could see the other two platoons of the infantry line company moving up.

Four olive drab UH-1D Huey slicks appeared over the rim of the firebase. As they hovered a couple of feet above the planking, the soldiers climbed aboard.

The helicopters bobbed in their hover as each man added his weight to the machines. Haynes sat next to the door, resting his pack against the back bulkhead. The helicopter gained a little altitude and then tilted forward, dipping slightly. It came out of ground effect and flew out over the jungle. The side of the mountain fell away sharply, and the helicopters were suddenly very high. The cold air and the vibrations of the bird relaxed Haynes. He sat back against his rucksack and laid his 16 across his lap. The gray-green jungle stretched from horizon to horizon. He found it ironic that it could be so beautiful from the air and so rotten on the ground.

Strong hands gripped Haynes and shoved him violently toward the open sky. He arched his back and twisted toward the interior of the ship. Prescott was pleased with his joke. He took his hands-off Haynes and grinned. "Be alert, trooper," he shouted over the roar of the engines.

Haynes took deep breaths to settle his jangled nerves. "Christ, I thought I was going out the damn door!" he thought furiously. Gradually his heart slowed. He wiped his palms on his fatigue pants legs.

The Hueys swung west and began working laterally across the mountains. A dense gray bank of clouds forced them down and between the gaps in the ridges. As the jungle walls sped by, Haynes hoped that there was not an extremely lucky NVA rifleman in the trees with an AK-47 and a lack of common sense.

Maxwell tapped Haynes' shoulder and pointed at a bombed-out spot on the slope of a mountain to the right. Haynes nodded his head in agreement. Maxwell pulled back on the bolt and armed the M-60 machine gun. Haynes pulled a magazine from a cloth bandoleer and shoved it into his rifle. Then he chambered a round and hit the locking mechanism with the heel of his right hand to seat the shell securely.

The helicopters turned again and began to drop rapidly toward the spot that Maxwell had pointed out. The nearness of the jungle brought Haynes back to the reality he had forgotten temporarily on the firebase. He concentrated on the rapidly approaching ground, trying to put everything out of his mind except the movements he would have to make in the next few moments.

The choppers leveled off and went into the LZ from the north. Haynes swung his legs out of the ship and positioned them on the helicopter's skids. The left-side door gunner opened up on the jungle, spewing brass cartridge cases. The bird stopped suddenly, nose high, and hovered a few feet off the ground.

Haynes jumped and landed running. He sprinted ten yards toward the edge of the jungle and dove for the ground. He panted, blood pounding in his ears. Suddenly another squad member dropped to the ground a few feet to his left. Saunders tripped over the man, his helmet and rifle flying. He landed with a "woof."

They waited.

Nothing happened.

The choppers were moving out of earshot, and the silence was growing. Haynes loosened his rucksack and worked it around in front of him. Then he turned and looked for Maxwell and the gun.

A man was lying in a heap ten yards behind him.

Kelly was kneeling over him.

"It's Maxwell," he said, sadly. "He's dead. I think his neck is broken."

The Lieutenant and his command group came up. He said, "I

saw it. The helicopter skid clipped him in the back of the head as it turned to leave."

FIREBASE BLAZE

The Squad—Routine Patrol

It was late when Kelly's men climbed off of the trucks into the rain at firebase Blaze. FB Blaze sat on the south side of Highway QL547, the road that led from the heart of the northern A Shau Valley to the City of Hue. The battalion's two other companies had arrived earlier. They spent the afternoon clearing the deserted base camp of booby traps and harassing the large rat population. The 101st Airborne Division troops would be operating in this area, and so the old firebase had to be re-secured. Because it was raining and because the company did not have perimeter duty, Kelly let the squad members sleep inside the bunker complex.

With flashlights and candles, they searched the abandoned underground caverns like archeologists exploring a lost city. Everywhere they found the marks of those who had preceded them. Stakes were driven horizontally into a dirt wall to support a makeshift bunk. A plywood partition that someone had constructed in an attempt to gain privacy.

In places piles of trash that the rats had chewed and sorted littered the floors. Finally, they found two adjacent bunkers that were relatively dry, and the exhausted men made their camp. That night the rats had their revenge as the scampered around and over the sleeping soldiers.

In the morning, without the sun to wake them, the men slept late. At six-thirty, Kelly came in and hustled them out to a mess truck sent out from Camp Eagle. They stood in line patiently for powdered eggs and powdered milk served on paper plates and paper cups. The hot meal was welcome, even if the eggs were runny and the bacon limp and greasy.

After breakfast, Kelly formed the squad up for patrol. He had an AN/PRC25 manpacked FM radio attached to a rucksack frame and decorated with several M18 soup-can shaped smoke grenades - yellow, red, and lavender—with him. "Drew, you studied engineering in college, didn't you?"

"Yeah, two years at Georgia Tech," he answered. "Old story. Ran out of money, ran into my draft board." He sounded bitter.

"Okay," Kelly said, "You're now the official RTO for this squad. Stay handy."

"Roger that," Drew said without objection. Picking up the radio by the shoulder straps, he walked off toward the bunker to transfer his pack to the radio frame.

◆ ◆ ◆

With Prescott, a small, gnarled Tennessee boy with a shock of black hair on point, they moved out in single file across the river and then turned south. The terrain was mostly flat and covered with scrub and occasional palm groves. The surface was broken here and there by weathered dike walls, collapsed wells, and abandoned hamlets. It had once been good rice land.

The squad moved slowly. Prescott was an experienced woodsman who insisted that the only differences between hunting deer and hunting gooks were that gooks shot back, and there wasn't any limit.

The game was different here than it was in the mountains.

Whenever American forces occupied Blaze, these trails were routinely patrolled. Instead of a Reconnaissance-In-Force, smaller squad-sized units patrolled widely in search of the enemy. They followed the routes the enemy would have to use if he intended to assault the firebase. He would have to assault the base if he intended to assault Hue. In theory, the constant reconnaissance made this impossible for the NVA.

Kelly pulled slack to Prescott's point, and Drew, in turn, followed him with the radio. Haynes, with the machinegun, followed Drew. Despite being a fire team leader, Monaghan also acted as assistant machine gunner instead of Prescott. Like Haynes, he was festooned with bandoleers of 7.62mm machinegun ammunition and his pouches of ammo for his M-16.

Monaghan was a large, taciturn individual who rarely spoke, but in his calm and steady way, he pulled more than his weight. Specialist Johnson led his team after Monaghan: Jones, Wood with his stubby M79 40mm grenade launcher. Lastly, PFC Saunders, pushing his glasses back onto the bridge of his nose as he walked through the heat. The soldiers maintained about ten feet between each other as the squad patrolled the area.

Kelly felt he had adjusted the squad well for this different type of mission. Prescott's almost supernatural ability to read tracks and signs made him a good pointman. Still, he tended to be slow and to waste time studying marks in the jungle that had nothing to do with the immediate problem of finding the enemy.

In a deserted NVA base camp, he had once spent almost twenty minutes in the brush and discovered the enemy's latrine. But now they had the time, and they wanted all of the information they could get, no matter how trivial, so Kelly tolerated his pace.

Giving the radio to Drew was another decision that Kelly considered sound. All of the men had a fundamental knowledge of radio procedures and map reading. However, Kelly felt that Drew, with his engineering experience, would handle the precise but straightforward mathematics of calling in artillery support better than any of the rest if needed.

Prescott held up his fist, stopping the squad. The men squatted down, facing alternately in different directions. Prescott had found a small clearing where someone had taken a lunch break. It was littered with rusted C-ration cans and scraps of wet cardboard. At first, Kelly was frustrated. It was evident that the site had been used by American troops. Then Prescott showed him fresh marks in the shallow mud. He told the squad to take a break while he and Prescott studied the marks.

Haynes sat down beside Drew and half-listened. The Southerner, speaking with his soft accent, reported their position to the company commander at the firebase.

Saunders sat down too and tried to make conversation. Haynes gave him a dirty look and turned away. His dislike for Saunders had increased sharply since Maxwell had been killed. The men in the squad were loosely paired by the buddy system, but no one wanted Saunders.

Now that Maxwell was dead, Saunders took the opportunity to

pair with Haynes. Mike remembered a saying they had in Advanced Infantry Training at Fort Polk about those trainees that just didn't seem to get it, "If I'm ever in a foxhole with him and we get attacked, he's the first thing I shoot."

Haynes grudgingly conceded that Saunders was getting better, but it did not change his attitude. What bothered him most was Saunders' daydreaming; he just didn't seem to understand the situation. He could hump, and he knew what he was supposed to do, but Haynes had the feeling that he was just going through the motions, his mind a thousand miles away. It made Mike really angry. He did not like to let his emotions rule him, but he couldn't help it in this case. Too much was at stake.

Kelly and Prescott decided that a single man had made the tracks. Whether he had been there by coincidence or as a lookout, they did not know. With Prescott still on point, they moved out again, slower now even than before.

Haynes stayed about ten feet behind Drew. After the months in the dense jungle, the relatively open terrain bothered him, and he did not like the slow pace. During the next half-hour, they covered no more than a kilometer.

Ahead of him, Haynes saw Drew stop for a trail intersection. He hefted the M-60 taking the weapon off "safe." He moved quickly to the intersection, relieving Drew, who moved on, antenna waving as he trotted forward. Haynes rapidly scanned up and down the intersecting trail and waited for Monaghan. The path seemed deserted, but Mike kept his eyes moving along it. It was several moments before he felt Monaghan's boot next to his. He moved out quickly.

Haynes heard a strange grunting sound behind him. Turning, he glanced back down the trail. He saw Saunders fumbling with his ammunition bandoleers and his rifle. It was apparent that he had dropped one. Mike turned in disgust and started to catch up to Drew, who was halfway across a small clearing ahead. There was a white flash, and the air cracked. The concussion lifted Haynes into the air and slammed him into a palm tree. Burning shrapnel tore into his left forearm, and something heavy landed on him.

Panic and fear drove a wedge into Haynes' consciousness and made it difficult for him to react. He thrashed at the dead weight on his legs, trying to free himself. Suddenly Kelly was beside him, crawling through the brush on all fours. His helmet had fallen off, and his sandy hair was plastered to his head with sweat. He said something to Hayes, but Mike couldn't understand him. It sounded like a record being played very slowly. Kelly pulled five feet of damp sod from Haynes' legs freeing him.

Rolling to his right Haynes caught a glimpse of Monaghan staggering to his feet, his chest crisscrossed with linked belts of M-60 ammunition. Haynes watched as Monaghan searched around in the vines and creepers for his M-16. For an instant, Haynes had thought he was looking at Maxwell.

Haynes sat up, turning to face the clearing. Clouds of yellow, red, and lavender smoke swirled among the bushes and trees. Cradling his wounded arm, he saw Kelly, still without a helmet, moving around in the rainbow fog. The rest of the squad was moving rapidly into the clearing, hastily establishing a small perimeter. Monaghan appeared next to Mike, yellow smoke tendrils coiling around his legs. "You okay?" he asked.

Mike held his left arm aloft with his right hand. Bright crimson blood smeared his forearm. Blood on his face trickled into his mouth. Carefully, he flexed his left hand's fingers to satisfy himself that the damage was not significant, but he could feel something foreign inside. "I'll make it," he said. "What in hell happened."

"Beats the shit out of me. A mine maybe... In any case, Drew's had it." Monaghan fumbled clumsily with Haynes' first aid pouch and pulled out a three-inch square compress bandage. Then he began to wrap it tightly around Haynes' throbbing arm, stanching the bleeding. "You'll be okay. Tell you what, I'll take the 60 and you take this." Monaghan said, passing his M-16 to Haynes.

Using the rifle as support, Haynes pulled himself to his feet. Rocking slightly, he felt his body stabilize; his balance return.

"Anybody else get it?" Haynes asked.

"I don't think so," Monaghan said as he retrieved the M-60.

"Hope everybody's okay," Haynes said, dreamily stooping to pick up his helmet. His stomach was queasy, and he was afraid he was going to be sick.

Like a tired old man, he slowly shuffled into the fog, dragging his weapon by the barrel. As he approached Kelly, he could hear him swearing viciously to himself. The bent and blasted radio lay at Kelly's feet. A few of the smoke grenades that had been attached to it were still sputtering. A small crater steamed where Drew had been. The dead man's chest still hung in the radio harness tossed into the brush on one side of the trail. Blood was everywhere, clotting in the yellow-brown dust.

Haynes felt a few drops, like the first of a summer shower, fall against his cheek. He looked up. In the tops of the palm trees were shreds of flesh and uniform. Haynes stared horrified. "What the hell did all this?"

"A mortar shell, I think," Kelly answered, kicking at the sides of the crater. "See those wires over there? They lead off somewhere to a small generator..., probably one of our claymore triggers. They wire a blasting cap into the shell and bury it." He looked off in the direction the wires ran and swore again. "Fuck! Command Detonated."

Monaghan got out a green plastic poncho, and he and Prescott began gathering up the pieces of Drew. Haynes realized that Saunders's clumsiness had probably saved his life. It made him uneasy.

"Kelly called the shaken squad together. "It's pretty obvious that this patrol is finished. When the fuckers blew the mine, they took the radio with it..., with Drew. We're gonna go out now, back the way we came."

Quickly the squad formed up behind Kelly, who took the point himself. They were a long way from home, and without the radio, they were vulnerable. Haynes felt a sharp pain in his ankle with each step he took. Monaghan caught up to him and offered to help by Mike declined. Monaghan had the lumpy poncho that contained what they could find of Drew tied to his rucksack. It leaked blood.

Haynes stuffed his left hand under his pistol belt for support, but after a while, the pain in his arm became unbearable. He then hooked his left arm around his right shoulder strap, elevating the wound and easing the throbbing pain somewhat.

Kelly, fearing an ambush, quickly led the nervous squad down the twisting trail they had traversed so slowly earlier.

Haynes adjusted his M-16, nestling it under his right armpit and holding the pistol grip. He ran the strap over his right shoulder so he could fire the rifle with one hand if necessary.

After nearly an hour, they came to a high mound of dirt, and old dike wall about seven feet high with its sloping sides covered with stunted grass. Behind it stood several tall palms. Motioning the squad to halt, Kelly moved up the dirt wall, peered over the rim, rolled rapidly over, and disappeared from sight. The team fanned out on either side of the trail, facing out and rearward toward an unseen but feared enemy. The sun was high in the sky. Salty sweat poured down Haynes' face, getting into his eyes and mouth. He rubbed at it with the fingers of his upraised left hand, and for the first time realized that he had a cut and a bruise on his cheek.

Kelly's head and upper body appeared over the top of the dike, and with a sweeping motion, he signaled the squad to advance. One by one the men went up and over the wall. When his turn came, Haynes scrambled up the dirt slope. At the top, Kelly grabbed him by the collar and pulled him over. He slid down the far side on his rump, pushing against the slope with his rifle butt.

Johnson's fire team was already positioned in a small depression surrounded by a small grove. The four soldiers, hugging the ground, rifles pointed outward in a wide defensive arc. Looking back the way he had come, Haynes saw the Prescott had taken the M-60 from Monaghan and was stationed atop the wall.

Kelly called his team leaders over. As an afterthought, he signaled for Haynes as well. The four soldiers squatted in a circle on the ground. Johnson unholstered a canteen from his pistol belt, took a long swallow and passed it to Monaghan.

"I don't know how much shit we're in," Kelly said. "The gooks could be right behind us or all around. I don't know if the bastard that pulled the trigger on Drew just didn't like radios or if they've got something planned, and they want us without communications. Either way, we've got to get back quickly.

"When we get close the firebase, we're going to have to be extra careful.
We'll be coming in unannounced. The battalion should be looking for us after we miss a radio check, but we can't count on it. We'll just have to play it by ear. I want to move out in three minutes. No longer."

Kelly's look was hard.

The team leaders left to take up positions on the perimeter, and Kelly turned to Haynes. "How you doing?"

Mike nodded his head. "I'll make it," he said.

"Sure you will. I saw you limping back there. Anything wrong with your leg?"

"Twisted it when I got hit," Haynes said. "It's feeling better."

"Well, we'll have to dust you off when we get back," Kelly took a small black notebook from his pocket and wrote with a government-issue pen.

"Can't they just stitch it up on the firebase?" Haynes did not want to be evacuated and risk being reassigned to another unit.

"There's probably still some metal in there, and it might get infected." Kelly patted him on the back. "You rest a little now. We've got a long hike ahead of us."

When they moved out again, Johnson was at the point with

Jones pulling slack. Haynes' arm continued to throb. He kept adjusting it to ease the pain. The best position was to hold his right collar with his left hand, but even that was good for just a few minutes. The ankle bothered him less and less, and soon his limp was barely noticeable.

Johnson held up his hand. The squad stopped silently, each man standing in a half-crouch in the burning sun. The seconds ticked slowly by. Haynes stood midway down the file, just in front of Monaghan. Sweat dripped into his eyes and off his nose. Rotating his head gently from side to side, he tried to determine what it was that caused Johnson to call the halt. His stomach was tight, and a muscle in his bruised cheek began to twitch. His thighs started to ache from holding the crouch. Slowly, he lowered his left hand from his collar to the foregrip of the M-16. His right index finger tightened imperceptibly on the trigger, taking in the slack, waiting.

Kelly worked his way forward to where Johnson stood. Everything on the trail stood out in sharp relief.

Haynes could hear shallow breathing behind him and the occasional clink of the M-60 ammunition. Sweat continued to flow freely down Mike's body. He pressed his lips together. They felt dry and chapped. He bit his upper lip gently, trying to pull away the crud.

Without a word or a signal, Johnson resumed the march. The squad took no breaks. When they approached the firebase, they swung to the west so they could go in along an old dirt road. Kelly figured it was safer. They would be in sight of Blaze when they hit the dusty road. The fear left them, and the soldiers began to chatter with relief. Monaghan caught up to Haynes and walked beside him.

"Hairy fuckin' shit, huh Michael m' lad?"

"Yes *indeed!*" Haynes said, relief evident in his voice.

Monaghan had less than two weeks to go before he DEROS-ed home to the World; to the States. He was walking comfortably despite carrying the heavy gun and Drew's remains. He walked with a half-smile on his face. The M-60 was balanced across his right shoulder, and he held it by the barrel.

A shiny brass belt of ammunition dangled from the gun's receiver. Monaghan pushed his helmet back with his left hand, and a lock of dark, sweaty hair flopped over his forehead. Drew's blood soaked the backs of his calves and boots where it had leaked from the poncho tied to Monaghan's rucksack.

"You sure are a sharp looking team leader," Haynes said, smiling. "A swell example to all."

"You look like shit," replied Monaghan with a grin.

Nobody ever mentioned Drew after that patrol.

HEARTS AND MINDS

Grey—35 and a Wakeup

It was morning when Grey snuck back into the MACV compound. He found MacEvy in the mess hall.
"Have a good time?" MacEvy said, looking up from his coffee.

Grey smiled as he put his tray down across from MacEvy.

"Love in bloom," MacEvy said. "Must be costing you a fortune.

"Some guys buy stereos; some guys buy cameras..." Grey said lightly,

Mac changed the subject. "Think you can handle a little hearts and minds work today?"

"What's up?" Grey said, digging into his eggs and grits.

"I've got to go wrap up some details near the coast for the story you're doing about the kid that's going to get his foot operated on out on that German Hospital ship."Grey ate slowly. He studied his tray: ham and eggs, real milk, pancakes, grits with butter. "Not such a bad life," he thought.

After breakfast, Tom went to Mac's room and retrieved his

cameras and a notebook. As an afterthought, he dug in his ruck and got an extra bandoleer of ammunition for his M-16.

MacEvy met him with the jeep outside the front of the compound. They drove north through the city, crossed the Perfume River, and then turned east toward the South China Sea. Grey lit a joint.

"You just stay stoned, don't you?"

"Yep," Grey answered, taking another toke, he leaned his head back, face to the morning sun.

"To hell with the war?" MacEvy asked.

Tom noted more than a trace of disapproval in his friend's voice. "What war?" he asked.

It was a clear day, and the light was good. Grey got out the Leica camera and loaded it with high-speed Ektachrome color slide film. He let his eye rove over the countryside. A man peddling an ancient water wheel, *click*, three small children on the back of an impassive water buffalo, *click*, and an old woman headed for a market with two baskets on a balancing pole over her shoulder, *click*.

"I'll tell you the truth, Grey, I don't have a lot of respect for you anymore. When I first met you, you knew what you were doing. You were cool in a fight, and you were good at your job."

The sky was cobalt blue, and they could smell the sea. Grey thought a moment before he replied. "Once upon a time, he began, "I was a pretty gung-ho combat reporter. I used to spend a lot of time in the field chasing the war and a lot of time on firebases writing up my copy in the middle of the night.

"There are two basic rules for a good Army journalist. The good guys never lose, and the good guys never get killed. If four of our guys get greased in a firefight, and we kill one gook, then you are expected to write up the one and forget the four." Tom took another drag on the joint before continuing. "You're not supposed to lie about the number of enemy killed. They do that back at headquarters."

MacEvy didn't seem impressed and said so.

"I don't give a shit," Tom replied. "You know, writing combat stories is like being a sportswriter," he said, "It's got the same aura of wholesome masculine sweat and locker-room-good-fellowship.

"Once, I was pretty proud of my work. It wasn't Pulitzer Prize stuff, maybe, but I managed to hit the wires once in a while. I got a lot of soldiers' names in their hometown papers. That struck me as a worthwhile endeavor, getting a little publicity and recognition for the dudes fighting this war."

Grey paused and took a shot from the canteen of whisky on his hip. Pot to get him high and Scotch to stabilize his head. It was a tricky trip, but he had learned to ride it. He tugged on his hat brim, partially to cover his eyes before he continued.

"Then I realized that a whole bunch of my readers were little boys—twelve, fourteen years old. Little boys were coming home from school and reading in the evening paper about what a lot of fun war is."

The jeep came to a ferry landing and had to wait.

A middle-aged Vietnamese woman approached Grey and motioned him to follow her. She did not speak.

"*Dinky Dau*," Mac said, tapping his head with an index finger. "Hangs around here and blows GIs for handouts. She's too ugly to fuck."

"Nice."

"Sha Na Na, life goes on."

The ferry returned to their side of the river. Mac gunned the engine and moved the jeep up the bent and rusted pierced steel planking than served as gangplanks onto the wooden-decked ferry. In a cloud of blue diesel smoke and creaking pulleys, the boat angled across the river.

Grey settled back in the jeep seat and let the rank odors of engine exhaust, sweat, mud, rotting canvas, dead fish, and decaying plant matter move over him in a redolent aroma.

After leaving the ferry on the other side, they passed through a relatively large village and turned onto a dirt road that led back into the jungle.

"Be kinda cool," Mac said, "From here on, it's more or less Viet Cong territory."

"What do you mean?"

"The fishermen," explained Mac. "They tend to support the other side. Something related to taxes, I think. They don't pay them."

"Okay," Grey said, sitting up a little more alertly.

"There's a sort of mutual agreement between the ARVNs and the villagers. You look the other way, and we'll look the other way," MacEvy elaborated.

"Is that how the kid got shot?" Grey asked. "Looking the other way?"

"The kid got shot a long time ago."

They came to an ARVN guard post. Mac dismounted and got into a discussion with the young South Vietnamese soldier. He called Grey over.

"Admire their B.A.R.," he said, "They just got it, and they're proud."

Grey examined the heavy relic of World War II and decided he preferred the M-60 that had replaced it in the U.S. arsenal. Still, it was a potent weapon. "Number one," he said, handing the weapon back, "Beaucoup kill VC."

The ARVN soldier looked a little startled. It occurred to Grey that the young man had not thought about the weapon in those terms.

Beyond the guard post, the road deteriorated further. Mac drove slowly. They lurched through the tunnel in the sparse coastal jungle.

The village sat on the other side of a small salt marsh stream. They parked the jeep and locked it with a padlock welded to a heavy chain that ran through the steering wheel and the driver's side seat frame, and then crossed the stream on an old wooden footbridge.

MacEvy led the way between the Vietnamese huts. The people looked at the Americans curiously. There was only one permanent looking building in the village. It was a single-story cement block and stucco cafe. It opened on one end by a garage door. Many boys played at a fooz ball table that stood under a thatched-roofed awning on the front of the building. Mac went into the cafe and spoke to a middle-aged man. After a few minutes, both men approached Grey.

"The Chief," explained Grey. "He's going to take us to the fisherman, the boy's father."

They crossed another footbridge, and then the brushy jungle ended, and the clean white dunes of the beach began. A group of about twenty Vietnamese followed, chattering. Grey remembered what Mac had said earlier. If this was Viet Cong territory, the two Americans were easy marks. His hand slipped onto the pistol grip of his 16.

The procession passed a row of old, but well-tended fishing boats, which had been hauled onto the beach and held upright with bamboo logs. The boats were multicolored above the waterline and had large eyes painted on their bows. Stretched across bamboo frames were large swatches of fishing nets drying in the sun.

In places, men stood reweaving holes in the nets while others worked on the boats, and still, others lounged in the shade. All of them were nut-brown from the unrelenting South China Sea sun. They were slim but hard-muscled. Their teeth were stained almost black from chewing betel nuts, which gave their faces a haunted look. Their hands were thickly calloused.

Their eyes followed the Americans as they passed.

The old fisherman's hut was halfway up the gentle curving beach of the village cove. He seemed genuinely happy to see them. A stray round from a firefight had crippled his only grandson, a boy about six-years-old, a year earlier. Like the fishermen on the beach, the boy was walnut brown from the tropical sun. His grandfather's tanned forearms flexed muscles like corded steel as his large, work-worn hands opened several bottles of cold beer.

The German hospital ship was due off the coast shortly. The boy would be airlifted via helicopter to the vessel for an operation that would, hopefully, restore him to something close to normal. It was this mission of mercy that guaranteed the GIs' safe passage through this VC village.

After MacEvy straightened out the details with the boy's grandfather, there was another round of cold beer, some flattery, and good wishes exchanged. Tom thought of the emotionally crippled orphans at Phu Bai, whose hearts and minds had already been won. Maybe it was just that sophisticated operations and therapy couldn't help them.

It was late afternoon when the jeep arrived back at the ferry. They had to wait about fifteen minutes for a small ARVN convoy to cross first. The smell of diesel exhaust hung sweetly in the humid haze. MacEvy turned the jeep off. The engine ticked a few times, cooling.

"You think you can do a story about the kid?" MacEvy asked.

Grey lit a joint, snapped his Zippo closed, and leaned back in the canvas seat. "Yeah."

"Won't compromise your principles or anything?"

The convoy's last vehicle was a two and a half-ton truck with quad-mounted .50 caliber machine guns mounted on a semi-armored gun mount. Several Americans crewed the weapon, and they had painted its name below the gun barrels. It was "Birth Control."

"I guess those guys drew a little escort duty," Mac observed.

"I did a story about quad fifties once," Grey said, laconically.

"Helluva weapon," Mac said as he started the jeep, put it raspingly into first gear, and drove with a lurch onto the ferry.

"Really?" Grey paused. "I thought it was a good story," Grey continued. "But it never got printed."

"Why not?"

"Well," Grey said, "It seems that according to the Geneva Convention, or something, the quads are strictly an anti-aircraft weapon consider too terrible to be used against personnel. The Army censors at MACV thought it more prudent to scrap my story than to give the Communists an air force."

"What are you trying to tell me?" MacEvy snapped.

"Hey, get the fuck off my back!"

They rolled off the ferry and pulled up the steep dirt bank to the edge of the blacktop road. Traffic was light, and they rolled smoothly toward Hue, the jeep's tires humming on the pavement. Mac topped the small vehicle out and about forty-five in fourth gear.

Grey relaxed and enjoyed the fresh evening air. He propped one foot on the low door frame. Dusk was the time of day that Grey liked best in Vietnam. The temperature dropped, and human activity slowed to an elegant, languid pace.

It made him think of gin and tonics on the veranda of a plantation, with fragrant breezes rustling in the palms.

"I'm worried about you, Tom," MacEvy said.

"Afraid I'm not holding up my end of the war effort?"

"I've got a feeling you're gonna slip a gear. You're not the same guy I used to know." He said, glancing at Grey.

"I'm short," Grey replied. "Everybody gets a little strange when they get short."

"I can see your point," Mac admitted reluctantly. "You figure you've done your part, and you've got a right to kick back and take it easy for a while. You've gotten around enough to see how many guys have cushy jobs like mine. You know how much better a deal the officers usually get, six months in the woods, and then an administrative assignment in the rear. But, amigo, what about the grunts on the line? A lot of those guys spend twelve months solid out there in the mud with their asses on the line every day."

"I know it's not fair, and so do you," Grey nodded his head in agreement. "But I've also heard that some poor college kids have to stay up all night studying for exams."

The road led them back into Hue. Grey liked the city. He often wondered what it would look like in peacetime, or what it was like in the Imperial days before the French came. Even dirty and cluttered with concertina wire and soldiers, the city has the distinctive marks of a very beautiful place. Saigon was the same way. Grey remembered that he had not truly appreciated Indochina until he went to Singapore on R&R. When he returned to Vietnam and gotten off the plane at Ton Son Nhut, it had felt like he had come home.

"Can I tell you something," Mac asked, "as a friend?"

"You've been telling me things all day," Grey snapped sourly.

"Yeah, but have you haven't been listening." When Grey didn't reply, MacEvy continued. "The dope over here is supposed to be some of the best in the world. You've been a junky ever since I met you, but you smoke a helluva lot more of that shit than you used to…"

"Mac."

"Okay, okay. I don't know anything about marijuana or what it does to your head. But I do know about booze, and I know what you've got in that canteen. You're getting some real bad habits, fella, and they aren't going away just because you get off a 707 in Oakland. It's going to be a couple of years before you get your head back together if you're lucky."

"MacEvy," Grey said, "Any guy that comes out of this war with just booze and dope to get over is damn lucky."

They arrived back and MACV and turned the jeep in. Grey was always depressed whenever he left Vietnam proper for the Army. He could not help but be grateful for a job that allowed him to see a lot of the country, if not always under the best circumstances. Most American soldiers spent their entire tours on massive bases like Camp Eagle or Long Binh Post. Except for the heat and the rockets, they might have been at Fort Leonard Wood, Missouri. The hours were longer in Nam, and the chicken shit was often worse, but it was the same Army.

The mess hall was closed, but they managed to talk one of the cooks out of some cold fried chicken. Then Mac went to make arrangements for a chopper to pick up the kid in a couple of days, and Grey went back to the room. He mixed himself a drink and sat on his bunk, reviewing the material he had on the kid. Propaganda writing to be effective required an angle, and he didn't have one yet.

Once you had the right angle or perspective, you could make the truth seem to be anything you wanted it to be. He studied the notes for a few minutes and then threw them aside, sick of the whole thing.

Despite the Scotch he had a horrible feeling in the pit of his stomach. The A Shau operation was not a joke. He had the feeling that MacEvy's tall, lean captain was moving heaven and hell in an attempt to get through the communications maze to USARV-IO and have Tom assigned to the operation. If the captain did get hold of Long Binh, and if Grey's few friends at headquarters did not sense the danger and manage to reduce the request to a tangle of red tape, he was lost. The Army had him by the balls.

If he went back south now and risked disobeying his orders, the Army could hold him in Vietnam virtually forever, pending judicial action. Grey had no doubt whatever that, given the opportunity, they would screw him thoroughly. A man on his way home and out of the service was a perfect choice to make an example. First, because he was no longer a real part of his unit and, second, because he suffered so visibly.

Tom knew that his only real hope lay in the intricate complexity of military administration and his resourcefulness.

Mac came in and mixed himself a drink and a fresh one for Tom. "I've got a bird laid on for 0800 day after tomorrow," he said. "Air America rather than one of ours. The Germans are a sensitive bunch."

"Good." Grey slid off the bed and started going through the tapes stacked in the wooded crate.

The crate was standing on end with the stereo on top, speakers to either side. He skipped over Johnny Cash and Loretta Lynn and found a Simon and Garfunkel.

"Sergeant Kolisch is coming over later," Mac said, sitting in the battered green vinyl armchair.

"Who's he?" Grey asked.

"Kolisch works with the Popular Forces, the PFs—an Advisor."

The second Scotch improved Grey's mood. He sat back down on the bunk, leaned against the cracked plaster wall, and listened to the music. *Cloudy, my thoughts are scattered, and they're cloudy...* There were a lot of good things in life, he decided.

The trick was being slick enough to catch the goods things and to duck the bad ones. The problem wasn't you; it was other people. If you could develop the knack of not getting involved in other human beings' lives, you would have it made. Cats were like that, he thought. They suffered alone and died alone. They didn't owe anybody anything. An infantryman told Grey once that the worst thing about Vietnam was seeing your friends get fucked up. The way to avoid that was not to have any friends.

Kolisch was a big, florid-faced master sergeant in his midthirties. Mac introduced them and mixed another drink. "How's the children's crusade?" he asked as he tossed aside an empty bottle and pulled another from the cabinet bar.

"Okay," Kolisch said. "The kids are pretty tough."

"What do they do?" Grey asked.

"Where's he been?" Kolisch said, turning to MacEvy.

"He's up from Saigon-way," explained MacEvy. "Public Information Office."

"Oh," Kolisch said, "a REMF."

"Trying his damnedest to be. But he ain't no real Rear Echelon Mutha Fucker."

Kolisch laughed and then became serious. "Since most of the young men are away in the Army, we've had a lot of trouble defending the smaller villages against terrorist attacks. Lately, we've been arming the older kids and giving them a little training. They really are good. They take things seriously, and they're not afraid of anything."

"Haven't got enough common sense to be scared," Grey observed.

Kolisch laughed again. "That's the best thing about most good soldiers." He handed his already empty glass to MacEvy and said, "Haven't you got anything but his fuckin' hippy shit music?"

"Johnny Cash, okay?" Mac said, pouring J&B into Kolisch's glass.

"Right on!" Kolisch said, pumping his fist in approval.

Mac gave Kolisch his whisky neat and began changing the tape. Grey was curious. "How do you feel about training fifteen and sixteen-year-old kids to kill people?"

"You got something against winning the war?" Kolisch asked

sharply,

"It's their country," Grey replied.

"Whose?" Kolisch asked.

"The Vietnamese," Grey answered cautiously.

Kolisch took a sip of the Scotch and settled down into a wooden chair by the table. "You may not have noticed but there are a lot of Vietnamese out there shooting at each other," he said.

"It used to be one country." Grey insisted.

"It was one country for about fifty years before the French got here." Kolisch seemed bored. "The Chinese for about a thousand years or so, freedom for fifty, then the Frogs until '54. Old Emperor Bao Dai was already having a lot of trouble keeping it together, or he'd never have invited the French back in after World War II"

"You think we've got a moral right to wage war here, then?" Grey asked.

"I don't think morality has anything to do with it," Kolisch replied. "Political power flows from the barrel of a gun, as Mao said."

"So, we have to kill to survive? Grey asked, a little astounded.

"Any nation that's not willing to fight for itself won't be a nation for long," Kolisch insisted.

"What about killing?"

"What about it," Kolisch replied, his dark eyes hard.

"And hate?" Grey asked, carefully.

Kolisch sounded almost philosophical. "Hate just makes it so much easier."

INTERLUDE

Grey—29 and a Wakeup

The lousy news Grey feared came much as he thought it might. He was drinking with MacEvy in the compound's small bar. There was a sign at the door that said, "CHECK ALL WEAPONS, and a guy behind a Dutch door who collected rifles, pistols, grenades, and knives and gave a claim check in exchange. Grey exchanged his .45 for a small, red disc with the number 32 on it.

The tall, thin Captain joined them for a nightcap.

"Good news, Grey," said the Captain. "We got hold of your office at Long Binh and had long heart-to-heart."

Grey felt his stomach turn.

"They were thrilled down there when they found out that you had stumbled onto this operation. It could be one of the biggest stories of the war."

"Great," Grey said acidly. "Who did you talk to?"

"Oh, my Colonel called your Colonel. Only took about five minutes," exclaimed the Captain excitedly. "It turns out they were at the Army War College at the same time." he continued.

"But what about the story of the kid and the German hospital ship?" Grey asked, still looking for a way out.

"Screw the kid," the Captain said.

"I think we already did," whispered Grey to himself.

The Captain bought a round of drinks and then spoke in a voice that was full of sincerity.

"Colonel down there says you're a damn good man, Grey. He said you're one of the best he's got, asked us to sort of look out for you." The Captain swirled his bourbon in his glass. "He said you were tapped by *Stars & Stripes*, but turned them down."

"Yep," Grey answered. The booze was good and tasted even better now that Tom had decided to get thoroughly wasted.

"We've arranged for you to be briefed by the brigade CO. That way, you can have immediate access to every level of the operation and cut through any red tape that might develop with the Brigade's Information Office or anyone else down the line."

"I appreciate that Sir, but I always work alone. It's my style. I just slip in and stay as anonymous as possible. It gives me..."

"That's great," the Captain said. "Mac's going to be plenty busy, and the less time you need, the..."

"What's MacEvy got to do with it?"

"He's going to be our liaison on this operation. You'll be working with him."

"Shit," Grey muttered while looking down.

MacEvy had been fighting to keep a straight face. Now he lost it and cracked up. Grey felt like shooting himself.

"You okay, Mac?"

"Yessir," Mac replied, trying to regain his composure. "I was just struck by the irony of it all. Tom and I have been friends for so long, and now we're finally going to get a chance to work on a major operation together."

"That's not the half of it," confided the Captain. "We were going to request some civilian press people for this business but decided against it because security is so tight. If Grey hadn't wandered in here when he did, there wouldn't be any on-the-spot reporting other than maybe some 101st PIO people, and God knows how much of the credit will remain after the story filters through higher headquarters.

"It was really a stroke of good luck for Tom," agreed MacEvy with a snide grin. "He'll be able to finish up his Army career with a big bang!"

"Finish up. You mean Grey's getting out?" the Captain asked, incredulity in his voice.

"I think so, Sir."

"No!"

Grey didn't like the way the two men talked about him as if he weren't there. In a tight voice he said, "Captain, I would like to point out..."

"You're not really getting out, Tom. Tell me you're not getting out."

"I'm getting out, Sir," Grey answered flatly.

"No!" The Captain seemed genuinely pained. "The Army needs young men like you. We old war horses can't carry on forever. We need young men, young ideas."

"Sir."

"Think it over, please. Think it over carefully." He got to his feet. "Talk to him, Mac."

"I will, Sir." Grey answered, continuing, "But I really want to work for NASA."

"That's good. National Security Agency, huh?" The Captain laid money on the table for the drinks. "You're a good person, Mac." Then he left.

◆ ◆ ◆

Grey was hopelessly hungover in the morning. He watched the blue and silver Air America Cayuse helicopter settle onto the pad at Field Advisory Element's headquarters two blocks from MACV. A rear echelon lieutenant with a briefcase and a pressed and starched uniform that belonged on the parade ground clamored aboard the helicopter. His only concession to the war was a .45 automatic hung from his immaculate pistol belt and the leather thong that tied it cowboy style to his leg.

Grey followed the officer into the rear of the small scout helicopter, tossing his rucksack and camera bag ahead of him. He noted with satisfaction that his equipment landed squarely on the lieutenant's spit-shined boots.

There was a subtle change in the Air America Cayuse vibrations, and Grey opened his eyes as the helicopter began a lazy turn. Tom leaned out of the open door. The cool wind rushing against his face with gentle pressure felt good.

Landing Zone Jane was a lone brown splotch amid a gently rolling terrain covered in scrubby grass-like tufts and was on the highest knoll in the area. It was located midway between Camp Evans to the north and Camp Eagle to the Southwest. Jane served as a base for a couple of Air Force Forward Air Control (FAC) aircraft, and as a refueling depot for helicopters from both the 101st Airborne and the 1st Air Cavalry divisions.

To Grey, it was a bus stop. He planned to catch a ride with a 101st bird to Camp Eagle and join up with the A Shau parade.

Jane was not much more than a mile in a rough, looping diameter. It was surrounded by concertina wire and low, carefully spaced sandbagged bunkers. Within the perimeter were a collection of tents, which housed an infantry unit based there for security, Quonset huts for FAC maintenance, plywood hooch's for the Air Force crews, and a large TOC bunker. There were two or three artillery emplacements; sandbagged for protection of the 105mm crews and other miscellaneous tents, bunkers, and sandbagged emplacements.

Running in a more or less straight line through Jane undulated a narrow black asphalt runway with a jerrybuilt control tower at its midpoint. Showers and latrines were clustered at the south end of the runway. Several large dusty black bladders of aviation fuel sat in the southwest section of the small camp. Everything was tinged that peculiar raw umber, streaked with brighter yellow ocher, common to army field operations in Vietnam.

About forty feet from the control tower was a large, white circle with an "X" painted in the middle. The pilot sat the chopper down with a gentle rocking motion on the pad. Grey climbed out and turned to drag his collection of equipment from within. Just as he slung his rifle over his shoulder, the REMF lieutenant put his boot against Tom's rucksack and shoved.

Grey caught his heel on the landing skid and stumbled backward, nearly falling. He recovered his balance, set his feet apart against the prop wash, and gave the officer the finger. The lieutenant looked outraged and quickly leaned forward and tapped the pilot on the shoulder, but the civilian had been monitoring the activity behind him and shook his head as he pulled pitch, twisted the throttle, and spun the Cayuse in the air.

Grey retreated through the surging wind and dust to a small sandbag wall. The helicopter hovered for a moment, swung slightly on its axis, then rose and flew away. Grey watched until in passed from view, headed Northeast toward the 1st Cav at Camp Evans.

It was not quite 8:30, but already the temperature was nearing ninety. Tom sat down near the sandbags, utilizing what little shade there was. He lit a Marlboro and rummaged in his rucksack for something to read. There was a rumpled, unopened letter in one of the pockets. In his haste to clear Long Binh, he had failed to read it.

Tearing open the envelope, Grey found a small piece of stationery with a light blue letterhead of a soldier with his rifle at high-point and his bayonet fixed. A three-inch diameter round patch fell out from among the pages and landed upside down in his lap. He picked it up and examined it.

Two concentric circles were embroidered in gold. On the outside band, backed in blue, were the words, also in gold, MOBILE RIVERINE FORCE · MEKONG DELTA. The center disk had a dark maroon background with a white anchor rampant. Stitched over the anchor was a gold symbol of a caduceus, the winged, snake-entwined staff of the god Hermes, which was now used as a sign of the medical profession. Holding the patch between the third and fourth fingers of his left hand, Grey read the letter.

It was from a company commander of the 9th Infantry Division's Riverine Force. The Captain wrote that he and his men felt that Grey had been a valuable part of their unit when he was with them at the fight by the dike. They were thankful for the medical aid he had given several wounded members of the company during a firefight. "This patch is in place of a bronze star. I wrote you up for it; however, the people at Awards and Decorations didn't think it was worth it. Well, we did, but this is the best we can do."

Grey wasn't sure what to make of it. He guessed it was because he had been a visitor who had when the shit was thick, pitched in and helped some of the "guys."

"The guys," Tom played with the phrase in his mind. Anywhere there were American soldiers in Vietnam, there were "the guys."

It was an emotional bond that went deeper than friendship or even love. If you were one of the guys or a stranger whom the guys chose to adopt as one of their own, they would do anything for you. They would give an arm or a leg, and they would cry inside when you died.

It hurt Grey because he knew that it was not the Army or

America or even freedom that he was betraying with his personal declaration that the war was over. It was the guys he was deserting.

But knowing it and feeling bad about it did not change Tom's mind. Just a few weeks ago, the 9th Infantry incident had been one of the things that pushed him over the edge.

They had been struck, very hard, and they had been pinned down. The medic was dead, and Grey, who had worked part-time on an ambulance crew while he was in college, had reacted naturally and without thinking.

The memory of it was a blur of images. Holding someone's guts in, trying to stop a pulsing chest wound with a dirty hand and being blinded by the crimson spray; looking down at his own arms and seeing them drenched in blood to the elbows; the anguished cries of the wounded and the pathetic pleas of the dying.

Grey had been very much the young soldier-journalist. He had worked hard to tell the true story of the war. He slowly realized that in Vietnam, the true story was a very complicated thing that he, Thomas Grey, didn't fully understand.

He saw, too, that the truth presented by journalists was, at best, one man's honest opinion. Often it was not even that. Every reporter had to slant his stories to please an editor, and editors, in turn, all worked for publishers. It became a question of viewpoint and a degree of truth. It was not that many reporters lied a lot but rather that most lied a little, and in so doing, the deception became massive.

And so, Grey quit.

He did not know who was right in Vietnam, and he was trying

not to care. He no longer wanted the prestige that journalism offered the successful. He disliked himself for even considering war as a means of furthering his career. His only goal was getting home alive.

Grey jumped, startled when someone tapped him on the shoulder. He turned his head and peered over the tops of his sunglasses. A soldier was standing to his left. He didn't have a shirt on, and his oxidized gray aluminum dog tags dangled in front of his tan chest. His fatigue pants were carelessly bloused into the tops of his well-worn jungle boots, and he too wore sunglasses.

"You waiting for a chopper?" the soldier asked.

"Sure am."

"Well, there ain't going to be any more today," the soldier said, bare-chested and with his hands on his hips.

"Why not?"

"Fuel's contaminated, so nobody'll come in here. No reason to." The soldier put his hands in his pockets, a gesture of finality.

"There is a God in heaven," Grey said softly.

"What?"

"Nothing... Is there anywhere around here a guy might get a beer?" Grey asked, now aware of the heat.

"Sure. We got some on ice over at the control tower," the soldier said, pointing.

"Well, lead the way, my man," Grey said as he got to his feet. "You've given me cause to celebrate."

The soldier extended his hand and said, "I'm Jeffers, air traffic controller. One of three up here."

Grey took his hand and shook it. "Name's Tom Grey," he said, "PIO."

Jeffers brushed a lock of hair from his forehead. "What the hell you doing at LZ Jane?" he asked.

"Trying not to get to Camp Eagle."

The two men walked toward the makeshift control tower. "What do you mean?" Jeffers asked, hefting Grey's rucksack onto one shoulder while Grey carried his camera bag and rifle.

"I've got 29 days left in-country," explained Tom, "and the bastards are trying to send me to the jungle to cover some op."

"Too bad."

Back where Tom had been sitting, the unfolded letter was lifted by a small current of air and floated a few feet before coming to rest against the base of the sandbag wall. The patch lay upside down in the dust.

The control tower was a low, two-story structure made entirely of old wooden ammunition boxes filled with sand. There was a sandbag wall around the lower level where the three Army air traffic controllers were housed. The upper level was open from about waist high but was shaded by a PSP roof supported on four wooden posts.

Windows had been fashioned in the lower level by taking

the bottoms off of wooden mortar round boxes and leaving the hinged side facing out as shutters. They usually were left open, but they could be quickly closed from the inside in case of rain or rockets. One of the doorways faced south and the other east. The room off the eastern door belonged to the two other controllers. Jeffers lived alone in the smaller south-facing room. He led Grey inside and had him put his stuff on the room's one empty cot.

"You can stay here 'til we find a way to get you out," he said.

"Thanks."

Grey replied as he looked around the room. The floor was of worn plywood, a luxury unusual in the field. Against the east wall was a green ice chest, and a Coleman lantern hung from a hook in the ceiling. Jeffers had nailed an olive drab painted wooden footlocker to the wall and then propped the lid open with a piece of a broom handle. The locker contained a few personal belongings; books and a bottle of Old Grand Dad bourbon. A couple of sets of fatigues were hung on nails driven into the wall next to the footlocker. Jeffers' bed was a standard metal GI issue with a thin mattress. The other was a wood and canvas folding cot.

Jeffers opened the cooler, pulled a couple of cans of Schlitz out of the water, and fished around for the can opener. When the cans were open, he tossed the opener back into the cooler and kicked the lid shut. Then he sat down on the bed and handed Grey a beer. "Welcome to LZ Jane," he said. The two soldiers tapped the rims of their cans together in salutation.

Tom leaned back against the wall and asked, "How long before I can get out of here?"

"Beats me. This's the first time we've had this problem. Got mud or something in the gas. If the choppers use it, it fucks everything up. Kinda gives 'em the dry heaves," Jeffers explained. "If you want, we'll try and flag down a passing chopper going your way."

"Nooo... I think I'll just wait it out. *'Sin Loi,* boss, sorry, I got marooned.'"

"I can dig it. No way I'd go to the boonies."

"How long you guys been up here?" Grey asked, sipping at the cold beer.

"About three months. We got some of the best duty in the Nam. Our NCOIC is down in Saigon, the bastard," Jeffers replied, spitting rolling the cold beer can over his forehead. "When he heard that this place was nearly overrun during Tet last year, he split," Jeffers said, smiling.

"No boss?"

"You got it. Just us three guys making do 'til we can go home." Jeffers opened the cooler and got two more beers. He splashed some of the icy water on his face and chest, gasping in the sudden cold. "God, that's great!" he spluttered. "Care to indulge?" he offered.

"No, not now. I don't want to spoil the effect of a morning's sweat just yet." Grey said, smiling.

"Come on," Jeffers said, "I'll show you our little operation and introduce you 'round."

The two men went outside and climbed the homemade ladder to the second level. There were two folding lawn chairs and a large plywood piece on which was tacked a plastic-covered map of the area. Next to the map table was a small field radio, the same type as the infantry manpack, which served as the landing zone's ground-to-air communications system. A scarred, olive-green wooden crate stood in the corner holding several batteries for the radio.

"Grey, this is Marlin," Jeffers said, introducing Tom to a tall blond headed soldier lounging on a lawn chair next to the map board.

"Glad to meet you," Marlin said. The mike to the radio draped over one tanned shoulder. He wore only a cut off pair of jungle fatigues, sunglasses, and a well-worn pair of jungle boots without laces. His olive-green socks sagged around his ankles. Beside him sat a couple of cans of beer, one open, one not. Next to the chair stood a tall brown plastic bottle of Copper Tone.

A slight breeze rustled the paperback pages of *Dandelion Wine*, Ray Bradbury's coming of age book that was open in Marlin's lap. The entire scene was mottled with sunlight spotting as it passed through the holes in the pierced-steel-planking that provided shade for the control tower.

"Well, here it is," Jeffers said, waving his hand in a broad arc. "The fabulous Landing Zone Jane."

Grey turned slowly, taking in the collection of jumbled tents and sandbagged structures. It looked like any other of the small desolate installations scattered over Vietnam. State, U.S., or Confederate Battle flags hung limply from improvised poles in front of several tents. A mud smeared jeep lurched between two rows of 25-man tents, which were bleached a soft olive drab in the tropical sun. The jeep's engine noise was barely discernible, and a tall radio antenna swung drunkenly in counterpoint to the jeep's movement. A dog yelped once from what Grey thought was a mess tent.

"Real nice," he said.

"Isn't it," Jeffers replied, sighing as he gazed at the sun-drenched somnolent vista.

Grey sat down on the sandbag wall, his back to the runway. Jeffers took the empty lawn chair. From time to time, the radio squawked to itself. After a pause, Grey asked, "Well, Mr. Marlin, what do you guys do for fun around here?"

"Well, mostly we drink beer, smoke a toke or two, and let Charlie walk on by. But mostly Jeffers has his mind on sweet memories..."

"There was this chick I used to date back in Jersey," Jeffers said, interrupting, "She was about 6 feet two and stacked like a brick shit house. Massive boobs," he said, cupping his hands in front of his chest in pantomime, his eyes were squeezed shut behind his sunglasses. "When I was screwin' her, my face would be right between those boobs, and she'd put her hands on them and rub them against my head." Jeffers paused and lit a cigarette. Exhaling, Jeffers said dreamily, "The smell. It was like nothin' else. Her skin, man, her skin was a smooth as glass, and she had the longest, nicest legs."

"Jeffers is quite a lover," Marlin said. "He's got athlete's foot on his dick from beating off in his dirty socks."

Grey laughed. "What's he got on his feet?"

Jeffers continued talking as if he hadn't heard Marlin or Grey. "I'd eat her out, and then I'd low crawl up her body. I mean it, really. It was like a beautiful mountain of flesh. I'd crawl up her body and pull myself up over those big boobs." The radio hissed and crackled.

"Does this place do this to everybody?" Grey asked Marlin.

"I should've married that chick," Jeffers said. "I was crazy not to marry that Catholic chick. I'd be home right now with three kids in the other room, a draft deferment on the dresser, and that massive, wonderful body under me. I was crazy."

The radio crackled again, intruding on Jeffers' reverie. *"LZ Jane... Air Force Two-niner, over."* Jeffers' eyes opened. He looked sad.

Marlin put the receiver to his ear and pushed the 'talk' switch. "Air Force Two-niner, Jane here, sir, go ahead."

"Jane, Two-niner. Ah, we got us something of a problem here, and it looks like we're gonna have to borrow your runway, over."

"Roger that, two-niner. State the nature of your problem, and type of aircraft, over?"

"Gotta engine on fire and the hydraulics are failing, over."

"We copy two-niner. State type of aircraft?"

"C-123K, over."

Marlin and Jeffers exchanged worried looks. "Sir, we copy engine fire and C-123 Kilo. Two-niner, be advised we have no emergency equipment, runway length one thousand feet of light asphalt, repeat one thousand feet... We recommend you divert to Phu Bai, over!"

"Jane, Phu Bai's a no-go. They advised you guys." A pause, just crackling on the radio. *"Jane, got any overrun on that runway?"*

Negative, Two-niner. One zero, zero, zero feet of light asphalt. The radio squawked in reply. "Two-niner, advise your plan?"

"Shit..., ah, Jane, we're about five miles out, from the north fifteen hundred and descending rapidly. We roger runway length one thousand, and no emergency equipment, over."

"Okay, two-niner, wind's five to ten from the east, altimeter is four five zero. Runway One Eight. Be advised, I don't think the runway'll be heavy enough for your bird, over."

"We copy, Jane, wind, altimeter and runway One Eight. With all the shit we got up here, we ain't got much choice."

"Two-niner, please advise when you have us in sight, proceed at your discretion, LZ Jane is all yours," Marlin said, paused, then continued, "We'll put Camp Eagle on alert to have Medevac on standby. Good luck, sir." Marlin dropped his hand to his side. He, Jeffers, and Grey stood looking north, Jeffers scanning with binoculars.

"Jane, Two-niner, we're about a mile out and have runway in sight, over."

"Roger, Two-niner." Marlin began to dial frequencies alerting any air traffic in the area of the emergency.

He checked with the TOC to confirm a monitor and alerted Medevac dispatch to have some choppers standing by at Camp Eagle.

"There she is," Jeffers shouted, pointing with his right hand. Grey could see Two-niner approaching, just a small dot smoke trailing from the port engine.

"Damn," Jeffers said, "Hope nobody's in the crapper!" All three men glanced toward the collection of latrines and showers at the south end of the runway.

The Air Force transport, one engine burning, seemed for a moment to hang in the air over the perimeter, as it made steep approach, full flaps and gear down. The flaming port engine was feathered and the right one spun in coughing spurts. The plane slammed onto the runway wings flexing. Huge chunks of dirt and asphalt were tossed into the air as it bounced up.

The pilot chopped the power, shoved aircraft back onto the runway as the copilot stomped on the brakes so hard, he was practically standing upright in his seat.

The tires and brakes began smoking and driving deep gouges into the thin layer of asphalt. The airplane careened by the tower; the right wingtip narrowly missing. Grey and Marlin ducked, and Jeffers dove over the side. Tom glimpsed the two pilots through the windshield wondering if he would see them alive in the next few moments.

The green-painted transport sliced through the cluster of showers and latrines like an out of control bowling ball, flinging pieces of latrines and plywood artifacts high into the sky. Then, it slammed into a sandbagged bunker. Two-niner seemed to shudder in its midsection; the nose gear disappeared into the crushed hull. A jet engine ripped from an under-wing pylon was sent spiraling in a crazy cartwheel into the shallow water of the rice paddy just ahead. The impact with the bunker shot Two-niner back into the air, trailing black smoke, orange flames, and tangled concertina wire. Then it drifted to the right, nose high, stalled, and bellied into the rice paddy with a *whumpf!* sending up a shower of brown water. Still not stopped, the right-wing tip caught the mud and spun the aircraft half around before it came to rest, its bent fuselage and wings like a beached whale taking its last breath.

Grey couldn't believe it. He found his hands gripping his belt, and his breath came in shallow coughs. His heart was racing. He glanced at Marlin, whose eyes were so wide open that the white folds around his eyes gave him a film negative raccoon look.

Marlin, after a moment, got back on the radio, "Two-niner, do you read, over?" He looked worried, "Two-niner, over" No answer. Just static.

"Shit," Marlin muttered to himself.

Grey saw Jeffers run to the destroyed latrines and begin a rapid search of the wreckage. The downed airplane smoldered and simmered about two hundred yards out from the perimeter. Jeffers, finding no one in the latrines, joined a small group of soldiers heading out into the paddies.

The rescue party was still a hundred feet away from the wreck, struggling in the paddy muck when a hatch opened on top of the C-123. Four men emerged, slid down the steep side of the aircraft into the water, and began running in a knee-high splashing shuffle against the mud and water. Tom cringed in anticipation of the explosion. His imagination writing arcs of flaming debris engulfing the straining crewmen.

But there was no explosion. "Helluva way to make a living," whispered Marlin.

"That's for sure." Grey lit a cigarette. His hands were trembling.

A few soldiers clustered at the base of the tower. The FAC crews joined them.

"Hey, Marlin," an Air Force lieutenant called up, squinting in the glare, "what 'n hell happened?"

"C-123 crapped out, Sir. Engine fire and some other shit, so they put her in here."

"Anybody hurt?"

"Don't know, Sir. Looks like they all got out. They oughta be up here in a minute," Marlin answered, looking down at the lieutenant from his perch atop the control tower.

Grey could see Jeffers approaching with the four crewmen from the C-123. All were soaked to the knees from the paddy water, and the gray flight suits of the Air Force people were dark with sweat. "That was some ride," the Captain said to nobody in particular as he approached the group at the base of the tower. "Say, where's the ATC?" he asked, dabbing at a bloody nose.

"Up there, sir." the FAC lieutenant said, pointing up at Marlin.

"Hey, man, thanks for your help." the Captain shouted up to Marlin. "I owe you one."

"That's okay, Sir. You buy the beer, an' we'll call it even," Marlin replied, smiling down at the crowd.

"Rubbing at his nose with his right sleeve, the Captain asked, "You gonna write me up for a Purple Heart?"

"Yessir. Just tell me where to sign," Marlin answered with a broad smile.

"You got a radio I can use?" the Captain asked.

"Sir, you'll have to use the one in the TOC. This's just a field radio." Marlin said.

"Do you think you were hit?" the FAC pilot asked.

"Beats me," The pilot answered, pinching his nose between thumb and forefinger. "I'm just glad it happened after we made our delivery to Quang Tri. We were carrying 80-millimeter mortar rounds and fuses from Da Nang. Would've been blown to shit."

Jeffers led the four airmen toward the TOC, and Grey could hear Marlin canceling the Medevac. The small crowd began breaking up, the men returning to whatever it was they had come from.

Grey spent the afternoon wandering around LZ Jane. He watched as ground crewmen loaded five-foot white phosphorous marker rockets in clusters of three under the FAC planes' wings. The aircraft, gray Cessna O-1's, were small, single prop, high-wing aircraft with Air Force markings. The two planes were parked in separate bays, shielded by high metal and sandbag walls. Overhead, camouflage parachutes billowed and flapped in the light breeze, providing a shimmering green shade.

Later Grey stuck his head into the TOC, but not much was going on. Two men were playing cards, another dozed by the large bank of radios, and a third sat leaning back in an old scarred wooden swivel chair, his feet propped up on a field table reading an overseas edition of *Time* magazine. The TOC was air-conditioned to a pleasant level but reeked of sweat, mold, and damp.

Grey spent some time watching a dozen GI's put the latrines back together and listened to them bitch about it as if the Air Force did this to them on purpose. A brief tour of the runway revealed deep gouges in the asphalt. The red earth underneath peered through.

Beyond the latrine detail, a group of men was restoring the perimeter and rebuilding the bunker. Someone had wised up, and they were relocating it about twenty meters to the right of the end of the runway. Someone and hand-painted a sign and tacked it over the entrance. It said, "Duck After Entering."

Jeffers joined Grey as he walked toward the control tower. "Want some chow?" he asked.

"Well, why not? I missed lunch." Grey answered, lighting a Marlboro with a snap of his stainless-steel Zippo lighter.

"Let's see. You can risk your life and eat in the mess tent or make do with some Cs. What'll it be?"

"Believe I'll stick with the C-Rations tonight. I'm too well wired for pilot society," Grey answered, pulling on his cigarette.

Back at the tower, Jeffers rummaged around and came up with a cardboard crate of C-Rations. He carried it up top, and Tom followed him up the wooden ladder. The third controller was there, and Jeffers introduced Grey to Bob Pearson, a lanky Negro from Chicago.

"Hey, Bob, where were you doing the all the excitement?" Jeffers asked, snapping the binding on the crate with a pair of wire cutters.

"I was over in the TOC playing blackjack with Captain Mac-

Donald. We got your transmission, so we monitored the whole thing. MacDonald was losing. He wouldn't let me leave," Pearson said with a wide smile, rubbing his thumb and fingers together, signifying beaucoup dollars.

"Well, you sure missed a show," Jeffers commented while handing a couple of boxes to Grey.

"Did you hear anything about the fuel," Pearson asked, opening a can of Beans and Franks with his P-38 can opener.

"It may be a couple of days before they can get to us," Jeffers explained. "I guess we aren't critical to the war effort.

"Looks like we are temporarily out of business," concluded Pearson.

The sky began turning a reddish-purple as the sun moved slowly toward the West. The three men watched as it flattened into a yellow-orange oblate blob before it abruptly slipped below the mountain ridges with an ocular flash, plunging the coastal plain into darkness. To the east, Grey could just make out the evening stars winking over the South China Sea. Pearson produced an Army issue flashlight from somewhere. It had a red filter to protect night vision, and he attached it to the metal ceiling with some wire apparently there for the purpose. The three soldiers silently ate their rations in the eerie red glow.

After collecting the trash and putting it back into the partially consumed crate, Jeffers lit a joint, and the three passed it around. After Pearson's second toke, he said, "I've had a long day at the tables, so I think I'll turn in." He stood up, took down the flashlight, and disappeared down the ladder. It began to get chilly, so Jeffers asked Grey to wait by the radio while he went for their shirts.

Tom felt awkward sitting alone with the radio as it crackled with far-away transmissions. It was like he was an unwelcome guest, or on his first date with his father up front driving. Other than the brief moment with the 9th Infantry, Grey had not once during his time in the Army had to use a radio.

"Well, I'll just fake it." he thought with uneasy bravado, lighting a cigarette.

Jeffers returned with the shirts in short order, and the two sat atop the control tower, rehashing the C-123's crash for a while, then fell silent. Jeffers turned the radio frequency, and they listened through the static of a far-away firefight; The *pop - pop - pop* of distant rifle fire coming through the radio speaker.

To the Northeast, 105mm harassing cannon fire sounded, *wump wump.., wump,* the sound muffled by the distance from Camp Evans, soon joined from the Southwest by artillery batteries at Camp Eagle. Grey leaned against the sandbagged wall where he could see distant flares drifting under their small parachutes from the Marine compound at Phu Bai to the Southeast.

Jeffers sighed and said, "Well, it's a quiet night," as red tracer rounds mixed with blue-green of NVA tracers arced into the blackness of the western mountains from another far-away fight. "I'm gonna turn in."

"What about the radio?" Grey asked.

"I'll take it to bed with me and poke the antenna out the window. Not like my girl back home in Jersey, but better'n nothing."

"Okay. I'll be down in a minute." Tom said, looking at Jeffers through the gloom.

He watched as Jeffers shouldered the bulky radio and vanished down the ladder. To the east, Grey caught the faint sounds of a helicopter. After a time, he located the green, red and white running lights and followed them as they moved south toward Phu Bai. Soon the glow faded from sight, and Grey listened for any sounds from the night, but it was uncharacteristically quiet. There was no light showing from the perimeter bunkers, not even a cigarette ember. Grey thought about going home, back to the World. Suddenly, a black, melancholy wave swept over him. He felt lost.

Finally, Tom climbed down the wooden ladder and entered Jeffers' room. Jeffers' had left the Coleman lantern burning low and had provided a pillow from somewhere. There was a poncho liner on the cot to serve as a blanket. Tom unlaced his boots and kicked them off, sliding them under the cot with one foot.

Insects fluttered about the lantern casting flickering shadows against the sandbag walls. Sighing, Grey stood up and turned off the lantern. He pulled the mosquito netting in place. Then, settling down on the musty smelling cot, tugging the nylon poncho liner over his body.

At 3:30 in the morning, the far-off rumble of an Arc Light raid awakened Grey. He felt the seismic vibrations more than heard the B-52 bombs. As he lay awake, staring at the less black rectangle of sky through the open window, he felt disconnected. After a while, he slept again—without dreams.

The morning dawned cold and misty. Shivering, Tom unpacked his field jacket for some protection against the weather.

Jeffers lay on his bed asleep, wrapped up in his sleeping bag. One bare arm and his head were all that was exposed. He snored very slightly.

Grey slipped his boots on quietly and pulled his razor, shaving cream, toothbrush and toothpaste, and an olive drab towel from his rucksack.

He wandered down to the partially rebuilt latrine area. He pissed into one of the three-foot pieces of six-inch diameter pipe protruding on an angle from the ground. He found a dented aluminum pan amid the rubble. He washed it out with some water from a large plastic container standing nearby. As quickly as he could, he stripped and gave himself a whore's bath, shivering in the cold. He shaved with cold water and without the benefit of a mirror. Toweling off, dressed and sat down on a pile of sandbags and laced his boots, leaving his pant legs untucked.

He sat on his sandbag perch for a while, watching soldiers materialize out of the fog one by one. Most of the GIs just washed their face, chest, and armpits, but a few stripped down for a chilly cleansing. It occurred to Grey that someone might get the wrong impression if he hung around the latrines too long, so he collected his gear and walked back to the control tower.

When he got back to the hooch, Jeffers sat up on his bunk, still wrapped in his sleeping bag. He blinked sleepily as Grey entered and yawned, scratching his tousled head. "Morning," he remarked.

"Morning. Sleep well?" Grey asked, repacking his belongings.

"Okay, I guess. See that thermos up there?" Jeffers said, pointing in the general direction of his locker.

"Yeah."

"Why don't you go over to the mess tent and get us some coffee?'

"Roger that," Grey said, taking the aluminum and red plastic cylinder. He crunched through the gravel, walking amid the swirling eddies of mist to the mess tent. Enroute, Grey tripped over a tent peg and sprawled on his hands and knees; the thermos skittered across the small rocks. He removed the bits of gravel pressed into his palms and brushed off his fatigue trousers at the knees.

Bending, he picked up the thermos and shook it by this right ear, testing to see if the glass liner was broken. It didn't rattle with broken glass, so he figured it was okay.

He entered the mess tent, pulling the flap aside, his head snapped to the right as he was almost overcome with the smell of powdered eggs and greasy bacon. Breathing very slightly through his mouth, fighting nausea, he took a place in line. When he reached the three large stainless-steel coffee containers, he drew off a hot thermos full, recapped it, spinning the red plastic lid with a single twist of his wrist. Nodding to one of the cooks, who stared at him sleepily and without interest, Grey hurried from the tent. Walking back to the tower, he rubbed his face with his right hand, convinced he had accrued a layer of grease.

He and Jeffers drank some coffee, letting the hot liquid warm their bodies. Jeffers finally climbed out of his sleeping bag, naked, and put on a pair of fatigue pants and a shirt. He pulled on a couple of worn socks and scuffed jungle boots, lacing them up, skipping every other eyelet. "While you were getting coffee, we were advised that they won't be able to resupply us with fuel for four or five days. It looks like you're going to be stuck here for a while," Jeffers said as he poured himself another cup. "We were lucky to hear it. The battery's about shot."

"Fine," Grey said, laying back on the cot, canteen cup of steaming coffee resting on his belt buckle, flanked by his warming hands. "Just fine with me," he breathed.

He spent the rest of the day quietly celebrating and staying out of the way of the men running the landing zone. He drank a little beer, snuck off twice for a joint, and finished reading Michener's *The Source*. As he closed the book, he tapped its worn and dirty cover with his right index finger. The finality of the book made him realize again that life back in the World was going on pretty much as usual. New books and records were being released. People still argued about the Super Bowl outcome. The war in Vietnam was just another topic of conversation at cocktail parties.

AN OPERATION

The 22d Surgical Hospital, Phu Bai

An infantryman staggered through the swinging doors of the dispensary. feet dragging, he made his way toward Haynes. He tossed his M-16 onto the cement floor, where it made a hollow plastic sound accompanied by a small clink from the metal clasp on the web sling. Then he shrugged slowly out of his rucksack and let it fall into a clumsy heap behind him. Turning slightly, he sat down heavily on the gray painted bench. With his right hand, he pushed his helmet back on his head.

Haynes saw that he had written the word "Short" and drawn a calendar on his helmet's camouflaged fabric helmet cover with a felt-tipped pen that showed he had only fifteen days left in-country.

Exhaling loudly, the soldier leaned back against the curved corrugated metal wall. His fatigues were dusty, as were his arms and face. His jungle boots were covered with gray mud from the soles all the way up to his ankles. Where he walked, he left a small trail of dried mud bits. His eyes were red-rimmed, and his mouth hung open, slack-jawed. The soldier's breathing was shallow but controlled.

Abruptly a medic came through a door marked "Authorized Personnel Only." He was a short black soldier dressed in a sleeveless and collarless gray pullover shirt with "326th Med BN," encircling a caduceus staff stenciled over his heart. He wore a gray surgical cap and around his neck dangled a white surgical mask on his head. In his left hand, he carried a clipboard. Watching him, Haynes felt his arm begin to throb again. The medic's boots squeaked slightly with each step.

Sitting down between Haynes and the other soldier, he said to the GI, "Well, what you got?"

Without opening his eyes, the soldier answered, "Nuthin really, Jus' some of Nam's jungle rot to take care of before I DEROS out of this goddamn country."

Shifting around on the bench, the medic said to Haynes, "Well, troop, what's your problem?"

"Took a piece of shrapnel in the arm here," Haynes replied, holding up his bandaged left arm. The medic sat the clipboard on his lap and took hold of the arm. Haynes watched as the medic carefully unwrapped the dirty white compress bandage.

His stainless-steel colored Seiko watch gleamed in the neon light. He pulled the stained bandage away. The medic grasped Haynes by the elbow and wrist and gently turned the arm laterally back and forth, examining the small wound. It had stopped bleeding, but the movement caused a small trickle of red to flow, and a jolt to Haynes, who grimaced at the twisting.

Dabbing at it with the bandage, the medic said, "This doesn't look too serious. We ought to be able to take care of you under a local."

"What's a local?"

"Local anesthetic," the medic answered. "But first, we'll take a couple of pictures and make sure we know where the piece is and see if there's any damage to the bones."

He picked up the clipboard and said to the other GI, "Okay, we'll take care of you soon's we're through with this guy." he said, nodding in Haynes' direction. "That is if we don't get busy."

Turning back to Haynes, he asked, "Your shot record up-to-date?"

"Beats me," Haynes answered with a shrug.

"Let me see it," the medic said tiredly.

Haynes pulled his wallet out of his back pocket and rummaged around looking for the three-fold white card. "Here," he said, handing it to the medic.

Glancing at it, the medic said, making a note on the top sheet attached to the clipboard, "Your tetanus is up-to-date." He then took down some information from Haynes' dog tag: Name, service number, and blood type. He then asked Haynes for his social security number, rank, and unit. "Here," he said, "Hold this bandage on the wound, Okay?"

"Okay."

The medic stood and motioned for Haynes to follow. They moved through a swinging door into a clean room in which there was some X-Ray equipment.

A technician had Haynes sit down next to the tan X-Ray table and positioned his arm between some small sandbags. He draped a heavy cloth over Haynes' chest and lap. Next, the tech took a film case from a cabinet and slid it into the slot below the table's surface. He then positioned the rectangular apparatus, which hung from a long multi-jointed armature. He stepped behind a large three-sided screen in the corner. The first medic joined the technician.

"Don't move!" Haynes held his breath, heard a soft hum, then click. The technician repeated the X-ray procedure, adjusting the arm for different angles.

"Follow me," the medic said, leading Haynes through another set of double doors into a room where there were several tables on large rubber wheels, a couple of chairs and swivel stools, medical cabinets, and other paraphernalia.

He had Haynes remove his shirt, and while Haynes was doing that, he puttered around with some equipment. He then took Haynes' blood pressure and temperature, noting them on the sheet on the clipboard. "What've you had to eat today?"

"Nothing." Haynes answered.

"Good," the medic said as he lathered Haynes' forearm around the wound and carefully shaved the hair, rinsed the excess lather off with a damp sponge. He then excused himself, saying he'd be back when the X-rays were finished. Haynes sat in a chair and wondered what was next.

He was just about to stand and check out the room in more detail when the medic returned with two other men. One of them, a doctor, took the X-rays, slid two of them expertly into the wall-mounted viewer, and flipped on the light. He studied the murky images for a few moments.

Turning to Haynes, he walked over and sat in a chair next to him and inspected the arm. The doctor said, "There doesn't appear to be any bone damage, and the piece of shrapnel is pretty small. From the looks of things, there wasn't a lot of energy behind this piece. Probably a ricochet. Now what we're gonna do is to debride the wound, which means we'll scrub away the damaged tissue, then we'll extract the metal piece, clean it out, sew you up, and put you in the ward for a couple of days of R&R."

The doctor stood up and said to the medic, "Okay, Dick, let's get ready." All three men left the room to scrub for the operation, leaving Haynes alone with his thoughts. His stomach felt a little queasy.

The second medic returned and helped Haynes mount one of the gurneys and wheeled it over next to a stainless-steel table containing several instruments and syringes on a white cloth. The medic snapped on and adjusted a sizeable circular light. Haynes squinted and felt the heat from the lamp.

He lay back, his head turned to watch what was being done to him.

The doctor picked up one of the syringes and raised it upward, depressing the plunger slightly. He held it there, the tip dripping fluid as the medic swabbed the arm around the wound with an orange-colored disinfectant.

Abruptly the doctor inserted the needle into Haynes' arm. Haynes jumped inwardly at the small, sharp prick. Tiny beads of sweat appeared on his forehead and upper lip. A prickly feeling itched his armpits and crotch. He watched as the doctor carefully injected some of the anesthetics into his arm, pulled the needle almost free, and reinserted it is a slightly different direction, injecting more fluid. The doctor used both syringes before he was through. The medic maintained his hold on Haynes' arm while the doctor sat back.

"We'll wait for this to take effect, the doctor said. "Then we'll begin. You might not want to watch. It looks worse than it is."

"I'll be okay," Haynes said.

"Okay, but don't move your arm."

"That's a rog."

The other medic moved over to observe the small operation. He adjusted the lamp, and the doctor picked up a shiny stainless-steel probe and poked at Haynes' arm a few times. "Feel anything?" he asked. Haynes told him he didn't, and the doctor said, "Now we begin."

Leaning well over Haynes' arm, he peered at the wound and inserted the probe about a few centimeters. "Feel anything?" he asked again.

"No, just some pressure." answered Haynes.

"Fine, fine." the doctor said, withdrawing the probe. He picked up a wire brush and began scrubbing at the wound briskly. Haynes shut his eyes and sighed. Before long, he heard the doctor say something about silk, and he turned and watched the medic expertly thread a small curved needle and hand it to the doctor.

The doctor closed the wound, stitching quickly. The skin puckered slightly between the black thread stitches.

When the doctor was through, the medic bandaged the arm lightly and moved it onto the table next to Haynes' side. He pulled his gloves off with two snaps that sounded like the sharp flap of a flag in a stiff breeze. He buckled a safety belt across Haynes' chest. "I'll take you over to the post-op section where we'll check on you every now and then for the next hour. If everything checks out, then we'll move you to the ward by dinner time, and write you up for a Purple Heart."

"Sure. Hey, thanks, Doc." Haynes said as the medic began to wheel him out of the room.

"Anytime." the doctor replied, smiling.

THE CITADEL

Grey—26 and a Wakeup

It was raining. The Monsoon drummed against the canvas top of the jeep and sprayed inside the doorless vehicle. Grey pulled his poncho tightly around his body and huddled back further into the seat. The jeep lurched slowly through water-filled potholes that pock-marked the white rock gravel road like miniature after-effects of a B-52 raid. The road ran arrow straight, splitting flooded rice fields that made up the gray countryside north of Hue.

Tran, a Vietnamese Army Sergeant who was some sort of intelligence liaison with MacEvy, was driving. He was impassively looking straight ahead, brown eyes like agate, unblinking. The feeble windshield wipers streaked painfully across the glass, smearing the ever-present mud of Vietnam.

"You like this war?" Grey asked.

"It's the best thing that ever happened to me," he replied, not taking his eyes from the road. "I hope it lasts forever," he said without enthusiasm.

"It might."

"It will," Tran said, his hand tightly gripping the steering wheel.

Grey sat up, straighter in the seat, and lit a cigarette. His hands were wet and cold. "Don't you have better things to do than run around the country collecting lost reporters?" he asked.

"MacEvy heard LZ Jane closed down, and he didn't wan you to miss the operation."

"Nice guy, MacEvy."

"He could run his own errands," Tran remarked. "This weather for shit!"

They came to a small iron one-lane bridge guarded by several bedraggled ARVNs. A young, good looking lieutenant appeared out of the plywood and tin shack that served as the guard mount. He was wearing tiger fatigues tailored almost skin tight. He had a red beret with a prominent ARVN airborne badge stitched in silver thread perched at a jaunty angle over his right eye. The Vietnamese version of *Love Potion Number 9* blared from the transistor radio he carried. The Lieutenant seemed unaware of the light rain and smiled as he talked with Tran. Grey pulled a canteen from his rucksack and took a pull. The whisky was warm and mellow.

After a few minutes, Tran and the ARVN lieutenant finished their business. Tran put the jeep noisily into gear, double-clutching the reluctant, maintained-starved machine. One of the soldiers raised the red and white striped barrier by pushing down on the cement-filled paint can that acted as a counterweight.

The jeep moved slowly onto the thin, warped wooden planks

that served as the bridge floor. The old iron bridge, a relic of the French occupation, was partially collapsed from Viet Cong sabotage during last year's Tet Offensive. In places, the cement roadway was replaced by wooden boards. Between the planks, Grey could see the weed-choked water, seemingly stalled forever, below him. Beyond the bridge, the road widened, and the road surface, although still gravel, improved.

"Where are you from?" Grey asked, glancing at Tran.

"Saigon," Tran said with only a trace of an accent.

"Ah, A rich Catholic neo-colonialist?" Grey asked.

"A warmongering elitist," admitted Tran with a grin. His first on the trip.

"Scourge of the people," Grey countered, smiling.

"Enemy of the proletariat," Tran answered back, also smiling, but appearing more grim than happy.

They lapsed once more into silence as Tran guided the jeep down the road toward Hue. By the time they got to the outskirts of Hue, the rain was letting up, and there were a few pedestrians on the streets. They passed a young Vietnamese soldier with his pretty wife, who followed several feet behind. Unconsciously Grey caught her eye, and they exchanged a sweet smile. Then the girl, remembering her station, turned suddenly away and quickly walked after her husband with only a hint of flirt in her walk.

Grey settled back in the canvas seat and watched the pedicabs, with their passengers almost completely concealed beneath black rain canopies. It was a good day for a GI to fool around in the off-limits city. "Maybe he could see Hoa. No. That had to be history," he thought.

The west wall of the Citadel ran parallel to the road. The long-wall, dark brown stone blocks darkened almost black in places by lichen, loomed over a lily infested moat between the way and it. The medieval fortress reminded Tom of a prison. "Have we got enough time to go inside for a while?" Grey asked.

"I must see a man downtown," Tran said. "We eat lunch there."

"We could spare half an hour. I've never been inside."

"Tourist?" Tran looked at Grey skeptically.

"The wave of the future," Grey smiled tightly at the Vietnamese sergeant.

They turned left at the *Song Hurong*, the languid Perfume River, near the railroad station, onto *Le Loi* Street that ran along the river. Suddenly Tran stepped on the brakes. "That's where your Marines died during Tet last year," Tran said, indicating the bridge where Tom and Hoa had met the old man.

Now Grey understood the significance of the bullet holes in the low concrete walls.

"The Communists were on the other side, inside Citadel. They had three—or four-gun emplacements set up to rake the bridge. A company of Marines with bayonets fixed tried twice to charge across." Tran continued solemnly.

Grey considered the effect of heavy caliber machinegun fire on the narrow concrete span of the bridge. It would be like firing a shotgun into a box. "Shit," he said flatly.

"They very, very brave," replied Tran. "They made the Communists fire their guns and reveal their positions.

"The Americans, on this side, called in artillery and knocked guns out. They took the bridge. Without it, the capture of Citadel would have been very more difficult."

Grey squinted his eyes, imagining the chaos, and concluded that the story was some after-the-fact Marine legend cooked up at the USMC Combat Information Bureau in Da Nang to describe irrational behavior. But, he thought, maybe it was true.

They turned left again and passed over the bridge toward one of the ornate gates to the fortress. A Vietnamese MP stopped them at the wall. He checked their identification and then motioned them on. The road led through a long tunnel to the interior of the massive fortress.

"This was once the capital of all Vietnam," Tran said. "The rulers of Annam conquered both Saigon and Hanoi and brought all the land under the rule of one man."

Grey was disappointed. The ancient imperial city was just another ruin. "A rather brief interruption in the hostilities as I understand it," he said.

"Vietnam is like a woman that is too beautiful. She attracts many men who are willing to fight for her." Tran replied, a rare smile on his face.

"A lot like California."

"California?" Tran asked, puzzled, staring sideways at Grey.

"Never mind."

Tran swung the jeep onto a narrow street and parked. They left the vehicle, taking their rifles, but leaving the other gear. Tran led the way into the temple complex to their left. Tran gave a few coins to two boys to guard the jeep and their equipment.

"We were once invaded by Kublai Kahn," Tran said.

"Is that right?" Grey said as much a statement as a question.

"Yes. The Kahn sent troops from China to conquer Vietnam, but they were defeated—in the A Shau."

"That's life and crumbled cookies," Grey replied, feeling surly and doubting the story.

"I don't understand."

"*Sin Loi*," Tom said. "Sorry 'bout that."

The two soldiers made their way through the deserted corridors of the building. In one of them, they discovered two Vietnamese schoolboys sneaking a cigarette. Grey, wise in the ways of schoolboys, realized that this must be a reasonably secure hiding place. He fished under his poncho and pulled out his pipe and a bag of marijuana.

"You Americans set such a good example for our young people," Tran said, sourly. Grey considered it, and then reluctantly put the paraphernalia away.

The temple complex itself was abandoned. Grey thought it odd. This fortress was Vietnam's claim to a unified history, the ideal stage for psychological warfare. It seemed to him that there should have been a few guards around to keep fanatical Viet Cong from scribbling graffiti on the walls. Such was not the case, except for the two schoolboys. He and Tran wandered in isolation through the abandoned temple of teak, stone, and tile, built in the Chinese style with unturned tiles at all corners, and now faded green pillars.

Tran found an open door, and Tom followed him into an enormous room. It was devoid of furnishings and wrapped like a womb with intricate overlays of gold foil on black and red painted wooden walls. The ceiling was supported by four wooden pillars with fantastically carved dragons snaking up their lengths; the floors bright in red and white tiles. It was beautiful, but he found it hard to believe that it was the capital of a nation or even a state, perhaps a county seat.

Grey sat on a small raised platform at the rear of the hall and watched as Tran tried the doors. He realized that three of the chamber's four walls were designed to collapse and fold away. The Vietnamese sergeant found one that was open and motioned for Tom to follow.

Grey got to his feet, shouldered his M-16, and lumbered slowly across the tiled floor. Kings and emperors had made decisions here. "Frogs and ponds," he thought without compromise.

Despite the misty rain, the light outside hurt his eyes. Grey crouched like a Vietnamese peasant on the steps of the temple. He held his black rifle held loosely between his legs, the barrel cool against his right cheek. He looked out over the parallel rows of waist-high cast-iron pots with exotic dragon motifs as handles. Two were toppled from the square stone bases they had once stood upon and lay in the weeds of the imperial courtyard. The scene with its medieval buildings was more rustic than imposing, but it stirred his imagination. *The small courtyard was filled with courtesans and courtiers who moved about in gay, colorful clusters.* His eyes wandered to the encircling walls.

The Communists had stood here for a fortnight, and they had died. Grey thought about all the soldiers that had fought since the Stone Age and knew that all the losers had struggled in vain. How many men had died for nothing on some bloody little patch of ground? The world was full of people who would slit your throat in a heartbeat for nice ideas.

Tran was heading toward the ceremonial gate. Grey sat in the rain and smoked a cigarette. He could almost see the way this place had been. The temple, with its walls removed and robed dignitaries moving around as if on stage. Old men dressed in silk brocade like the one he and Hoa had seen on the bridge that day long ago moved in a stately procession. Laughing innocent people with petitions in hand. But the idyll was a fantasy. They had fought then with the same petty bitterness that they struggled with today.

Tom walked through the gray morning, across a small footbridge at the end of the promenade toward the gate. A yellow and red Vietnamese flag flew from a tall pole at its top.

He found Tran on the third floor, at the top of the wall. Below them, they could see the river and beyond it, the familiar buildings of the city. The too modern Catholic cathedral from which the Communists had taken two hundred boys and old men for reeducation during Tet stood out. Reeducation ended for them in a mass grave about than five miles outside Hue. They could see the University, and also the High School where legend said both Ho Chi Minh and the murdered President Diem of South Vietnam had attended. The Sportsmen's' Club on the opposite river bank with the whorehouse nestled across the street, and the bulk and barbed wire of the MACV compound dozed in the hot, tropical drizzle.

"You like Hue?" Tran asked.

"It's okay," Grey replied. "Reminds me a little of Waterloo…, the rivers are a lot alike."

The Vietnamese did not understand.

"Iowa," explained Tom, "Waterloo, Iowa. In America."

"Oh."

"Nice little town on the Cedar River. Like the Perfume."

The two soldiers worked their way back toward the ground. The wooden steps inside the gate towers were largely blown away. The gouges in the mortar made by bullets of various calibers were evident everywhere. "This is called the Gate of Heavenly Peace," Tran said over his shoulder.

"Makes sense," Grey said ironically.

The schoolboys who had been smoking were now examining the jeep. Tran spoke to them briefly in Vietnamese, while Grey checked to see if they had liberated any of his belongings. All seemed in order, and Tran started the jeep while Grey mounted up. The boys smiled and waved goodbye.

Tran drove out the way they had come. The same MP was still on the gate. This time he motioned them through without a stop.

The rain had let up, and the streets were once again filled with a gaggle of people and vehicles. Tran and Tom turned east at the river and headed downtown. Grey took off his poncho and rolled up the sleeves of his fatigue shirt. Along the road, he occasionally saw pictures of an oriental infant with a halo. At first, he thought it was the Christ Child. He asked Tran who told him it was the Baby Buddha. Tom mused on the universality of images.

The river was lined with sampans lashed together to form a ghetto. Hoa had lived on the boats before her mother had died. Tom tried to imagine her as one of the skinny children playing along the muddy bank.

Traffic downtown hardly moved at all. Pedestrians crowded the sidewalks and the small open-front shops. A poster for a Samurai movie dominated the central intersection above the marquee of a turquoise-painted theater.

Tran drove a block beyond it and then turned left down a narrow, busy side street. They parked the jeep again and went into a small restaurant. Tran paid another two boys to guard the vehicle.

Grey did not like Vietnamese food, so he did not order. It was extremely impolite not to eat the native cuisine, but he didn't care. He figured bridging cultural gaps was a two-way street.

Tran gave him the "Ugly American" look as the waiter hurried away.

A man joined them at the table, and he and Tran spoke at length in Vietnamese, pointedly ignoring Grey. Grey had a cigarette and listened to the soft singsong of the language and the clinking of dishes. The lined faces of the older men in the cafe were set in stoic frowns. He wondered how many years it took to etch an expression permanently into the flesh.

Tran finished his meal, and the mysterious companion left without acknowledging Grey.

Grey leaned his forearms on the table and peered at Tran through the cigarette smoke. "You get around, Tran. Big business at Saigon MACV. Have to see people in town. Now you're on your way to the A Shau. You're pretty active for a sergeant."

Tran smiled but said nothing.

"You speak excellent English," Grey said mildly.

Again, the Vietnamese was silent.

"Fuck it," Grey said as they rose and left the restaurant.

The jeep moved across Hue's main bridge and into the now heavy stream of military traffic headed down Highway One. Old women in conical hats hawked sodas, sandwiches, beer, and dope to the passing GIs. After they passed the peasant market's square, the flow of traffic thinned out, and they picked up speed. Grey filled his pipe with marijuana and lit up. In half an hour he would be back in the Army, and in a few days, he would be back in the jungle. "Is there any way you're going to win this war? He asked suddenly.

Tran steadied the jeep with his elbows and lit a cigarette, a mentholated Salem brand cigarette favored by the Vietnamese. Grey was glad to see some sign of personal weakness. "The other side has all the advantages," said the Vietnamese soldier. "We build something, and they blow it up. It is much easier to knock things down than it is to put them up. We must guard everything, yet they can strike wherever they choose. The Communists blame everything wrong in South Vietnam on our government. They have no government for us to blame.

They can promise anything."

"And they have the desire to win," added Grey.

"Yes, there is a difference between people who want to change the world and those who only want to live in it."

On the right, the road was lined with flooded rice paddies. On the left, the Saigon to Hue railroad ran along the top of a high earthen wall. Once, under the French, it ran all the way to China.

"They'll never give up," Grey said.

"Neither will we."

"The Americans will go home," Grey predicted.

"Why?"

"Because of the money."

"In World War I, Vietnam sent men to fight the Germans. In World War II, we fought the Japanese."

"So did the Russians and the Chinese."

"The West will not desert us. Nixon will fight," Tran said with a sharp slap of his hand on the steering wheel.

"And if he doesn't?"

"Then we will live in the jungle and fight like the Viet Cong. We will become the destroyers."

Tran turned the jeep right onto one of the dirt roads that led to

Camp Eagle. The area reminded Grey of small-scale Wyoming bush, except the landscape was dotted with the concrete rings and rectangles of Vietnamese graves. The tiny low-set shrines made Grey think of birdhouses.

"You do not believe in our war?" Asked Tran after a while.

"I don't believe in anything."

"Not even yourself, I think..." Tran said flatly.

The MPs at the gate to Camp Eagle wore the Screaming Eagle patch of the 101st. Two manned an M-60 machine gun emplaced on the left side of the gate, protected by three cement-filled oil drums reinforced by sandbags. The emplacement was sheltered by a large piece of corrugated steel, covered by two layers of sandbags. The machine gunners smoked and talked to each other as they idly scanned the jeep. Two others stood to the left of the gate near a sandbagged guard shack. There was a sign above the guard shack that read, "Welcome to Camp Eagle, Northern Home of the 101st Airborne." The sign looked professionally painted and included the gold, white, and black of the division insignia. An MP by the shack waved the jeep through.

Eagle had changed since the last time Grey had seen it. The roads were graveled, and wooden buildings had replaced most of the primitive brown canvas tents.

"I have to check in with the Division Information Office. It used to be up there at the top of the hill." Grey said, pointing.

The GIs they saw along the road wore pressed fatigues and had newly shined boots. Their uniforms all had proper insignia, and their haircuts were according to regulation.

On the right was a large, relatively attractive chapel that would not have been out of place in suburban Chicago. A dead GI's name was memorialized on a sign in front.

Tran parked the jeep by the Information Office, and Grey went inside. He was a little off-balance. Six months ago, these troops had been at war. Now they seemed to be an occupation force.

The building was clean and filled with neat, busy soldiers. Grey stood in the doorway until he spotted a familiar face. The man was bent over a typewriter, struggling to get his story down on paper.

"Cole!"

The writer looked up, angry that his concentration had been broken. Then his face relaxed into a grin. "Grey, you fucker. How you been?" he asked as he rose from behind the machine.

Cole was an ordinary-looking man of twenty-four. A graduate of the University of Kentucky school of journalism, he stood just about six feet tall and weighed about 160 pounds. A bit heavier than the last time Grey had seen him. Brown hair, brown eyes, and lightly tanned skin.

"Okay, man, what's the hap?" Grey said, shaking Cole's hand.

"Shorter and shorter and shorter," Cole said, having his hand back and forth as he bent toward the ground.

"Dig it!"

"Really." Cole snagged an extra chair from a neighboring desk. "What are you doin' up here?" he asked.

"MacEvy's arranged something for me."

"I didn't know that spook was still around, and whatever he's got, it will not be a good place to be going right now," Cole said, spitting out a bit of tobacco.

"No shit."

"Those assholes down at G-3 don't know the war is over."

Grey lit a cigarette, "I doubt you know the war is over when you are planning the war." Grey observed. "How is the war, anyway?"

"A drag. This place is getting worse that Ft. Campbell. Spit shined boots and 'Yes, Sir—No, Sir.'"

"You seem to have done okay. Specialist Five and your own desk in the main office."

"I've got an important job," Cole said conspiratorially. "We've got a General running for Congress when he gets out."

Grey laughed. "You're putting me on."

"Nope. We don't cover the troops anymore; we cover the General."

"Well…, Eisenhower did all right."

Cole's voice was flat. "Forty-one more days of this bullshit, and I'm going home."

"For sure."

"How long are you going to be around, man? I get off in a few hours, and the partying sure has improved. We got everything but women."

Grey got to his feet. "From the way things look around here, I'd say you'd have to keep the noise down."

"Yeah, well, there is something to that. But drop around anyway."

"That's a rog." Grey said, looking around. "I've got to get going now. My ride is waiting outside."

"Your ride?" Cole asked, leaning back in his chair.

"Yep. One of Mac's boys. He thinks I might escape." Grey answered, smiling. "Say, anybody in charge around here?"

"You might try Lieutenant James," he said with a gesture, "over there."

"Thanks. Look, maybe I'll catch you later."

"If not, I'll see you back in the World." Cole said, returning his attention to his typewriter.

"You got it." Grey said, turning toward the Lieutenant.

He was a small, precise man, and he was bent over his plywood desk, reading a copy of *Ramparts*. "What's the problem, soldier?" he asked, carefully noting Grey's casual appearance and sparse insignia.

"I'm from USARV-IO. I'm going down to one of your infantry companies."

The Lieutenant was mildly impressed. "The civilian media usually works out of here." he said.

"The civilian media usually works out of the bar at the Phu Bai Press Club... if they ever get this far north."

"True," the Lieutenant smiled. "What's your name?"

"Specialist Four Thomas Grey."

The Lieutenant wrote it down. "Good luck," he said.

"Thanks," Grey replied.

"Hope you don't need it," the officer said, turning back to flipping through the pages of *Ramparts* magazine.

Tran started the jeep and backed onto the road. The sun was going down, and the gold of evening softened the base's mining camp atmosphere. The chopper pad was larger than the last time Grey had been with the 101st and had been planked with PSP. A big expensive sign proclaimed it Eagle International.

"What a crock of shit," thought Grey.

CAMP EAGLE—INTERSECTION

Grey—24 and a Wakeup

Rain drummed with a sweeping sound as it passed in rhythm against the faded brown canvas of the brigade PIO tent. Water leaked through in several places where the repellent had failed. The small shaded 60-watt bulb swung slightly from its cord, vibrating in gentle counterpoint to the swaying tent. Smoke from Grey's cigarette curled upward and clung near the ceiling in a silver-white cloud.

Tom rocked the folding chair back onto two legs and took another slow drink from a can of beer on the scarred portable green field table. Then he leaned forward again and resumed his struggle with the dirty, battered old typewriter.

Rivulets of water reflected the light with a dim silver glow as they meandered down the tent's inside. In places, the water pooled, upside down lagoons of rainwater, and dripped onto copy paper, old newspapers or photographs, or the worn plywood flooring.

The air smelled musty from the mildewing canvas, decaying and moldy wood.

The tent flap snapped open in a spray of fine droplets, and Mike

Haynes came in hunched over against the weather. He pushed the hood of his poncho back and shook the water from his floppy bush hat. Grey was startled by his appearance. In four months, the angry young man he had known in Saigon had aged. While he hadn't exactly gained weight, his facial features were thicker and heavier. Haynes put his hat back on and turned to survey the tent. When he saw Grey through the gloom, his mouth dropped open.

"Tom? Damn., what in hell are you doing here?"

"It's a small war," he answered, standing.

"God, I guess so," Haynes said, advancing toward Tom. "How've you been?" Excitement was evident in his voice.

"Okay, you?" Grey said diffidently.

"Fine," Haynes was recovering his composure. "Jesus, man, it's good to see you."

"For sure." Grey took Mike's hand, and both men laughed. "You old fucker!"

Haynes struggled out of his poncho and accepted the can of beer that Grey offered. "You the one that called down to the Company for me?" he asked.

"Yeah. Figured that'd be the easiest way to find you," Grey answered, taking a pull of his beer.

"It's just coincidence I was there. The rest of the guys are still in the field."

"The arm?" Grey asked, nodding at Haynes' bandaged forearm.

Mike grinned, "Got a little close to a mine," he said ruefully.

"Too bad."

Haynes shrugged and then asked, "Worse for the other guy." he said quickly. "You up here for an Op."

"Sure," Grey said. "Just like a vulture. Death is news."

"Maybe we'll be lucky." Mike got a chair and lit a cigarette. "Although things seem to be heating up out there."

"Bad enough," Grey said carefully.

"Yeah, but not like it used to be." He was silent a moment and then changed the subject." "You're pretty short, aren't you?"

"About two weeks, plus two or three maybe."

"Bummer! It takes that long to do the paperwork to get you out of this country."

"They're making an exception in my case," Grey said. "Express checkout lane."

"Lucky you," Haynes said, sitting on an empty chair.

"Really." Grey opened a drawer in the desk and took out another beer. As an afterthought, he pulled out a large plastic bottle of pills. "Want some Darvon?" he asked.

Haynes shook his head, "When'd you start on those?"

"Not mine," Tom said as he put the thousand caps back in the drawer. "Somebody here's got a habit and a friend both.

"Careless, too."

"Maybe he's just generous," Tom said.

"You about through here? I got a case of beer on ice down at the hooch. I'm trying to make the best of my little vacation."

"I can finish this anytime," Grey said. He pulled the piece of yellow copy paper free of the aged Remington typewriter. "Creative journalism."

Outside, the dark night was periodically lit by the artificial novas of parachute flares sent aloft along the perimeter. Tom and Mike made their way down the mud-slippery Headquarters Company street to the main road, rainwater sluicing from their hats and ponchos. Muffled light escaped the tents on either side of the road, and country-western music floated faintly from a transistor radio in a mess tent.

The two GIs walked in silence through the gravel and mud. The rain was cold, and the wind picked up, chilling the friends. In the distance, a machine gun rattled briefly, and someone blew a claymore with a sodden "woof" sound. To their left, the flares revealed the pale white circles of concrete Vietnamese graves.

In some of these, they could glimpse the dull orange glow of soldiers smoking dope. Eagle, it seemed, had been built in the middle of a vast cemetery.

Mike's company area was on the flats below the graves, and it was a virtual sea of mud. They went inside the darkened tent, and Haynes lit a short, thick candle held in place on a wooden crate by a pooled of hardened wax. Both men shed their rain gear, and Mike dug out two olive drab towels, while their shadows cavorted on the canvas. He smelled one of the towels and tossed one to Grey saying, "Not too rotten."

"They used to issue white towels back before '66," Grey said, sniffing the mildewed air.

"Really."

"Yeah. Couple dudes must have got their dicks blown away." Grey said, toweling off his head and neck.

"We didn't know much about guerrilla warfare when this started," Haynes observed.

"We didn't know much about a lot of things," Grey said.

"Well, we're learnin'," Haynes got two beers from his cooler, opened them, and sat down on his bunk.

Grey took one of the beers and sat down on the cot facing him. "Here's looking at you, soldier," he said, his voice pitched in a Humphrey Bogart imitation.

"Roger that," Hayes said, offering to tap rims in a toast.

"How bad is the arm?" Grey asked, tapping Hayne's can with his.

"Nothing much. Little shrapnel is all. Did a real number on the dude in front of me, though." Haynes glanced sadly at the plywood floor.

"*Sin Loi*," Grey said gracelessly.

"Say, you guys have been in the A Shau, haven't you?" Grey asked.

"Yeah, once," Haynes eyed Grey carefully. "Why?"

After a pause, Grey said, "What'd you think of the valley?"

"A little spooky. Maybe because the A Shau's got an evil rep, or maybe because we got hit."

Grey nodded, "Sorta like the first time you fall off a horse. It's not easy to get back on."

"We're going back in?" Haynes asked, staring at Grey. He dreaded the answer.

Grey sat on the facing bunk, water trickling down his neck, his eyes in shadow. "Yeah…"

"Shit!" Haynes spit, stomping a booted foot, mud flaking off, scattering across the plywood floor.

Tom fished a pack of joints out of his field jacket, "Can we smoke in here?"

"Sure, what're they gonna do? Send us to the fuckin' A Shau?" Haynes said, bitterly.

They each lit a joint and smoked in silence for a moment. "Pretty nice weed," Haynes said finally.

"I got it in Hue, I think there's some opium in it," Grey said while flipping the lid on his Zippo lighter over and over with a metallic *Snick, Clink, Snick, Clink, Snick, Clink.*

"Is that right?" Haynes said, leaning back on his bunk.

"Ever smoke much 'O'?" Grey asked exhaling.

"No," Mike said.

"I've never done it on purpose. But, I hear it just nails you to the floor. I can see how a guy could get into heroin." Grey said, leaning back on the bunk he was sitting on.

Over the sound of the rain pounding on the tent, they heard outgoing artillery begin to fire.

"Makes you wonder, doesn't it?" Haynes remarked.

"About what?" Grey asked.

"About where the world's headed." Haynes looked away, slowly rolling his beer can between his palms.

Grey sat up in the bunk and carefully threw his empty beer can at a rat that had been eying them from under a neighboring cot. "Sometimes, I feel that there really is life after death, and this shit goes on forever."

Haynes laughed mirthlessly. "You're okay, Grey," he said. "Here, have another Schlitz."

◆ ◆ ◆

Haynes and Grey had met on a flight south from Hue/Phu Bai to Bien Hoa, the rear area of the 101st Airborne Division. Grey had been in the A Shau with the 1st Cavalry Division, and Haynes was fresh from the woods with the 101st. Both of them were bound for the R&R processing center at Tan Son Nhut.

They agreed to meet at the gate to the 101st Division (Rear) and catch the bus to the R&R Center. It was Grey's idea, and by the time they got off the bus in Saigon, he had talked Haynes into going briefly AWOL.

Tan Son Nhut was, at that time, the busiest airport in the world. The two soldiers got off the bus, turned left instead of right, and simply walked back out through the main gate.

Half a block beyond it, they caught a cab. "Continental Palace Hotel," Grey instructed the driver, stashing their sparse luggage in the front passenger seat.

"Sure thing, GI!" the driver responded enthusiastically.

Haynes pulled several times before the door opened with a pronounced creak. They climbed into the rear seat of the aging blue and cream-colored Renault. The cabbie slipped the vehicle into gear, and off they lurched into the mayhem of Saigon traffic.

"What's the Continental?" Haynes asked, eyes wide as he stared out the window. "A whorehouse?"

"No, not for us anyway," Grey said. "It's one of the few places in Saigon where you can still get 'Paris of the Orient' vibrations. The civilian press people spend about half their time there."

"Where do they spend the other half?" Haynes asked, turning to look at Grey.

"Down the street at the Caravelle Hotel roof-top bar."

"All of them?" Haynes asked. He didn't know if Grey was putting him on or not.

"Occasional expeditions are mounted into the interior. These are manned for the most part by fearless and/or foolhardy freelancers and lowly young reporters desperate to get ahead in whatever organization, paper, network, or wire service they work for.

"There also seems to be a fairly large pool of Asiatic cameramen that the TV networks have hired," Grey said, continuing,

"They do this in an attempt to disseminate technology and create jobs within the Vietnamese economy," Grey said, sarcasm etching the tone of his voice.

"Nice of them," Haynes said, wondering how many other things were going on of which he was clueless. From his perspective, as a lowly infantry grunt, he didn't see much other than the back of the guy on patrol.

"They're really nice people," Grey agreed, lighting a cigarette with his Zippo lighter; *snick, click, snick.*

Haynes had never seen a sizeable Asian city. He was intrigued by the mass of people who crowded and surged along the sidewalks. It was so different than the sedate streets back in the World. He assumed that the traffic pattern was European in origin. It consisted of small cars, bikes, small motorcycles, jeeps, and two and half-ton trucks plunging down the narrow streets with total disregard for anything resembling lane designations. The signal for a left turn, an arm extended abruptly, did not mean I am planning to turn. It said; *I am in the process of turning now!*

About half of the vehicles on the street were those of the American and South Vietnamese military. A veneer of dust lay on everything. The crippled people and pockmarked buildings the war continued to create were evident everywhere. A light blue pallor of diesel exhaust smoke hovered over the thoroughfares to a height of twenty feet or more. The overwhelmingly sweet diesel smell in the humid heat was one of the signatures of Vietnam.

As the taxi hurtled along, Haynes was amazed to see Conoco and Shell Oil gas stations scattered about. A billboard proclaimed *You have a friend in Vietnam—The Chase Manhattan Bank.*

The taxi threaded its way toward downtown, and as it did so, the scenery began to improve. The buildings were more substantial and more imposing, and most had had their bullet holes plastered over. There were parks, one with a zoo nestled amidst the shade trees. The streets were wider and less crowded, and the people were clean and relatively well dressed.

"That's the National Assembly," Grey said, pointing at a structure on their left. "Sort of like the capitol building in Washington. President Thieu's palace is a few blocks that way," he said, motioning straight ahead.

"City Hall in Chicago is bigger," Haynes observed chauvinistically.

"But, probably about as corrupt, too."

The dinted and wheezing cab stopped in front of the hotel, and the two men paid and got out. After collecting his gear, Haynes felt a sudden memory pang as he stepped onto a genuine city sidewalk. He stood there for a moment and tested the cement by rocking lightly on the balls of his feet. Grey led the way onto the open-sided veranda of the hotel and found a table.

"*Garçon,*" Grey said, motioning toward a man in black and gold livery.

"Sir?" the waiter said with just the hint of a bow.

"Scotch, *avec de la glace*." He looked at Haynes, who nodded, not knowing what the French words meant, and trusting that Grey wouldn't poison him.

"A pair," he said. Haynes sat back in his wicker chair and surveyed the plush accouterments of the open-air bar. The floor was of dark red unglazed ceramic tile, and stucco archways marched around two sides of the large "L" shaped room. Wood and wicker four-bladed fans studded the chocolate-colored tin ceiling. They stirred the tropical air and creating seductively shifting patterns of light and shadow across the patrons.

Most of the customers were either Americans or Europeans in their middle twenties. They wore civilian clothes or the khaki-colored military-like jumpsuits favored by the civilian press. Their hair was styled, and they looked tan and fit. The hotel had an air of elegance that Haynes could not for the moment assimilate.

Haynes knew that men were struggling against the hot primitive jungle, or in the less primitive but equally hot rice fields and villages within fifteen miles of where he was sitting.

Up north right now, his friends in the platoon were probably humping up some bitch of a mountain. The paradox made him angry. "Nice way to fight a war," he said finally, bitterness clear in his tone.

"They're not fighting a war." They're civilians." Grey said.

"They're Americans."

"You don't understand, Haynes," Grey said. "America's not at war. The rest of the Army's not even at war. It's just us, the United States Army Republic of Vietnam, the Marines, the Air Force and some Navy"

"These guys are Americans," insisted Haynes.

"It doesn't matter. Most of these guys wouldn't shoot at a Viet Cong if they saw one…, interview him if they could, take his picture…, but not shoot at him. It's not their responsibility."

The drinks came, and Haynes turned his attention to the Vietnamese passing on the street. The crowd was sprinkled with young girls wearing American clothes and too much American makeup. Grey, noticing Mike's interest, said, "We'll go down Tu Do Street later."

"I'll drink to that." Haynes said, saluting the famous street of bars and brothels whose name translated into English as "Freedom Street." A place he had heard of, even up in I Corps.

The Scotch was smooth and crisp and included real ice cubes—without bugs trapped in them, as in amber. The taste was nostalgic, and he could feel the alcohol fumes smart his eyes. Haynes hadn't had a drink of hard liquor for three months.

"To the ladies of Saigon," toasted Grey.

"Saigon ladies."

A barefoot Vietnamese boy wearing a clean white shirt and navy-blue shorts stood on the sidewalk and spoke to the GIs over the low partition of the open-air cafe. He was selling hand-painted Christmas cards. Haynes bought a package of four and tipped the boy double the price.

"Sucker," Grey said as he ordered another round of drinks.

Smiling, Haynes replied, "A poor orphan, no doubt."

"Who has just had another lesson on the great American handout." Grey rejoined.

"You're a sweetheart, Grey."

Tom smiled and settled back with his drink. He liked the veranda of the Continental. Sitting there with his Scotch, he felt like a character in *Casablanca*. Here was a trace of the exotic adventure that an Asian war had held for a bored journalism major. He volunteered for duty in Vietnam, thinking it would be a great adventure. In some ways, he thought, it was one with too much mud.

"Let's get something to eat," Haynes abruptly said, breaking Tom's reverie.

"We can eat here, but it's pretty expensive."

"I'd like some real American food."

Grey order more drinks. "I know just the place," he said.

"Well, let's go."

"They don't serve drinks there," explained Tom. "We'll have to build up our alcohol content first."

"Naturally," Haynes agreed.

"Do you ever get to Hue?" Grey asked.

"No," Mike said. "It's off-limits. When we're in the rear, we're damn lucky if we can get to the Marine BX at Phu Bai. Why?"

"It's quite a place. A friend of mine from Cu Chi is up there with MACV now. I spent a couple of days with him before I went to the 1st Cav. Some town."

"What'd you think of the Cav?" Haynes asked.

"They were pretty impressive. Grey slid his chair back from the table and lit a cigarette. "They're as aggressive as hell, and I think the discipline and extra weight they carry gives them an edge. They go something like three days between resupply..."

"Four days. We work in the same way." Haynes affirmed.

Grey nodded. "I think that's better. If Charlie sees those helicopters every day, he can't help but know pretty much where everybody is. It's hard to believe that those guys can carry as much weight as they do and still move effectively. Discipline, I suppose."

"We have that—airborne training and all," Haynes said a little defensively.

"Well, airborne *esprit* then or unit pride. Either way, they're pretty tough.", , t"For a leg division, "Haynes snapped, contempt in his voice.

"Oh, of course," Tom mocked, "But they've got golden crossed sabers on the noses of their helicopters, and they move like cavalry."

"Okay, so they're okay. But they still can't do the same stuff we can. They've got different priorities and training. They have rivalries. You know, pilots vs. legs. They can't be as tough because they're not as tight."

"As, say, the 101st?"

"Or the 173rd." Haynes was trying to be open-minded.

"Now that we've solved that, let's go eat," Grey said as he counted out a stack of piasters, his last, and handed them to the hovering waiter.

Stepping into the bright sunlight, they caught a cab to a modern five-story office building in the city's diplomatic quarter. On the second floor of the U.S. Government office building was a cafeteria. They order fried chicken dinners at PX prices. Mike fell on the meal with an almost savage relish. When he had finished, he ordered another one. Grey had coffee. Finally, the younger man was sated. The two caught another cab back to the area around the Continental and started a pilgrimage down *Tu Do* Street.

Prostitutes and B-girls loitered in front of small bars from which loud jukebox rock'n'roll poured into the sunny afternoon. The neon signs flickered *Hollywood Bar, Miami Club, Crazy Horse Saloon, Mimi's* Haynes and Grey turned into a joint labeled both *Las Vegas Casino* and *Paris Bar*. After their eyes adjusted, they found an empty booth. They were joined by two attractive young B-girls before they had a chance to order a drink.

"Hi, GI," one of the girls said, sliding expertly onto the red Naugahyde seat, draping an arm around Tom's shoulders.

"Hi, honey," Tom said as he tried to get the bartender's attention. Personally, he preferred the Continental.

"You buy for me one tea," she asked with practice ease, rubbing

Tom's chest through his shirt.

The other girl was similarly attending to Haynes. Mike was taken. She ran her hand under his uniform shirt, the light touch of her nails as erotic a feeling as he had ever had. She said," I love you too much, GI."

"Sure," Mike squeaked, and the bartender miraculously appeared. Grey bit his tongue, ordered a round, and hoped this establishment didn't water all the drinks.

The girls were pretty. The one who sat next to Haynes had Suzy Wong features and hair to her waist. The other was stockier and carried quite a set of tits. Haynes thought he was back in the World.

"You girls come here often?" Grey asked with mock seriousness.

They giggled.

The Johnnie Walker Black wasn't watered, and Grey sat back to enjoy the music and the perfume. The bar was dark and cool. A small shot glass filled with a dark caramel-colored liquid sat before each girl. Haynes started to reach for it, but Grey stopped him, saying, "Don't taste that."

"Why not?" Haynes asked, puzzled.

"Because it's probably Coke and it cost you five bucks.

"*What?*"

"That's a rog," Grey confirmed. "They call it Saigon Tea, and it goes with the girls."

"Oh, what the hell," he said, knocking back his Scotch.

As Grey shut his eyes, he heard Haynes ask, "You like Americans?"

"They're exchange students," Tom said, "from San Francisco."

Haynes ignored him. "What's there to do in this town?" he asked.

Everyone but Grey had finished their drinks. The slender girl next to Haynes swirled her glass to emphasize the situation. "What you got in mind, GI?" she asked.

The bartender was back, and another round of Johnnie Walker and Saigon Tea was placed in front of them.

"Those aren't real," Grey said suddenly, sitting up.

"What?" chorused the girls and the alarmed bartender.

"Her tits," Grey said, indicating the young lady's chest who sat next to him. "Vietnamese don't have tits like that." he continued with conviction.

The Orientals relaxed, and the bartender again disappeared.

"I'll bet they're fakes," continued Grey.

"No," the girls were amused, "they real. True."

"Naw," Grey said, "Vietnamese have little tits, *ti-ti* tits.

"She not Vietnamese," said the girl next to Haynes. "She Chinese."

"I don't believe it," Grey said. "Show me."

Without appearing to think about it, the Chinese girl unbuttoned her blouse, exposing her breasts. Grey studied them a moment and then reached forward and cupped a hand under each one. "Well, they feel real," he said, slowly, hefting the fleshy weights. "What do you think, Mike?"

Haynes reached across the table and began toying with the girl's chest. "Seem real to me," he said, grinning broadly, a young man's grin.

"Only one way to tell for sure." Grey leaned forward and sucked one of the large brown nipples into his mouth.

The girl leaped angrily to her feet; her face twisted with disdain. *"You foul, GI! You numba fuckin' ten."* She spat before she turned and stomped away with her friend, arms akimbo, as she tucked herself back into her bra.

"That's the trouble with these people," Grey shook his head sagaciously. "No sense of humor."

Haynes appeared angry. "Bitch. It was worth twenty bucks for Chrissake."

Suddenly the bartender appeared. He, too, was angry, and his face was set in a theatrical mask of emotion. "You go, you go now, or I call MP."

Haynes' left hand darted out like a whip. He caught the bartender by the throat and pulled him into the booth. With his right hand, he freed his knife and held it menacingly over the frightened man. "My friend and I are going to finish our drinks," he said in a slow, deliberate voice. "We're going to drink them quietly and peacefully," Haynes shook the bartender. "And you're going to stand here and see that we enjoy them."

Several Vietnamese toughs were moving about in the rear of the bar.

Haynes let the bartender up and sat back to finish his drink, his right hand with the knife rested on the table. Grey threw off his drink in two or three awkward gulps, amber liquid ran from one side of his mouth and down his neck. Haynes stood up and took the bartender firmly in his grasp and walked to the door. Grey followed.

They parted company at the sidewalk. Haynes put his large folding knife in a pocket. Hayne's eyes seemed to glitter as he stared at the bartender. The two Americans turned and had not gone five feet when the Vietnamese turned and ran back into the bar, screaming.

Haynes and Grey bolted into the street and flagged down a taxi. "A whorehouse," Grey shouted, "and quick!"

Tom sat back in the seat and tried to relax the adrenalin surge as the city's ambiguity crept around them. Haynes was still trembling with rage. "God damned fuckin' people," he said, tightly, "We get our asses blown off so they can run their little racket, and then they gotta fuck with us, *man!* We get a little ahead of their game, and we're assholes. We're assholes, man!"

"Ah, driver," Grey said, leaning forward, forearms resting on the back of the front seat, "Cancel that whorehouse and take us to Tan Son Nhut."

"Why?" Haynes snapped.

"Because we ain't neither one of us in any mood to be fuckin' around in this town.

"By God if the bastards want to fuck around..," Haynes said, angrily.

"That's what I mean."

"Shut your damn mouth, Grey!" Haynes snapped.

Grey did.

It was late afternoon, and the bustling throngs of people going about their business struck a discordant note in Haynes' boozed and angry mind. He had wanted to kill the bartender. Now, as the emotion drained from him, he was glad he hadn't. "Let's go somewhere for a drink," he said.

"This driver's going to think we're nuts."

"The meters running." Haynes gestured fitfully, turning to gaze out the window.

"Where can we get a nice, quiet drink, driver?"

"I know just the place," the cabbie turned in his seat and smiled at Grey. "It's close to Tan Son Nhut, so if you change your mind again, you can walk."

Grey noticed then that the driver had blue eyes and no left arm. "How come you've got blue eyes?" he asked.

"My father was a French soldier; my mother was Vietnamese. When the French left, I went with my father to live in Paris, but I returned because I missed my mother." The cabbie turned again and grinned, "I pretty fuckin' dumb."

The cab passed through a gate in a long white-painted wall, turning into the Vietnamese Air Force Officer's Club, driveway. The building was a two-story, white building with an orange tile roof. Baking in the sun in front of the building was a dilapidated Grumman Bearcat fighter. It had Vietnamese Air Force insignia painted on the fuselage. It was a sad and undignified end to an excellent World War II vintage airplane. There were no other Americans around the club where he dropped them. "You sure we can go in here?" Grey asked, doubtfully looking at the two-story white stucco building.

"It okay. Nice place," the Taxi driver said.

"What the hell," Grey said, paying him.

Bright Asian flowers tumbled down the side of the building in a white and lavender cascade. The tall, wrought iron adorned windows were shaded by small roofs that mimicked the tile of the main roof. A white curtain fluttered languidly from a second-floor window, maybe an invitation to surrender.

Grey and Haynes strode up the gray steps and through an incongruous aluminum revolving door. Inside, the two-story atrium floor was covered by black and white patterned marble. A plush burgundy-colored carpet swept up a staircase that curved from the left up to a marbled balcony. Two uniformed Vietnamese airmen lounged over the railing, leaning on their elbows. Cigarette smoke drifted toward the beamed ceiling as they gazed dispassionately down on the GIs.

Under the balcony, off to the right, was a door with maroon Naugahyde held to it with hundreds of brass nails fixed around the edge. Grey, followed by Haynes, who staggered slightly, strode purposely toward it, confident that the concession to tawdriness must be the entrance to the bar. The Americans went in through a double door, like an airlock. The bar was dark and crowded. After a bit of searching, they found a booth in a corner. The room was full of soldiers, airmen, and a couple of sailors in their whites and Vietnamese hustlers and scam artists.

Scattered among them was a hoard of B-girls. Several girls tried to sidle into the booth, but Grey sent them away, explaining that both men were married to Vietnamese women in Cu Chi. Later the mama san came by, bought them a drink, and said they were good men and heroes.

Haynes was silent for a moment after she left. Then he said, "You know what bothers me?"

Grey ignored him. The music from the jukebox was early sixties rock'n'roll, and he felt mellow as hell. Maybe it was the weather, the lush yellow sunshine flowing down on Saigon. Perhaps it was the booze or the cabbie or the two joints they had fired up on the way to the club, but he felt encased in a pleasant reverie.

"It's unnecessary."

Tom did not like the statement intruding on his semi-consciousness.

"These are really nice people. I mean, there are assholes like those people back at the bar, but there are assholes everywhere. These people are just like us. They just want to live." Haynes paused a moment and realized how ridiculous he was sounding. "Fuck it," he said finally.

Grey did not want to think about it. He ordered a couple of hamburgers and lit a Marlboro. "This friend of mine in Hue. Name's MacEvy..," tapping his lighter on the tabletop.

"Uh huh," Haynes said, glad for a change of subject.

"When he first went up north, he flew on a C-130 with a bunch of Vietnamese civilians, Officers' families, or something. They had the nylon seats down on the sides, and the civilians were in them, and the GIs were on the deck. It was a pretty lousy day… you know how a 130 is anyway."

The food came, and Tom dug in, putting the possible original species of the meat our of his mind. Dog was a local favorite. "Well," he continued, "Most of the Vietnamese had never flown before, so a few of them turned a little green before they got off the ground. Things were okay, though, until they hit the usual bit of turbulence where you cross the mountains west of Da Nang." Tom paused for effect, his hamburger dripping condiments, "One kid about twelve got sick. Puked all over about three GIs. Then the kid's mother got sick, and after she let loose, a chain reaction started. Everybody got sick. The Vietnamese, the GIs, the crew chief…, everybody."

Haynes shook his head and smiled a little blearily, his hamburger untouched in front of him.

"MacEvy said it was the worst thing that ever happened to him. Everything was covered with puke. There was about an eighth of an inch of vomit on the floor, and the troops had to sit in it. It was all warm and smelly…"

Mike felt the booze turn in his stomach and realized that he'd better eat something, too.

"But," Tom said, "When it was all over, when everybody had puked their guts out, and they got used to the smell, they got to laughing. Laughed their asses off. Some of the GIs started smearing it on each other and throwing it around. The NCOs put a stop to that, but MacEvy said people were just fuckin' hysterical. The women, especially. All those demure little Vietnamese ladies cracking up and laughing so hard they pissed their pants."

Haynes was picking slowly at his hamburger. Then he realized that Grey was fucking with his mind. He purposely took several large, sloppy bites from his sandwich and, chewing, asked testily, "Are we going to get laid or not?"

Grey had not really thought about it since the cab. Still, this night on the town in Saigon had been his idea. "Sure. Why not?" he said.

"Where?" Haynes asked, mollified.

The mama san was sitting at the bar drinking tea, real tea, with several Vietnamese soldiers. Tom motioned to her, and when she came over, he put the question to her directly. She thought it over. "Blue Swan Hotel," she said. "You go Blue Swan, say Mama San Di send you." The old lady was obviously disappointed in their infidelity.

They did not find a cab. Instead, Grey and Haynes caught two blue cyclos, motorized rickshaws. They resembled three-wheeled cycles with a wicker basket and a seat set between the two front wheels, and the "driver" who sat on a bicycle type seat behind the passengers. They were cheap, and they were convenient, but they were also easy to hit. The fact was not lost on either of the soldiers. Grey could just imagine how neatly a grenade tossed into the basket he was in would eliminate one-half millionth of the U.S. war effort.

In the heart of the city they began to spend long periods waiting for traffic lights. At one red light, Haynes saw an expensive chauffeured car idling next to them. He raised up, as best he could, and gave the startled diplomat and wife a jaunty salute.

The light changed, and Haynes was forced back into his seat as the cyclo, in a blue exhaust cloud, sped off, with Grey's in hot pursuit. The last thing Grey saw of the limousine was the startled look on the matron with the beehive blond hairdo seated in the back, her mouth formed a wry, knowing smile.

Finally, the cyclos, seemingly having exhausted their careening nature, pulled up before a narrow four-story light blue stucco building. Tottering slightly, they gazed up at the building. "You think it's really a whorehouse," Grey asked.

"Beats the shit out of me," Haynes answered, putting his hands in his pockets.

Just as they turned to go inside, a hulking MP stopped them.

"Let's see some ID," he demanded.

Grey began searching nervously through his pockets. He found a shorthand notebook, which he surreptitiously gave to Haynes. Eventually, he fished out his USARV press card and showed it to the MP. Satisfied, the MP turned to Haynes.

"All he's got is his notebook," Tom said, babbling, "He's down here from the 101st, and they don't issue press cards. We're doing a story on the Vietnamese government for his unit's paper."

The MP took the notebook from Haynes and flipped through the indecipherable shorthand notes.

"We missed our bus," Grey said. "We had a few drinks and missed our bus. We got talking to some people about the pacification program." Grey ran on. "It may be a story I can do something with. It's my fault, really. Mike here wanted to get going."

The policeman was intrigued by the shorthand. He had never seen it outside of girls' notebooks in high school. That a grown man would be walking around this city with a notebook full of the scribbles astounded him. The fact simply did not fit into any of the categories for normal behavior that he had learned to recognize.

Besides, if he ran them in, it would take all night to fill out the paperwork. And it was late, and the two drunks stood a pretty good chance of getting shot if he didn't run them in. "Where you headed?" he asked, staring hard at Grey.

"Ah, right here, Sir. The Blue Swan. The Blue Hotel is what the guidebooks call it." Grey said, hopefully.

"I call it a mangy whorehouse," The MP stated. "But go on in," he said, "but don't come out till morning and don't cause any trouble, and don't forget to use your rubbers. If there's any trouble, I'm the one who'll have to come in, and I'll remember you," the MP said, staring intently at both soldiers.

Haynes was amazed by the MP's decision. A break from a cop is a little like an act of God. "Thanks, man," he said. "I mean, really..., thanks a lot, man."

"It's okay. Take the elevator to the top floor." the MP instructed them knowingly, handing the notebook back to Haynes, turning without a further glance.

The hotel lobby inside the blue building was dusty. The plaster on the walls was cracked and broken in a few places exposing the bricks underneath. To their right, next to the iron stairway, was an old French elevator; the open birdcage type. The two soldiers entered it, the floor sagging under their weight, then floating back level with the floor. Haynes closed the grate-like door as Grey pushed the worn black plastic top button among those on the brass plate's verdigris.

Slowly, as the ancient hydraulics began to function, the two men rose in faded majesty through the ceiling. The elevator eventually bumped to a halt at the top floor, exhausted, the tread of the elevator not quite matching that of the hall. The two soldiers stepped up, exiting the contraption. Like the corridor on the street, the upper level was musty and painted a teal blue to about the four-foot level, and a yellowy cream above. Down the hall, to their right, was a wooden door painted red.

"Must be the place," Grey said, turning to lead the way.

Raunchy live music and a haze of cigarette smoke greeted them as they walked inside. Vietnamese men and American GIs shuffled with Oriental girls on the minute dance floor. A small, attractive, elderly woman welcomed them.

"Mama San Di sent us to you," Tom said.

"Very good." She bowed slightly and showed them to a small table off the dance floor and asked if they would like a drink.

"*Ba Muoi Ba*," Grey said.

"*Ba Muoi Ba*?" Haynes said, leaning across the table. "What the hell is *Ba Muoi Ba*?"

Grey was amused. "You've been in Vietnam for four months, and you don't know what *Ba Muoi Ba* is?"

"How in the hell would..."

"I don't know about you, Haynes. Get you all dressed up and

can't take you anywhere.

The Vietnamese woman spoke in very polite and precise English. "He means 33, it is one of our local beers; a nice beer." She smiled warmly at Haynes, who felt he had just had his hand patted.

Mike nodded, blushing, and thanked the woman.

"It is said," she went on, "that if the Honorable Ho Chi Minh and Honorable President Nuygen Van Thieu sit down and drink thirty-three of them together, there would be peace in Vietnam.

Both men laughed, enchanted by her elegance.

Then she smiled again and said, "I imagine you young gentlemen prefer the company of ladies younger than myself."

"Not so," Grey gallantly protested.

"You are kind." She nodded her head briefly and then disappeared toward the back of the bar.

After a while, a white-aproned waiter brought two bottles of beer and two large glasses with correspondingly large chunks of ice. Haynes poured half a glass and took a tentative sip. The beer had a vaguely familiar smell and left a strong aftertaste.

"They don't pasteurize it," Grey said, grinning. "I have been told that instead, they use a little formaldehyde as a preservative. It's not bad once you get used to the taste." He filled his own glass and watched the beige head form on top of the reddish liquid.

He took a long drink. "There's no quality control either, so the alcohol content ranges from plus or minus five percent to about fifty percent," Grey added, wiping foam from his upper lip.

Haynes took another sip and turned his attention to the bar. The men who lined it were of various nationalities. They stood, invariably, with one foot on the long brass rail, and all wore some sort of military uniform. Most were unarmed, but sidearms, suspended from leather or canvas belts, were spotted about. Here and there, pairs engaged in quiet conversation. But mostly they drank alone, either watching the dance floor or sullenly concentrating on their booze or their images in the large mirror behind the bar.

Grey tapped a fingernail against the glass ashtray in time with the music and sighed. "This band is pretty good for Vietnamese," he said.

"I wouldn't know," Haynes replied testily. "I haven't heard too many bands lately."

"That's life," Grey said with a broad smile.

Presently two young girls appeared through the crowd and took seats opposite each other and between Grey and Haynes. My-Duyen, who sat to Haynes right, wore American style clothes and cosmetics. Her blouse, knotted over the soft curve of her belly, was thin, and he could see her brown nipples through it. Her red shorts were short and tight over a small bottom and sleek looking legs. Her black flats were scuffed. She was beautiful.

The other girl, Linh, was smaller and slim. She was dressed in the traditional Vietnamese au dai. The black slack outfit and sheer white blouse with close-fitting sleeves and high-buttoned collar accentuated the soft brown of her face and hands.

Her long black hair shimmered in the yellow, smoky bar light as it framed her face. She glanced at Grey and Haynes and dropped her eyes demurely.

Perfume enveloped the two soldiers.

"You wish that we stay with you tonight," My-Duyen asked Grey without preamble. Her voice was soft but carried easily over the music.

"You bet!" Haynes said without hesitation.

"How much?" Grey asked, leaning back in his chair as if in no hurry to conclude the transaction.

"Seven hun'red pi." My-Duyen said, smiling as she took one of Mike's hands in hers as she regarded Tom easily.

Haynes took out his wallet without releasing My-Duyen's hand. Because he didn't have piasters, he paid the seven dollars in pink and green military pay certificates. Sighing, Grey gave Linh MPC as well. Mai passed the small bills over to My-Duyen, keeping her eyes down. The waiter placed two cocktail glasses on paper napkins in front of the girls.

"Shall we have one room or two?" My-Duyen inquired.

"One," Grey said quickly, thinking about R&R costs in Singapore.

"Five hun'red," She said.

Grey paid placed a five dollar note near My-Duyen's hand. Slowly she reached out and took the bill. Standing, My-Duyen smiled at Haynes as she pulled free. "I'll get key," she said.

Suddenly, inspired by who knew what, Tom asked Linh to dance. The music had slowed and had a hollow bluesy quality that hung in the smoke-filled barroom. Windows lined one wall. Grey shuffled in sadness with the other dancers he could see out across the darkening city as long blue shadows filled in the bright stucco surfaces. The girl seemed hesitant in her step and said nothing.

My-Duyen returned and motioned them to the table. Grey sat down, but Linh remained standing, near My-Duyen. "Go to the room, and wait for us there," My-Duyen said.

Grey wondered briefly if this was a rip-off, but decided not. Hynes held up an old-fashioned key attached to a worn, oval brass fob with the number 6 engraved on it, and let it swing like a pendulum. "Ready to get laid?" he asked, rattling the key.

"Let me talk to the bartender first, and get some beer," Grey said, standing.

The room was narrow and small. Twin brass beds with a small night table between them jutted from one wall. The off-brown color of the faded decor reminded Haynes of old jeep tops.

"We'd better stash our money," Mike said, "I got an uncle that claims some whore ripped him off for three hundred bucks one night after he fell asleep."

"Bummer."

"Yeah, it was my old man's money."

The went over the room quickly and discovered that the brass knobs on the bedstead were removable. They rolled up their money and jammed it into one of the hollow posts. Then they went into the white-tiled bathroom and opened the only window. Haynes put down the lid on the stool and sat on it.

Grey experimentally straddled the bidet and took two cigarettes from a pack of Salems. Clever and industrious Vietnamese had worked all of the tobacco out of the cigarettes. They replaced it with fine, stemless, dynamite marijuana known on the street as "Saigon Red." The pack had been carefully resealed and sold on Long Binh Post for two dollars. Haynes lit one and leaned back against the pipe that led up to the tank of the old toilet. The white ceramic handle of the pull-chain rested on his shoulder. The smoke was rich and thick, fresh with the taste of menthol.

Just as the two soldiers were finishing their joints, the girls knocked on the door. Haynes, a little wobbly, went to let them in. Each of the girls carried a few items, which they stacked on the bed stand.

"We brought some good things for you," said My-Duyen, motioning toward a jug of bottled water, several Cokes, and a few small round cardboard boxes of cheese. My-Duyen took small triangles of foil-covered cheese from the box while Linh poured Coke into foggy glasses from the bathroom. Grey sat on the edge of the bed and examined the top of the cheese box. It was printed with a tiger and Vietnamese words. The label reminded him of the colorful packaging of firecrackers and the Fourth of July.

Haynes stopped Linh from pouring the third Coke and pulled two *Ba Muoi Ba* from a cardboard box next to the bathroom door. My-Duyen was displeased.

"You drink too much," she said with a pout.

Grey, eying the tableau, wondered if she really gave a damn. "If she did," he thought, opening the bottle Haynes gave him with a worn metal bottle opener, "She was one rare whore."

"What 'n hell do your care?" he asked.

My-Duyen looked at Grey sternly with her left hand on her hip. With her right, she jabbed the air in his direction, waving a red-painted nail under his nose. "You drink too damn much! You plenty *Dien cai Dau!*"

"It's just me face, Luv," he replied in his best Ringo Starr accent.

Linh then knelt on the bed beside Grey and began unbuttoning his shirt. She removed it, then folded it carefully and put it in one of the drawers of the nightstand.

My-Duyen poured their beer into glasses and served the cheese. As he did so, Linh knelt at Tom's feet and began untying his boots. Embarrassed by the attention, he motioned her to stop and did the work himself.

He put his right hand under her chin and tilting her face up said, "You sure are quiet."

Linh stood awkwardly, and stood before him, eyes again cast down.

"She new," explained My-Duyen. "She only be prostitute for few days."

"My father…," began Linh. They all knew the story. In a good year, a peasant could clear about fifty dollars raising rice and produce. A pretty daughter was worth five or six hundred in the city or wherever GIs congregated. Grey covered her mouth with his hand and stared for a moment at the girl's delicately featured face and luminous eyes. "I'm an asshole," he thought. Then he reached for the old Empire-style lamp and turned out the light.

Her body was small, almost tiny. Grey took her carefully. Even so, the girl did not respond, and he could only kiss her lips by holding her head with both hands. It should have been a beautiful experience or a rollicking experience, but it was not. Necrophilia entered Grey's mind.

Haynes apparently did not have any such problems. My-Duyen was pretty hip and seemed to enjoy her profession. Mike had a lot of love stored up, and for two hours, it seemed, the bed creaked and groaned as he explored Vietnam.

After a time, Grey said, "Mike, let's swap."

"What?" Haynes mumbled.

"We are," Grey continued, "At the end of the earth conducting drug-induced debaucheries in an oriental whore house. Why not?"

My-Duyen struggled free of the blankets, her brown arms flailing, and half sat up. Her makeup was smeared into a clown's mask, and her pretty young face was set with determination. She succinctly informed Tom that most GIs would be happy to have a new girl and that most would, furthermore, be gentlemen and do their best to make sure that the evening was a pleasure. Grey had a suspicion that the Hotel Mi Lan was mostly an officers' hangout.

He turned back to Linh, and it was then he realized he had hurt her feelings. In the half-light, silhouetted against the white sheets, she was small and beautiful.

He kissed the soft, smooth skin of her neck and moved his

body gently against hers. With his left hand, he found the blanket and pulled it over them. As the night progressed, he saw her smile a few times, and he thought that if she was laughing at him, he was a least getting her attention.

Haynes woke him once during the night and called him into the bathroom. My-Duyen was using the bidet, and Mike felt the strange phenomenon worthy of observation.

"Mysteries of the Orient," Grey mumbled and returned to bed. He lost himself in the warm, gentle flesh of the Vietnamese girl.

THE SQUAD—RE-FIT

Grey—23 and a Wakeup

Grey left the brigade headquarters area and walked slowly toward the battalion. The rain had stopped during the night, and already the heavy traffic along Camp Eagle's main drag had packed the mud back into a smooth, hard surface.

Helicopters moved quickly through the clear sky, and although the morning was chilly, Grey knew that the day would be hot. This was Vietnam. He crossed the road and started down the sharp embankment for the Company area. Everything in the large depression below him was a burnt umber color, the tents, the vehicles, and the mud. There were, as at LZ Jane, flags posted in front of some of the tents; American, Confederate battle flags, and some state flags. Grey smiled at the lone skull and crossbones pirate flag that puffed out above one tent.

The members of Kelly's squad sat on a collection of lumber and sandbags next to their tent. The glint of dog tags contrasted sharply with the skin of their bare chests.

"How's it going, Michael?" Grey asked, walking up to the group.

"Okay, considering it's the morning after."

"That's a rog," Grey said, smiling while wiping his red-rimmed eyes with the back of his hand.

The other squad members looked up briefly from their tasks and nodded at Tom. Then they returned to the job of weapons maintenance.

Haynes was cleaning rounds of M-16 ammunition with a green cloth torn from an old tee shirt. Grey noticed that Mike's knuckles were skinned, and the wrist below his bruised forearm was slightly swollen. Schilling and Jones were ejecting shells from magazines into a wooden crate sitting at Haynes' left side. They then tore down the empty magazines, cleaned each one, and tested the spring. If the spring was weak or the case dented, the entire thing was tossed into an empty C-Ration carton.

Johnson and Saunders took the rebuilt magazines and reloaded them with cleaned ammo. Eighteen rounds in each magazine; every fifth one a tracer. Tracer rounds were identified by a touch of red paint on the tip of the bullet. They were piled together between the two soldiers. Grey noted that Saunders' face was bruised, and his left cheek slightly swollen. He sat quietly, head down.

Bayaban was sitting cross-legged on a sheet of plywood assembling belts for the M-60. Grey watched a moment and then sat down to help. He took a belt and, being careful not to damage the links, disassembled the entire belt. Grey cleaned each round separately, paying particular attention to the rim at the base of each cartridge. He then soaked the metal links in some gasoline. The reporter dried the small metal bits on a clean rag and then reassembled the belt's entire length. He did the job quickly and efficiently, and he knew that the others would notice. It was a small thing, but Grey knew it would help establish his bona fides with the squad.

"Trying to show me up?" asked Bayaban with a grin.

"You're not bad for a rookie," Grey replied, smiling back at the larger man.

Prescott and Jennett came around the corner with crates of new ammo. They sat them down, and Jennett worked the lids loose with his black hands. When Jennett folded back the buff-colored paper, the new brass glittered in the sun like gold.

"I hear we're going in from Firebase Blaze," Prescott announced.

"When?" Haynes asked.

"The day after tomorrow. The whole Brigade's going in. Gonna be some show."

"We getting any jets?" asked Johnson, hopefully.

"Everything," said Scotty. "They've got artillery up on two firebases on the rim of the Valley, and they'll be B-52s if we need them."

"I think maybe Kelly was right." Johnson shook his head slowly. "The big shots know something we don't."

"You know," Jennett said, "If we get in that Valley and it starts raining again, we could get our asses in a sling."

"Maybe that's what they've got in mind," Haynes said, wiping another round with the rag.

"What do you mean?" Johnson asked, worry evident in his

tone.

"Maybe," Haynes suggested, "They think that if it starts raining, the NVA will think we've got troubles and come across the border to have at us."

"Yeah... that's cool," Jones said. "Sucker them in and then kick the shit out of them." He laughed, his face shining in the morning sun.

Kelly came around the corner of the tent with a can of Pepsi in his hand. "You guys doing okay?" he asked.

Everyone nodded.

"Good." Kelly briefly examined the work that had been done. "Why don't you take fifteen minutes and relax a little?"

Nobody argued. Haynes and Grey drifted up the hill toward the Enlisted Men's Club and a cold soda. Tom took off his shirt in acknowledgment of the rising heat and humidity. They walked up the hill in silence. There wasn't time to drink the pop in the Club's cool interior, so they brought the cans with them as they started back toward the company area.

"What's with you and Saunders?" Grey asked.

"You noticed his face, huh?" Haynes asked in reply.

"Yeah," Tom said, "And your hands."

"He didn't do anything," Haynes said, inspecting his right hand as he flexed it. "He was really happy because he got his Combat Infantryman Badge, and I really laid into him."

"Everybody was pretty drunk," Grey said in consolation.

"It wasn't the booze. It was all this fuckin' hate I've got in my guts. It's like having a bomb inside you," Haynes said, squinting in the afternoon glare.

Grey hesitated before he spoke. "Hate's the only thing you really learn in war. Dehumanization."

"Dehumanization my ass," snapped Haynes. "It's human as hell. That's what makes it so God-damned bad. It happens to everybody. Human beings are real assholes."

"We should've gone to Canada." Grey mused.

"I did." Haynes said.

"You're kidding," Grey glanced quickly at Haynes.

"Nope. I got my draft notice, and I split," Haynes said, spitting into the dust at his feet.

Grey lit a cigarette. He was intrigued. "What happened?" he asked.

They two soldiers walked in silence for several moments. Haynes not wanting to speak, Grey feeling he should not. Finally, Mike began, "I packed up my VW, guitar, socks 'n all. I went up through Detroit," he said. "And into the tunnel under the lake toward Windsor, Canada.

"The guard on our side asked my nationality, and I said 'U.S.', and I went through. The guy on the other side asked me the same question. Only that time, I said 'American.' The guy looked at me and said, 'Are you sure?' I sat there at a turn-around that is right after the Canadian border guard's post, listening to WIL on the radio, and then I turned the car around and came back." He tossed the empty soda can into the air with one hand and snatched it back with the other. "It was that simple."

They turned off the main road and down into the Company area. The camp on the muddy flats was active beneath the tropical sun.

"Kinda reminds you of Vietnam, doesn't it?" Tom asked with a lopsided grin.

Haynes nodded his head. "Did I ever tell you about the time me and my old buddy Grey went to Saigon?" he asked.

They both laughed.

Kelly was waiting for them in the squad area. "Did you gentlemen have a pleasant sojourn?" he inquired politely.

"We just went up to the EM Club for a quick soda, Kel." Haynes said, looking sheepish.

"I said fifteen minutes, Haynes. Fifteen minutes means fifteen minutes."

"Sure, Sarge."

"Come on, I want to talk to you." Kelly turned and walked toward the orderly room. Haynes looked around at the others and shrugged his shoulders in inquiry. Nobody knew anything, so Mike started after the Sergeant. Grey went back to cleaning ammunition.

"What's up?" Haynes asked when he had caught the squad leader.

"Monaghan's gone, rotated back to the rear, then home to the World. That means I need a new fire team leader."

"So?"

"So, you're it."

Haynes was surprised. "Kelly," he said, "I don't want to be fuckin' fire team leader."

"I didn't ask if you wanted to be a fire team leader. I told you you are the fire team leader."

"Why me?" Haynes asked. "There are lot better guys in the squad than me..."

"No there aren't. You're good, and you know it, so shut your mouth. Department of the Army's getting generous as hell with promotions. If we get over to the orderly room quick, we might get you made at least an acting corporal before they give it to some fucking cook."

"Shit." Haynes said, without conviction.

"You love it," Kelly said. Then he added with an air of finality, "Somebody's got to help me with those knotheads back there. Besides, it's worth about fifty-bucks extra a month."

Haynes got his stripes, or rather Sergeant Kelly knew somebody who knew somebody who got the stripes for him. They were actually two small black collar pins in the shape of two chevrons. When they got back to the squad, the men congratulated him with evident sincerity. That cheered Haynes and removed the uncertainty that comes with a promotion.

After lunch, Grey lied about having something to do at the Division Public Information Office and went away to get ripped. Mike turned his attention to his personal gear and went into the tent to get his M-16.

◆ ◆ ◆

In the gloom of the tent interior, Jones and Prescott were stretched out on adjacent bunks sharing a joint. "Care for a toke of the herb?" Scotty asked, smiling.

"Not right now," Haynes said as he sat down on his own bunk and lit a cigarette. "Why'd you guys come over here?" he asked.

"Stupidity," Jones said flatly.

"Prescott agreed, although tentatively. "It was more *naïveté*, I think. They tell you you got to go to school, and so you go to school. They tell you to go to work, and you go. When they told me it was time to go to the war, I figured, what the hell, school, and work weren't much fun, and things might pick up in the Army."

"If you feel that way about it," Haynes inquired, "Why don't you blow a foot off or something and get sent home?"

Jones pointed out that he had only two feet and that he had a deep affection for them. "All for one, and one for all," he said.

Prescott took the question seriously. He rolled onto his side and propped himself up on his elbow. "I kinda like pulling the trigger on the sanctimonious little bastards," he said. "I mean our side tells us a bunch of shit, and their side tells them a bunch of shit. But those fuckers believe it! They're just chock full of pride and self-righteousness…"

"You forgot *dignity!*" Jones added.

"Oh, Lord, yes. Their profound fuckin' *dignity*." Scotty paused. Then he said, "At least we know we're mother fuckers. There's a certain honesty in that."

"And dignity, too." Jones added again.

"Yes, by God, *dignity*."

Haynes quietly finished the cigarette and collected his M-16.

He met Johnson just outside of the tent.

"You seen Jones?" asked the Black soldier.

"Yeah, he's in the hootch."

"What the hell's he doing in the hootch?"

"Kickin' back."

"Great fuckin' bruther I got." Johnson barked.

Johnson left Mike and quickly ducked through the tent flaps. Sitting with the rest of the squad, Haynes sat on the plywood sheet and removed the canvas sling from his rifle.

Behind him, he heard Johnson and Jones approaching.

"You ain't got no fuckin' brains, have you Jones?"

"Oh, man," Jones whined.

"You could have at least found a place to hide. Kelly'd have your ass in Long Binh Jail before breakfast."

"Kelly knew we were smokin' last night." Jones whined.

"That was then, this is now," Johnson said. "And you knows it."

Haynes turned his attention to the M-16 on his lap. He removed the plastic foregrip, opened the rifle, and unhinged the stock from the firing group and barrel. Carefully, he removed the bolt and disassembled the entire mechanism.

Seated across from him, Wood was doing the same thing. Haynes watched as the slender Kentuckian worked lovingly on the small parts with a clean piece of rag. Wood always looked sad. Haynes didn't think the sadness had anything to do with real events. It probably had to do with something cosmic.

Mike put the firing mechanism back together and tested the trigger for its sharp, solid snap. Next, he cleaned the barrel—the inside first with patches and then the outside with solvent. A little rust had developed, and in places, the bluing had worn away to expose the steel below, especially around the flash suppressor. Lastly, he covered the weapons with a thin coat of oil and put it back together. It felt good in his hands, smooth and dependable.

Haynes remembered a story his father had told him about his service in the Second World War. They had taken a German position and found the body of one of its defenders. The man's teeth were rotting in his head, and he was emaciated with hunger and disease. One of the few things they found in his pack was a spare bolt for the machine gun. It was immaculate and freshly oiled, carefully wrapped and stored away in a piece of oilcloth.

The sun was edging westward in the sky, and in a few hours the temperature would start to fall. Kelly came around the tent's corner with a half-case of cold sodas and called a break. While the men drank and joked among themselves, he inspected the weapons and ammunition.

Haynes leaned against the sandbag wall that surrounded the sides of the squad tent and thought about something Kelly had once said about not losing any more men than were necessary. He had been tempted to ask how you decided what was necessary, but he had not. In other wars, there were objectives to take, a position, or control of an intersection, or forcing a gap in the enemy's line. You could think of those things in terms of minimal losses because they were tactical decisions taken against the backdrop of a strategic whole, and made sense at all levels.

But Vietnam was not like that. The geography was only the stage. It was a war of extermination. Search and Destroy. Hunt down and kill. They walked the fine line between soldiers and bait. Both sides played the game, stalking and maneuvering to gain the best position for bargaining a life against lives. It went on, and it would go on until the bulk weight of human blood finally tipped the scales.

THE A SHAU VALLEY

Grey—19 and a Wakeup

It was dark and cold, the last few moments before dawn. Hayes felt the muscles of his chest tremble with the chill. It reminded him of duck hunting, waiting in the brisk morning with his father before entering the blinds. He shifted his gear higher onto his back and rubbed his hands together for warmth. In the darkness, he could hear the whispers of the other soldiers waiting with him next to the long line of trucks.

The truck driver, standing behind Hayes, pulled the metal pins holding the tailgate, and the heavy piece of steel dropped open with a slam and a clattering of chains. The rhythmic idling of the trucks filled the air with heavy diesel exhaust. Kelly moved along the line of men with a red filtered flashlight, taking a headcount. He exchanged a smile with Haynes and then nodded to Grey as he passed.

Haynes' feet were cold and despite a hot breakfast less than an hour before he was hungry. He fished a cigarette out of the pack in his shirt pocket and began looking for a match. The sudden *click-flash-burn* of Grey's Zippo startled him. Peering over the flame at Grey, he couldn't read any expression in the dancing light. Maybe, he thought, there was nothing to see.

Down the line, men were boarding the trucks. Kelly gave the

word, and the squad members got to their feet. Haynes tossed his rucksack onto the bed of the deuce and a half and then climbed up. The rest of the team followed. Bayaban, Schilling, Saunders, and Prescott. Grey came last. His pack was lighter than those of the other men, and he boarded without taking it off. Haynes and Prescott lowered the benches on the sides, and the soldiers settled back, their rifle butts and rucksacks between their feet.

Johnson's fireteam came up next—Modeland, Wood, Jones, and Alvarez. A few moments later, Kelly crawled over the back and helped the driver close the tailgate. Haynes put his cigarette out on the steel floor. He concentrated on the chill air and the steady vibrations of the engine.

There was a slight commotion behind the closed tailgate. A man put his foot in the iron stirrup on the rear end of the truck and swung his head and chest up over the tailgate. The appearance of the officer startled the men. He quickly motioned them to stay seated.

"This is going to be rough," he began, "Maybe the roughest we've had in a while. There's a pretty good chance that we're going to get a solid shot at them." The officer paused for a moment. Then he said, "You guys are the best. Don't ever forget it. Good luck." He snapped them a salute as he swung back to the ground and started down the line for the next truck.

The men were silent for a few moments before Modeland said, "Goddamn, the Boss saluted us!"

"He's okay," added Schilling.

"You think we're gonna see much shit, Sarge?" Wood asked."

"Yep," replied Kelly, lighting a cigar. "We're going into the A

Shau."

Ahead of them, they heard trucks begin to pull out. Their driver revved the engine, double-clutched, and slipped the deuce and a half into gear. The driver managed to get the large truck moving with only a gentle protest from the transmission. It lurched ahead, the soldiers moving in counterpoint, and swung onto the road. Grey whispered, "And so it begins."

Haynes, with the rest of the squad, craned his neck to look up at Grey, whose eyes were shadowed as dark as if he wore a mask on his helmet. He stood above them, leaning against the cab's steel roof, as still and as watchful as a crow.

The convoy passed through Camp Eagle's north gate, crossed the sandpits, and swung west toward the mountains. The sky was turning gray, and there was a glow of pink in the east. Haynes heard Schilling snap the breach of his M-79 grenade launcher open and then, after a moment, snap it shut again with a hollow shotgun-sound clink. Someone coughed. The truck continued to lurch and sway through the ruts. The soldiers did likewise to the truck's motion.

Grey rested his arms on the cab of the deuce and a half, enjoying the wind rushing against his face. In the half-light, he could see the overgrown rice paddies and the untended graves that marked the boundary of the free-fire zone further west. They passed a pastel ruin of a Nguyen Dynasty tomb.

Tom thought of Hoa. It would be nice to do on a Sunday. The two of them could bring a picnic lunch and spend the day exploring. But he supposed that fried chicken, deviled eggs, and hotdogs were things she wouldn't understand. He smiled when he caught himself thinking of snatching some C-rations.

Dawn revealed the clouds of dust the convoy was raising amid the already rising temperature. Firebase Blaze sat on a low cluster of hills at the western edge of the coastal plain. The trucks pulled to a stop along an abandoned airstrip beneath the dusty base. The tailgates slammed open, and the men spilled out onto the road. Kelly led his squad down a steep embankment to the decayed asphalt. They gathered in a small cluster at the edge of the strip. Kelly went off to check with the Lieutenant. Grey got out one of his cameras and began taking pictures.

"Gonna make us famous, Grey?" Modeland asked, grabbing his crotch and making a cross-eyed pose.

"Gonna make Grey famous," Prescott stated, shouldering his pack.

"I sign all my work 'US Army'," Grey muttered.

"The papers back home really print this shit?" Wood asked

"Sure do," Grey answered, taking shots of the GIs. *Snick-snick-snick.*

"I'll be damned," said Schilling.

"It sells newspapers, Prescott muttered sullenly.

"Something wrong with that?" Grey asked. "We are fighting for capitalism."

"Yeah, and capitalism's doing just fine. Everybody's making money on this war but us." Prescott sat down, leaning on his rucksack. "Even the god damned peace movement's making money."

Kelly came back and told them to relax. They were where they were supposed to be, and there was nothing to do but wait. He checked his own equipment and then walked out onto the airstrip, scanning it in both directions.

Haynes watched his squad leader for a moment and then realized that Kelly was nervous. "Well, how about that," he thought.

"Grey," Johnson asked, "Why is the A Shau supposed to be so bad?"

Grey intended to wander around the airstrip shooting pictures before they went in. Instead, he squatted like a Vietnamese with his knees in his armpits. He lit a cigarette while he worked on his answer. Exhaling, Grey said, "You know how you get a feeling about a place or a situation? If you just slow your mind down real quiet like you can get a feeling of what it's all about?"

Johnson nodded tentatively. "Well, the A Shau's like that?"

Grey continued. "I went into the A Shau Valley last summer with the 1st Cav, and I got this feeling that..., well, it's Asia. I mean, Vietnam is just a beach, but back in those mountains, back in the A Shau, it's really Asia."

"The dark continent," added Wood solemnly, his young eyes wide.

"Precisely," Grey said softly, his eyes going from one squad member to another. He spit into the dust as if to ward-off a voodoo spell.

Kelly, overhearing the conversation, walked back off the strip, and lit a cigar. "The choppers'll be here in about half an hour. If any of you guys can find a little shade, take advantage of it."

Grey picked up his cameras and worked his way down the edge of the airstrip. The infantrymen were gathered in clusters ready to board the helicopters for an air-assault. They looked grim but competent. "Well, if you're scared," thought Tom, "you can't blame it on your comrades-in-arms."

Grey did not need his watch to tell him when the time for the assault neared. Sensitive to the small signs, he began moving back toward Kelly's squad among the slowly animating men. A magazine being loaded into a rifle, another sling tightening, or a last pull on a rucksack strap alerted him. When he returned to the squad, he found that Kelly had already told the men to saddle up. They had put their gear on and split into the two fire teams, one on either side of the runway. He caught the sergeant's eye, and Kelly motioned him with a nod to the right, where Haynes stood.

The Hueys came in from the south, swung in a long line over Blaze, and then flew in low over the airstrip, settling down finally in single file. "Damned efficient," though Grey as he scrambled onto the aluminum floor of the Huey.

The correct number of choppers for this number of men. The proper distances between the groups of men on the landing zone. The right amount of fuel in each aircraft and the right amount of food, water, and ammunition on each man's back. Everybody with a place and somebody to make sure they were in it—a self-contained group of fifteen hundred men. Drop them anywhere, and they would fight. When the fighting was over, they would build towns and roads, and in time there would be beer tents, traffic cops, and girlfriends. Even a little newspaper for Grey to pound out.

When they were airborne, the troop carriers squared up into groups of four. Through the large open hatch, Tom could see the sky filled with olive green potbellied Hueys, small egg-shaped observation helicopters, and the flat, sinister profiles of the Cobra gunships. The helicopters stayed close in a group like migrating birds, high up in the sky away from enemy small arms fire.

No one in Kelly's squad spoke. Men leaned back against the bulkheads, their rucks, or each other. Some had their eyes closed, others stared blankly, deep within themselves. A few, like Grey, absently studied the jungle terrain beneath them.

It was a long flight. The helicopters climbed higher above the mountains. The thin air was chilly, and Jennett, sitting opposite Grey, shivered and wrapped his arms around his body. They changed directions, sought a narrow passage between the mist-shrouded peaks. The mountains were long slender ridges running parallel like the Appalachians. Limestone and granite escarpments probed the sunlight from within the triple-canopy jungle as they sped by. Suddenly the formation flew out over the open valley.

From the air, it was possible to locate the major trails and intersections of the enemy's supply lines by the shell craters. There were thousands of them, some large, some small, all filled with water that reflected the rising sun like flashbulbs as the choppers flew overhead. They had been hammered into the earth over the years and looked like penciled dots on a terrain map. Large areas were as barren and pock-marked as the moon.

The men stirred and shifted their positions to see the A Shau. The chartreuse green floor was half a mile across and widened as the airmobile army continued north up its length. Jones, his black face ashen with cold, pointed to a faint brown geometric pattern on the grounds. "What's that?" He yelled.

Grey cupped his hand around Jones' ear, "The old Special Forces camp," he shouted over the noise of the chopper. "It was over-run a couple of years ago."

Grey nodded to himself. They were getting close.

Suddenly the gunships broke out of the formation and began flying long looping circles around the LZ. The Loaches, egg-shaped light observation helicopters, pulled back out of the way, and the Hueys went in fast. They held their formation, and when Kelly's squad hit the ground, they found themselves amid the platoon—where they were scheduled to be.

The prop blasts from the choppers flattened the tall, sharp elephant grass as the men fanned out and hit the dirt. When the helicopters were gone, silence descended on the Americans. The grass swung back up, and the soldiers were submerged in a yellow-green sea.

"Hello. *Helloooo.*" It was Haynes.

The laughter was interrupted by the throaty *braap* of a Cobra's electric Gatling guns. Kelly got the squad to its feet and moved the men out along a small section of the developing line of troops. The gunship was working a small knoll that jutted out of the elephant grass a hundred meters in their front. The tracers from the mini-guns formed a solid, dim-red fluorescent stream that poured into the jungle. A second Cobra joined the hunt and sprayed the knoll with the steady *pop, pop, pop* of its electric grenade launcher. The Lieutenant shouted for Kelly, who threw off his helmet and sprinted in a half-crouch for the platoon command group.

Haynes looked up at the sky. High up, almost out of sight, he could see the jets. Lower, nearer the ground, prop-driven two-seater Forward Air Controller, FACs, worked in widening circles away from the perimeter. Little brother looking for targets. In the same type of aircraft, Cessna L-19s, the PsyOps teams flew low over the jungle. They blared melodramatic Vietnamese chatter and tinny funeral music at the unseen enemy.

The gunships pulled away from the knoll, and one of the FACs began nosing around. He made a few passes, circled once, and then fired two white phosphorous rockets.

"Here comes big brother," said Prescott, sucking on an unlighted cigarette, sweat beginning to run down his face.

"There goes the man that's got my job," Johnson said. "He'll be back in Da Nang at the O-Club with a cold Martini inside a hour."

"Yeah," said Prescott, "but he's sure gonna bring some shit now."

The jet peeled out of its holding pattern and began a long swooping dive. Flashing like quicksilver in the morning sunlight. Its size and speed and roar grew as it approached the crouching GIs. The pilot put her in low over the perimeter, nosed up a little for the knoll, and dropped his load.

The pilot threw the Phantom jet into a tight loop that sent him skyward like a water skier hanging far outside on a tight turn. There were a flash and a crack. The air was filled with debris, and the knoll was burning. The fighter, a small silver dot, began to fall again toward the earth. This time the line of attack was perpendicular to the perimeter. He shot past the men in a screaming, tooth vibrating blur. The second explosion sent up a wall of orange flame and thick black smoke.

Kelly was back and struggling into his gear. "Let's go," he shouted. "Prescott's point."

"What!" Prescott exclaimed.

"Move, damnit!"

Haynes found his ruck, sat down against it, and leaned back into the metal frame. He hooked his arms through the canvas straps and rolled off the pack onto his hands and knees. Using his rifle as a crutch, he pulled himself to his feet. If Prescott was first, then he'd be second. The two of them had agreed to work point and slack together since Drew bought it. Haynes switched his M-16 from safe to automatic.

The squad was ready, and Kelly signaled them to get going. Prescott bounced a few times to settle his ruck before he started across the valley floor. The ground beneath the grass was soft, and Prescott moved slowly and in a wary crouch. With his right hand he held the sixteen next to his body and used his left to push aside the elephant grass. It was sharp-edged and would slice his forearms if he hit it at the wrong angle. Prescott stopped and rolled his sleeves down. Haynes and the others followed suit.

Scotty worked in roughly a straight line toward the knoll. The grass, crushed under his boots, made the track easier for Mike, and he concentrated on pulling slack. Covering those things that the point man couldn't. Whenever Prescott had to turn, he waited until Haynes caught up with him so that they never broke line-of-sight. Mike scanned the grass, but he had no doubt that the trouble would come from the knoll. Biting flies and clouds of mosquitos found the soldiers.

Prescott was getting close, and he passed back the hand signal to halt. He could see a small opening in the jungle that covered the knoll, and he did not want to go in there. It looked like a trail, and if the NVA had anything set up, that's where it would be. To his right, about halfway around the small hill, was the smoking hole the airstrike tore in the foliage. He decided to angle right and then come in straight through the crater. If they were going to fight for it, Prescott knew that they would be aiming at the main body of the platoon. His oblique movement would put him out of that line of fire and through the gap where anything Chuck had planned would be improvised. Grey was fourth in line, just behind Saunders. Tom was crouched low and moved carefully, watching the knoll and ready to hit the dirt. "Fucking infantry," he thought. "If they were using nukes, they'd have to have the infantry mop it up."

Prescott paused and waited for Haynes. It was twenty meters to where the knoll jutted sharply out of the ground, and the elephant grass gave way to dense jungle. Mike's first inclination was to get down and wait for Kelly. But he was a fire team leader now, and he had to get something going.

The situation was not good. Here, there was little cover on the flats, and bunching the men up would be inviting fire. To the left of the clearing, the fighter created was a rock formation. He pointed it out to Prescott and had him move about half the distance and wait. Bayaban was through next with the M-60, and Mike moved him and Saunders about five meters to the right. Then came Grey, and Haynes was now ready to move his team at Kelly's order.

"Prescott's going to try and make those rocks," he explained. "You're his slack." Grey started to protest. He was a reporter, not a fucking Army infantryman. Suddenly he shrugged his shoulders and turned toward Prescott.

Kelly and Johnson's fire team moved to Haynes' right in support. "Rock' n' Roll," Haynes said.

Tom frowned and switched his weapon to automatic.

"Scotty," hissed Haynes. "Go!"

Prescott got to his feet and began moving toward the rocks. Grey followed him. Behind him, Tom heard Haynes ordering Schilling to get down where he was with the M-79. Prescott was in a hurry to get to the rocks. He had taken several long strides before Grey saw the black muzzle of the AK. It was protruding from the jungle and tracking on Scotty. Tom fired from the hip and fell sideways as he let his knees buckle. Scotty dove for the earth, and the air erupted with fire. Grey dumped his ruck and scrambled behind it. Bullets tore into the ground near him. Prescott had made the rocks. Tom crouched and came up like a sprinter out of the blocks. For an instant, he was straight up. Then he dove head-long into the rocks and Scotty.

Haynes was on the ground next to Schilling. He counted three guns firing from the hillside. Rolling to his right, he landed on Saunders. "Up there," Mike shouted, waving his arm. "The ledge over Prescott and Grey!" Bayaban nodded and shifted his body to bring his machine gun into play. Red tracers began hammering into the jungle. On the left, Schilling was thumping M-79 rounds into the knoll with care and concentration.

With the rest of the squad behind him, Kelly broke from the trail and ran straight into the hill. They hit the jungle fifteen meters to the right of the rocks, flanking the NVA position. A squad to their left provided covering fire, trying to suppress enemy fire.

"Can you see anything?" shouted Kelly.

"Fuck no," Prescott yelled back.

"Try some grenades. We're going up here and get behind them."

"Shit!" Prescott sat down and began unhooking grenades from his web gear. He tossed one on Grey. "You throw em," he said.

"Why?"

"Because I'm left-handed," Scotty explained.

"Bullshit."

Prescott smiled.

Grey held onto the rocks with his left hand and leaned out carefully. He quickly gauged the location of one of the enemy positions and then ducked back. He pulled the pin, released the spoon, and immediately counted to two. Then he leaned out from the rocks and lobbed the grenade gently up the hillside. He was back, tight against the limestone before the dull womp scattered small twigs and dust over him. "Shit!"

"Hey, Grey," Prescott said, "Toss them higher, will ya? That one almost rolled down on us." He tossed Grey another grenade.

Without answering, Grey worked his way a few feet down the wall of broken stone and quickly tossed the second grenade. This time a little harder and higher onto the hillside.

Haynes was flat on the ground and firing around his rucksack. He felt a momentary flush of admiration for the doomed Communists. He decided that they didn't have any choice now and that they were just trying to take a few guys with them—him for one.

The rest of the squad had quietly worked its way behind the North Vietnamese positions, and now Kelly swept across them from the rear. The assault was quick, efficient, and vicious; M-16's and grenades.

When the firefight was over, Haynes got to his feet. Slowly his ears adjusted to the silence. Schilling was moaning in the grass a few feet to the left. Mike walked quickly to him. An RPG round had hit Schilling's ruck a glancing blow, and small pieces of shrapnel had torn into his face and upper body.

The soft mass of the pack had broken the blast force, but the man was a mess. A piece of high-velocity steel the size of a dime had broken his cheekbone, and the right side of his face sagged at an odd angle. One eye was closed, but the other leaked tears, few millimeters below its normal position, and stared out toward Schilling's feet. Haynes did a quick survey and saw that the pain would be the immediate problem once shock wore off. He knelt down beside the wounded man and spoke softly, "How bad is it?"

Shilling paused a moment for breath and said, "It hurts. Jesus God, it hurts."

Someone yelled, "Medic!"

"There'll be some morphine in a minute. You're going to be okay." Schilling fought again for breath and dignity. "My eye's fucked up," he said. "I can see, but it's weird... It's fucked up, isn't it?"

"Yeah," Haynes admitted, patting Schilling on the shoulder. While Prescott applied a compress bandage to Schilling's face. Cruz, the platoon medic, slid to Shilling's side and took the bandage from Prescott. He dropped his pack and immediately checked Schilling's airway. Almost simultaneously, he fished around for a morphine syringe.

The squad stood in a cluster about 15 feet away trying not to look.

The rest of the platoon was moving up, and the Lieutenant approached. Taking a quick look, he said to Haynes. "You take your people up with Kelly. We'll take care of your guy."

Haynes gave Schilling a gentle pat on the arm and then stripped the belts of M-79 ammunition from his shoulders. At the same time, the medic carefully held the wounded soldier's head.

Haynes, carrying his own weapon and the short, thick barreled M-79, started slowly through the heat toward the knoll. He passed Grey, who was retrieving his rucksack, without comment. Saunders and Bayaban had their rucks on and were standing beside Schilling. "I'm sorry, man," Bayaban said.

Schilling grinned oddly with the left side of his face. "It's okay. I'll be okay."

"Take care of yourself."

"Sure."

The two young soldiers turned and followed Haynes and Grey up the hill. Mike knew it wasn't his fault. He had handled the situation just as he should have. But it wasn't Schilling's fault either. He, too, had done everything just as he should have.

There were twelve dead NVA on the knoll, seven from the airstrike plus the five the squad had killed. Kelly had his men strip the bodies and sort their weapons and personal gear. There were a lot of souvenirs. He had Johnson tag the items for the men.

"Schilling's out," Haynes told Kelly when he reported.

"Bad?"

"He's going to have a plastic face."

Kelly nodded, saying "Shit!" He spit into the dust, then said to Haynes. "Well, get your guys ready to move. The second platoon is going to take point, and we'll be pulling drag for the Company," he said. "The Captain wants to keep pushing."

Jones found a Viet Cong who wasn't shot up too badly and sat the corpse up against a tree. He and Prescott had given the man a lighted cigarette and a jungle hat. The body wore only black shorts, and the infantrymen were striving for a beachcomber effect. Flies were already buzzing around the dead man. They were trying to talk Grey out of his sunglasses when Kelly said, "Leave him alone, or I'll make you bury him." Kelly spat and turned away, saying, "Get your shit and get ready to move."

The squad leader moved away. Jones spoke softly, "Watch him a minute."

"What?"

"Just watch Kelly a minute."

"Shit."

Slowly Jones took his knife from his scabbard and cut an ear from the dead enemy's head.

"Hey, man!" Prescott was not happy.

The lifeless ear felt strange in Jones' hand, like wax or plastic. The second wave of the assault was coming in now, the Hueys sweeping low across the grass like Mongol cavalry. Jones, suddenly feeling sick, tossed the ear onto the dead man's lap.

Kelly was walking back toward them. Prescott retrieved his jungle hat. Jones grabbed the still-burning cigarette from the dead man's lips and stuck it between his own. They pushed the body sideways, behind the tree.

Kelly stood in front of them with his legs spread and his hands on his hips. "Get your shit and get ready to move…Now!"

Prescott and Jones walked away. Grey stood up and faced Kelly.

"I'm pulling out," he said. "I'm going back to the battalion CP and riding out with the Colonel."

Kelly looked over Grey's shoulder at the bloody Vietnamese and asked, "What went on here?"

"Wouldn't know, Sarge," Grey said lightly, not feeling it.

If Kelly was angry, he did not show it. He said, "This kind of crap gets started, and guys get flaky."

"I suppose sane people make better killers," Grey said, cinching up his rucksack.

Kelly stared at Grey for a moment. "Give the Colonel my love," he said finally.

FUNERAL

Grey—21 and a Wakeup

Grey sat on the hood of a jeep and looked down the small knoll's slope at the formation of men below. The four companies of the battalion were drawn up in neat rectangles facing the makeshift reviewing stand. The soldiers stood at parade rest with helmets cocked under the left arm.

A lean graying Colonel, the brigade commander, addressed them from the platform. Bright streamers and flags curled around the guidons like multicolored eels. Between the four hundred men and the general were arranged almost thirty M-16s. They were stuck into the ground and held there by the bayonets affixed to their barrels. A helmet capped each of the rifle butts.

The symbolic graves cast long, fading shadows in the morning light.

Tom snapped a picture as the brigade adjutant stepped forward to read the names of the dead. The lieutenant colonel's voice boomed clearly across the improvised parade ground, "...PFC Kline, Nathan A.; Specialist Four Kosticheck, Robert M.; Sergeant Larse, Clarence H.: PFC Lavino, Anthony G.; Second Lieutenant Margrave, Donald H.; Specialist Four Maxwell, Peter C.;

Private Mason, Douglas B.; PFC Nakamura, Keith T...."

This would be about all there was in military honors for the dead men at the Division level. Grey's eyes slowly wandered to the horizon and then back to the small formation below him. The unit, the United States Army of Vietnam, standing in the tropical furnace, burying its dead.

Back in The World, in scattered National and private cemeteries, there would be taps played, flags folded and given to mothers or wives, and 21-gun salutes fired by local VFW or American Legion honor guards. The winds would blow cold through the trees, adding to the gulf between Vietnam and The World.

The chaplain stepped forward to pray. The men continued to stand bareheaded in ranks, motionless.

Grey got into the passenger seat of the jeep and looked at Cole behind the wheel. Then he too leaned back and closed his eyes. It was pleasant in the shade of the vehicle's canvas top.

◆ ◆ ◆

There was a breeze. It came easily through the vented slats of the barracks wall. Grey lay comfortably on the soft, nylon poncho liner that covered his mattress.

Briggs came through the door at the far end of the barracks. Outside, the night was silent and calm.

Briggs walked the isle of empty bunks and stood over Grey. "Let's go get a drink," he said.

Briggs was plump and neat and always looked like an officer to Grey.

"No, thanks."

"What's the matter, you sick?" Briggs asked with credulity.

"Just thinking."

"That's no good. Come on; let's go get a beer." Briggs insisted, leaning against a wall locker

"I've been drinking too much beer lately," Grey said.

Briggs flipped up the mosquito netting on the bunk next to Grey's and sat down. "Getting religious?"

"Getting tired of hangovers," Grey said, shaking his head slightly.

"Drink Scotch."

"Sure." Grey sat up on the cot. There was a pack of cigarettes on the cement floor of the hooch. He picked them up, tapped one from the package, and pulled it out with his lips. He lit his Zippo lighter with one snap of the wrist, which both flipped open the top and rolled the roughened steel wheel against the flint, lighting the fuel-soaked wick. Exhaling, Grey looked at Briggs and asked, "What are you going to do when you get out?"

"I don't know," Briggs said, thinking. "Get a job, I suppose. I've got my degree, and I had some fair offers from some newspapers before I got drafted. Probably get married."

"Sally?"

"Yeah," Briggs did not sound particularly enthused. "I should probably spend a couple of years philandering, but..., ah, I don't know."

Tom pulled the cooler from under his bed and got out a couple of beers.

"Thought you were quitting," Briggs said.

"Just cutting down," Grey said sardonically.

The building was neat and clean, and cool. Grey was always a little surprised by the comfort and sophistication of Long Binh Post whenever he returned from the field. It was like returning from the frontier. The closer you got to the line and the infantrymen fighting there, the more primitive things became. Coming home to Long Binh was always nice. Grey liked floors and doors and hot showers and clean clothes. But, he also had an affection for the guys on the line.

Briggs took the can of beer Tom offered. "What about you?" he asked. "Gonna go after the big time, the *New York Times*, AP?"

"No." Grey shook his head again.

"You've done some pretty good work, man. I mean, if there's anything I hate to do, it's to admire somebody else's work, but you really have done some good stuff."

"Don't mean shit." Grey sounded more resigned than angry. "I don't think I want to be a journalist anyway," he said.

"So?" Briggs said, raising his eyebrows and cocking his head to one side.

"So what?"

"So, what are you going to do?"

Grey hesitated. "I'd like to get into the space program," he finally said.

"What?" Briggs asked, incredulously

"I'd like to go to work for NASA. Grey said.

Briggs began to laugh, rocking back onto the bunk.

"What's so fuckin' funny?" Grey snapped.

"That's ridiculous," Briggs said, dropping his feet back to the floor.

"Why?" Grey's voice was sharp.

"Man..," Briggs looked at him and laughed again. "There ain't no way."

Grey got up and walked to the screen door at the end of the building. The night sky was clear, and he stared up at the unfamiliar stars of the tropics. "I'm serious," he said.

"Sure, you are."

"I am."

"How are you going to get a security clearance?" asked Briggs, trying to reason.

"I've already got one."

"You won't when you get back to The World. The Army knows all about you now. The government knows you're a fuckup."

Grey returned to his bunk and lay down. "I thought you said I've done some excellent work here.

Briggs took one of the cigarettes from the pack on the floor and lit it. "Okay," he asked, "Why the space program."

"None of your Goddamned business," Grey snapped petulantly.

Neither of them spoke after that. Briggs finished his cigarette and snuffed it out in an ashtray that someone had fashioned from a beer can. He sighed as he got to his feet, opened his mouth as if to say something to Grey, and then seemed to think better of it. Instead, he turned and walked toward the door and the humid Vietnamese night.

"Ass kissing son-of-a-bitch," Grey muttered, shutting his eyes against the ceiling light.

The sirens began a few seconds before the first rocket hit.

Grey instinctively grabbed the mattress with both hands, and turning, fell to the floor with the mattress, as a shield—on top.

"Goddam," he thought miserably, "I can't get away from the war even on Long Binh." He flattened his body against the cold concrete.

FIREBASE BERCHTESGADEN

Grey—17 and a Wakeup

Outside, the rain was coming down in sheets. Tom Grey sat cross-legged on an air mattress on the tiny bunker's floor and wrote in a shorthand notebook. A small C-ration can he had fashioned into a crude coffee cup sat on a patch of bare earth at his side. Water dripped through the sandbags and PSP into the dim interior of the hootch.

MacEvy lifted the poncho that formed the fourth wall of the structure and crawled in along with a blast of cold wind and misty rain." The Old Man'll see you in about half an hour," he said flatly.

"Good," replied Grey. "Did you hear anything else about the NVA officer that D Company captured?"

"He's dead."

"You're kidding," Grey said, looking up.

"Nope. Somebody at the hospital killed him." MacEvy said, shaking water from his poncho.

Grey laid his notebook down beside him and lit a cigarette.

"The guys in D Company will be pissed," he said. "They wanted to kill him pretty bad themselves."

MacEvy got some heat tabs and started to make coffee. "You got any sugar and cream?"

Grey fished around in his rucksack and found two paper and foil packets. "What's the Colonel doing?" he asked.

"Worrying, MacEvy said, "The rain is letting up, but this weather is for shit."

"Has Chuck been active?"

"Not yet." Mac got into his own gear and dug out a few cans of C-rations. The bunker was low; the ceiling less than four feet from the floor. One wall was the stone side of the mountain. The front was sandbagged with an opening that was covered only by a poncho. The other two were sandbag partitions that separated the hootch from its neighbor's. The bunkers sat in a row against the base of a small cliff, like Anasazi apartments.

Mac opened a can of boned chicken and began eating it cold. "How's the newspaper business?"

"A little slow. I wrote up everything I had in the TOC last night. They said they'd get it out when they get a regular bird in."

"Could be a while," MacEvy observed.

"Could be."

Mac stared at Grey for a moment, but the empty ration can down and said, "You're going back in."

"The Valley?" asked Grey.

MacEvy nodded.

"That's a crock of shit, stammered Grey. "I can do my job from here just as well."

"Your fucking job." MacEvy got to his knees and flipped back the poncho. Light, cold air and rain gusted into the dark cubbyhole.

"You're a shithead, Grey. Do you really think anybody gives a damn about the sophomoric crap you write? You're here because soldiers function better when they think they might get their names in the paper. You're a God-damned morale factor—just like the Red Cross girls." Then he turned and grinned. "Don't forget the Colonel," he said as he left the room.

Grey sat silent for a moment. Then he shouted at the gray-green plastic wall, "What's his fuckin' morale problem?"

"Bastards!' Tom threw his make-shift coffee cup against the sandbags. "Fuck all of them." His hands were trembling. A low rumble of thunder underscored Grey's tantrum. Finally, he shoved his feet into his boots and laced them up. He stuck the notebook into his belt and put on his field jacket. The rain had not let up, and it took Tom's eyes a few moments to adjust to the fragile daylight.

The Berchtesgaden firebase extended two hundred meters across a bare stone ledge before the mountain dropped sharply away to the narrow notch where the chopper pad had been built. It spread across the saddle between two hilltops about a thousand feet above the valley floor.

Beyond the helipad, the ridge rose to a small knoll. The combat engineers were still working on completing the firebase. Above the cliff, behind the bunker, was another knoll. From this, the highest point for miles, the brigade's artillery pounded the jungle below. Mud, gray rain and running water dominated the scene. Around Berchtesgaden, the mountains plunged sharply. Cold mist clung to the installation. Grey set his face against the sharp wind and headed across the ledge toward the TOC, the brigade Tactical Operations Center. He felt sorry for the troopers who were out in small, miserable, wet listening posts that surrounded the fire base. Antes in the gamble against a surprise attack.

An olive-drab Huey appeared out of the clouds in the Valley below and struggled for altitude. Its red cross, set in a white square on the nose, was visible to the men on Berchtesgaden. A gust of wind caught the chopper as the pilot tried to thread the notch's steep stone walls. The craft twisted, rocked in the air, and then retreated back out over the A Shau.

The second time he came in low, avoiding the choppy winds along the crest. He barreled hard at the mountainside and then pulled the bird up at the last second into a near stall, laying it on the pad like a dolphin powering itself out of a swimming pool.

Grey moved to the lip of the cliff. He stopped; the cold sank deeply into his body when he saw the cargo through the misting rain. Six or eight bloodied and mutilated infantrymen were being carried from the helicopter. They were severely injured, and the men who moved them in the rain to the medic's bunker at the side of the LZ were silent. A tall Black sergeant, naked to the waist, stood at the bunker door and directed the placement of the wounded. Two were left on the sandbag roof of the dispensary. A couple of off-duty artillerymen took up positions over them with ponchos, keeping off the rain. The ponchos snapped and flapped in the gusting wind. A kettle-drum of thunder swept over the firebase.

Another Medevac hovered in the mist off the firebase. The first lifted off, scooted low across the pad, and disappeared over the edge into the clouds below. The second ship came straight in, chanced the wind and won.

There were two more loads of wounded. One man, one who had stayed on the bunker roof, was a dull red color. His skin had been blown off. He was not the victim of anything solid. He had been struck by the heat and force of an explosion. A medic, blood-stained, scrambled up from the hidden field hospital with a couple of other and knelt in the rain, blood streaking off his body as if it were his own.

The last Medevac brought in body bags, six of them. Plastic olive drab envelopes, six by two, and bulging in places to the width of a man. They were stacked neatly, like logs, at the edge of the jungle.

A Huey slick hovered briefly above the pad and shoved out stacks of equipment; helmets, rucksacks, and weapons. The fabric helmet covers were emblazoned with the things men write to mark their individuality: good luck signs, calendars, jokes, and the names of wives and girlfriends.

Grey turned away and realized for the first time that he was in a crowd. "What happened?" someone asked.

A young lieutenant was standing next to Grey, his aluminum dog tags glittered against the pale white skin of his chest. "An airstrike," he said.

"What?" someone asked.

"An airstrike missed. They were trying to bomb through the fog, and they missed. Some of the guys were standing up. They thought it was for Charlie," the lieutenant replied.

Most of the men on the firebase had stopped working to watch. Even the artillery was silent. Slowly, after the last helicopter had departed, the men returned to their tasks, bent over in the rain. The 105s were back in action first, their low bark ripping through the camp. Then came the loud, deep rumble of the 155s. Grey followed the lieutenant down the stairway into the tactical operations center.

Down in the pungent, musty-aired bunker, Grey spoke to a staff sergeant seated at a cluttered desk. "I'm from PIO," he said, "I'm supposed to interview the Colonel."

There were two rooms in the large underground headquarters. One was devoted to communications, the other filled with maps and staff officers. "In there." the sergeant said to Grey without looking up.

Grey walked into the map room and repeated that he was from public information. As soon as he was identified to the brigade commander, a remarkable thing happened. The Colonel was effusive in his welcome and sent his officers scurrying out of the room. On instruction, Grey got both a cup of coffee from a dented aluminum pot and sat down on a metal folding chair in front of the Colonel's field desk. He was a slender, good looking man in his mid-to-late-forties. It seemed to Tom that he had been used as an excuse to clear the office.

"I'm afraid there's not much to tell you," began the officer quietly. "The weather is dominating the situation right now." His hair was a salt-and-pepper grey-brown, and his ruddy face looked worried as he massaged his temples with his fingertips.

"Is this the Achilles heel of airmobile warfare, sir?" Tom asked without preamble. "The weather."

The Colonel shifted in his seat and paused to light a cigarette. "Weather is a factor in any combat situation. The problem with airmobile is that you depend on the choppers for resupply and major troop movements. This close to the rainy season," he continued without irony. "There is a certain amount of risk involved in operating here. On the other hand, if it weren't for the choppers, it's pretty doubtful that we'd be here in any kind of force. The A Shau is damn near inaccessible from the coast."

"The North Vietnamese don't seem to have much trouble getting in and out of here."

"It's not quite the same, soldier. They come down on the other side of the border, through Laos. They cross the Plain of Jars and filter in through a couple of pretty easy passes. Except for the B-52s, it's a nice walk. Getting from here to the coast is tougher, but they've got something we don't. Time. They've been fighting this war for twenty-five years, a couple of months setting up an attack doesn't mean much to them."

"How much danger is there if the weather stays bad?" asked Grey.

"Not so much, really. Helicopters can't fly IFR, but the Air Force can…"

"What were those chopper pilots flying just now?" Grey asked.

"Courage." the Colonel said simply. "If worst came to worst, we could re-group our guys and establish a major defensive position, and resupply by airdrops until the weather lifted. Before you say 'Dien Bien Phu, let me remind you that we have a real Air Force to support us. Besides, we still have the arty up here, and those shells go where they're pointed. The only real problem with the rain is that it might prevent us from carrying out our mission as planned." He stubbed out his cigarette in a C-Ration can, "But, things rarely do go as planned."

The officer paused and lit another cigarette. "Actually," he said, "I'd like nothing better than to have the NVA come out and have at it. "I've got a pretty rugged bunch of boys down there."

"That's sort of the way we felt about Tet, wasn't it?" Tom asked.

"Whose side are you on?" the Colonel asked, squinting at Grey though the cigarette smoke.

"Just curious," Grey said honestly. He got up to refill the coffee cups.

"We beat them at Tet," responded the commander. "We really hurt the Viet Cong; pretty much wiped them out. It was over a year ago, and the VC hasn't done much since.

"That's not what Walter Cronkite said," Grey observed.

"Cronkite is, militarily speaking, an ignorant amature. He and the newspapers are saying that this constitutes a subtle move toward peace by the Communists… that's a crock of shit. We kicked their ass, and the only reason they haven't done anything is that they can't." He reached for the refilled ceramic coffee cup emblazoned with the 101st Airborne patch.

"But politically…"

"I'm not political," the officer snapped. "I'm just a soldier. All of us are. If we were political, there'd be some jerk from your office around to keep me in line."

Grey had to laugh. But still, it wasn't quite what he was asking. "Don't you think," he said slowly, "That in this particular war, politics is really the major issue?"

The Colonel studied Grey for a moment. "Off the record?" he asked, finally.

"Sure," Grey flipped his notebook shut.

"Really... Off the record?"

"Yessir"

"I think militarily we've got the war won. The enemy can no longer conduct large scale conventional, or otherwise, operations. We're starting to put a real crimp into his ability to wage guerrilla warfare. The fact that we're back here sniffing around in the boonies along the border indicates that the coast and the cities are pretty safe. We can hold South Vietnam as long as the American people want us to."

Grey liked the man. He admired his manners and his professionalism. Still, he pressed the interview. "If we've won the war militarily, why are we back here sniffing around? A lot of guys are getting killed; those guys they just brought in upstairs."

"That was a mistake," the Colonel answered sharply. Continuing, he said, "The weather was a contributing factor, but basically the FAC made a mistake. Friendly fire mistakes are costly, but they happen." The Colonel rubbed his forehead and said in a whisper to himself, "Friendly fire. Can you imagine we call it that?"

"Yes sir, but it's a mistake that wouldn't have occurred if we weren't here in the Valley."

The Colonel didn't like Grey's comment. Not, Grey thought, because he didn't want to respond to it, but rather because he didn't want to think about it. "They keep coming," the Colonel said, "We beat them in Hue, we pushed them through the mountains, and now we've got them here in the A Shau. If we don't fight them here, we're going to be fighting in Hue again."

"Are the NVA really the best infantrymen in the world?" Grey asked.

"Shit," the commander laughed. "They're good, but they're not anywhere near that good. Their reputation was earned in the columns of the *Washington Post*. Paper tigers." The Colonel laughed again. "Truth is, they get very little training, and most of them have only fired their rifles once."

Grey got to his feet. "You got a story?" the Colonel asked, standing, as well.

"No," Tom said frankly, "Not one the Army will print. I guess I sorta wasted your time."

The Colonel shrugged. "Depends on how you look at it," he said, standling and offering Grey his hand.

"Have Sergeant Randolph send my people back in, will you?"

"Sure, Sir." Tom stopped at the door and turned to face the Colonel, "Good luck, Sir."

The lean officer smiled. "You too, Grey."

Outside, the rain had increased again. Tom stood in the doorway and looked across the slate gray stone ledge. To his right, a first sergeant made a blood and guts speech to a mix of cherries and ragged looking veterans. Grey surmised that they had probably been scrounged up in a hurry. They were going in as replacements to the unit that had suffered from the airstrike.

He turned into the wind and fought, his poncho flapping in the suddenly strong winds, his way to the small bunker at the base of the cliff. Inside it was dark, and Tran was reading by candlelight. MacEvy reclined against the sandbag wall. The Colonel's driver, to whom the bunker technically belonged, sat dozing against the stone back wall. Grey found some coffee and heat tabs and started a small fire. "What's so interesting?" he asked Tran.

"Captured enemy documents," said the Vietnamese sergeant with a smile, his eyes a dark, shining agate. "Letters from home."

"Really? How's everybody in Hanoi?"

"In love, apparently," replied Tran. "Struggling and hoping for the day when their families can be reunited in peace and glorious victory."

"Anything dirty?"

"Dirty?" Tran asked, puzzled by the euphemism.

"Sexy."

"No, just love and a fervent desire for victory," Tran said, smiling.

"Pure hearts, huh?"

"No." Tran said, "Their government censors the mail." Grey looked in his rucksack for something to read, then changed his mind and threw out the water he had heated for coffee. He took off his boots and laid down on his air mattress. As he pulled his dirty poncho liner up around his shoulders, he felt a tightness in his lower back.

Vietnam had cost him the ability to shit with any regularity. When he could, it was usually the runs for two or more days at a time. He had lost so much weight that he had stretchmarks across his pelvis. His body was as hard as a rock, a hardness that melted everything out of him. Tom did not sleep well. He was sweaty and drifted between semi-consciousness and blurred snatches of surreal dreams.

Finally, Tran shook him awake. "You okay? "Tran asked, shaking Grey awake.

"What?"

"You okay, Grey?"

"Yeah... fine." Grey rubbed his eyes and discovered that he had been crying in his sleep.

It was still dark outside. Tran looked worried in the guttering candlelight. MacEvy, sitting cross-legged at the other end of the bunker, was studying Grey carefully. Tran politely looked away and began rummaging around in his gear.

"I'm okay," Tom said.

Tran nodded his head and turned his attention back to the helmet full of rice he was cooking. Grey pulled on his boots and slipped under the wall of ponchos.

The rain had stopped, but the firebase was covered with a thick fog. It caught the faint moonlight refracting it to silver mother of pearl. Tom turned to his left and followed the narrow path up along the perimeter. The cold wind felt good. He lit a cigarette and leaned back against the damp wall of the cliff. The urine ran from his body in a warm, steaming stream. He shivered with a sudden chill. He moved further up the trail, found a place to sit down, and smoked another cigarette.

He had to get a hold of himself. He was childish. "Shrug your shoulders and tough it out. Shit, it's only war, not even a big war; just a nasty little foreign misunderstanding. A little mistake the government made. You're whole. You haven't bled. You're alive. Back into the Valley for a few days, and then everything will be over. Go home with your medals and the GI Bill. Just a hamburger and a shake, a couple of beers with the guys and a piece of round-eyed ass; that's all you need. Everything will be just like before." He thought. But he was pretty sure it wouldn't be.

A lone figure came up the trail towards him. It was Tran carrying two canteen cups. "I brought you some food," he said as he approached.

Grey took the cup tentatively. "Worried about me," he asked.

"No," said the Vietnamese sergeant. "The others," he made a gesture back toward the bunker. "They talk too much."

Grey spooned some of the rice and C-ration Steak mixture into his mouth, not believing Tran's protest. The food was excellent. Really good. Tran had simmered a few cans of sliced beef with gravy in the rice and had added some spices from his pack. It was the first thing Tom had eaten in a long time because it was good and not because he was hungry, and he was grateful for the Vietnamese soldier's thoughtfulness.

"They talking about interrogation methods," Tran said. "They agree that if you have several prisoners, the best method is to shove a couple of them out of a helicopter before you even talk to the others."

Tran sucked on his white plastic spoon for a moment before continuing. "With women, MacEvy says that the best way is to threaten to shave their heads. That is correct and very effective." Tran took another spoonful of rice and beef. "In Vietnam, this is the way we punish prostitutes.

"Young VC women who would die for their cause," continued Tran, "Will betray it rather than live with the contempt our people have for whores." He tapped his teeth a couple of times with the spoon and added, "That is strange, is it not?"

Tom said nothing.

"Don't you think that is strange?" Tran persisted.

"I'm going home in a couple of weeks," Tom said at last.

"I don't blame you for that," Tran said seriously.

"Big of you," Grey snapped.

"America has many soldiers. You have done your part. Now it is another's turn," Tran said, turning and walking back through the fog toward the bunker.

DAY IN THE LIFE

Grey—16 and a Wakeup

Ground fog hovered over the position, tendrils lacing between the trees in lacy filaments. Men moving about in it had a flat, ghost-like appearance. Tom lay on his back on his poncho. His head rested against his rucksack while watching the dawn evolve through purple to blue as the mountain emerged black against the brightening sky. He listened to the small birds calling, crickets, and the other soft sounds of the awakening jungle.

The smell of his body mixed with that of the damp jungle floor. Small twigs and leaf particles had gotten inside his fatigue collar and itched his shoulders and upper back. Resisting the urge to scratch, he burrowed deeper into his field jacket. His legs made a slippery sound against the plastic poncho as he slid them up, making himself into a ball against the morning chill.

He could hear the members of the Company beginning to stir. Behind him, Haynes rolled over and kicked him lightly in the shoulder. "Sleep well, soldier?" Mike asked.

"Yeah. I really did," answered Grey. "Why is that?' Why do you sleep so much better in the open?"

"Is that why you came back? To get a good night's sleep?" Without waiting for an answer, Haynes got to his knees and began rummaging around in his gear. "You got any heat tabs?"

"Sure." Tom rolled over and searched through his rucksack from the prone position. His fingers were stiff, but he found the olive-green aluminum foil packets containing the blue-white tablets. He tossed a couple over to Haynes and lay his head back down on the cool poncho, and watched Haynes work.

"Want coffee?"

"Sure," Grey replied, rubbing his hands together to warm them up. He thought about a cold-water shave, but he did not see anyone doing it so, he decided against trying.

Haynes pulled his canteen and cup out of its canvas case and then did the same with Grey's. He filled one cup two thirds full of water and sat it on the stove they had fashioned from an empty C-ration can the night before. Then he slid two heat tabs into the stove and lit them. Blue flame clung to the tablets like burning alcohol. Grey shifted his head and saw other members of the platoon moving about, heating coffee or opening Cs for a quick breakfast.

The heat tabs burned themselves down to a viscous scab. Mike stirred in instant coffee and divided the hot coffee between the two cups. "Here," he said, passing the cup to Grey.

Tom grunted his thanks as he struggled into a sitting position, trying not to spill his coffee. Haynes opened a can of peaches and took a nylon spoon from his shirt pocket. "You'd better eat something," he said, "It could be a long time till lunch."

Instead, Grey lit a cigarette. The coffee was good. There were a few hours in the early morning when he actually preferred it to whisky. Mike finished the peaches, followed them with a can of crackers and cheese, and then started packing his gear.

Tom grasped the frame of his rucksack with both hands and gently rocked it off the edge of his poncho, where it had served as his pillow. Beneath it was his canvas pistol belt with a canteen, a bayonet, and two forty-five magazines. He slid the handgun into the scarred brown leather shoulder holster and snapped the retaining strap. He reached for his helmet, which was upside down a few inches from where his head had been. In it was his wallet, an extra pack of Marlboro cigarettes, his pens, sunglasses, and his notebook. He filled his pockets and then re-laced his boots. Perhaps it had been careless to have left them untied.

His M-16 was lying on the poncho next to where he had slept. Tom propped it against his ruck and then· spread the plastic sheet out as well as he could on the rough ground. Next, he spread the nylon poncho liner evenly over it and folded the bedding lengthwise into thirds. Carefully he rolled it into a tight cylinder, like a skinny sleeping bag, and attached it securely to the bottom of his rucksack. He replaced the canteen and cup and spent a few minutes making sure the entire rucksack was snug and firm.

He grabbed Haynes' well-worn spade, an entrenching tool in Army parlance, and began filling in the fighting hole they had dug the evening before. It seemed to Grey that war was digging a lot of holes and then filling them in. He thought to remember the line. He could use it in a story someday.

Haynes got to his feet and began checking his men. Grey took his sixteen, a bandoleer of ammo and a small C-ration toilet paper packet and headed for the perimeter. Jones was on guard and nodded when Tom displayed the tissue paper.

A few meters into the woods, Grey slung the ammunition belt over one shoulder, dropped his pants, and held onto a small tree with his left hand. He squatted with his rifle across his lap. After a few moments, he gave up and climbed back down the hill.

Kelly was bent over a plastic-covered map talking to Haynes and Johnson when Grey got back to his equipment. Buckling on his pistol belt, he joined the group without invitation.

"We'll hit the Ho Chi Minh trail about here," Kelly was saying. "If Chuck's got any caches left around here, they'll probably be along the trail. I want you on the point, Johnson. Take your time and check everything out. Our friends might have something along there worth fighting for."

Tom studied the map for a moment and found the circle of dense topographical lines that marked the Hill 937, Dong Ap Bia. The grease penciled mark Kelly had drawn lead obliquely toward it. Grey figured they would probably veer from the Ho Chi Minh Trail tomorrow and cut across the valley floor toward the jungle-covered massif.

"Mike," continued Kelly, "I want you to stay close to Bayaban. There's a good chance we're going to be hitting some shit, and I don't want my sixty fuckin' up."

Haynes shifted his weight and paused a moment. Finally, he said, "Then why put a cherry on it?"

Kelly was going to ignore the question. Then he decided that Haynes deserved an explanation.

"He's got the size," Kelly began, "That's obvious. But he also seems to have some brains. He did okay on the assault when we came in here. But..., why let him get bad habits?"

"He could be assistant gunner for a while," Haynes replied.

"He could, but he won't," Kelly said, "So, stick close to him." After Kelly and Johnson had moved off, Haynes called to Bayaban. He was a tall, rangy young man about twenty, and he ambled when he walked. The glittering belts of linked ammunition crisscrossed over his chest, and his swarthy complexion made Grey think of a Mexican bandit.

"How's everything?" Haynes asked.

"Okay," said Bayaban. The 27-pound M-60 machine gun was balanced easily over his left shoulder. He held the weapon by one of its extended bipeds near the end of the barrel.

"You remember what I told you about using that thing?"

"Sure do," Bayaban replied without guile.

"What did I say?"

The patronizing tone of the question would have bothered Grey, but Bayaban answered readily. "Get down and don't commit the gun until I get orders. Fire short bursts so I don't run out of ammo or attract too much attention or cook the barrel. and make sure I know where the assistant gunner is." The tall youth grinned broadly, pleased with himself.

"Definitely a Bandito," Grey thought.

Without orders, the men began sliding into their rucks and getting to their feet. Tom carried about 30 pounds, half the weight on the backs of the other men.

Because he was not officially attached to the command, he was not required to tote a share of the extra ammo, claymores, or LAWs—Light Anti-tank Weapons. He could have done so voluntarily, but he chose not to. He had heard the tale of a straggling cherry abandoned in these mountains. Besides, he had to carry his camera gear, pens, steno pads, and the other paraphernalia of a reporter. "Not exactly and offset," he conceded to himself.

Haynes adjusted a small, white plastic bottle of insect repellant in the elastic band that encircled the camouflage cover on his steel helmet. He fine-tuned his rucksack, tugging on the shoulder straps for a good fit.

Grey bounced a few times to settle his equipment and wrapped an olive-drab towel around his neck. A few yards away, the platoon sergeant, Edison, was talking over the radio. His map was spread out on the jungle floor. He was surrounded by the three squad leaders, the medic and his RTO, the radio operator, and the new Lieutenant. He signed off the radio and held a last-minute conversation with the sergeants before the group broke up. Edison headed up the rise toward the CP, followed by his RTO, the antenna waving in counterpoint to the steps as he walked, and the Lieutenant.

Kelly returned to the squad. The men gravitated to him. Johnson, who was walking point, started down a small trail into the jungle. Jones let him go about fifteen feet and then started after him. Kelly stood aside and gave a brief inspection and nod to each soldier as the squad filed by.

When Modeland, pulling drag, came up, Kelly turned and walked down the trail. He worked his way along the slender column until he caught up with Saunders. He held his place for a few moments, whispering something to Saunders, before moving farther ahead and fell in behind Wood.

Johnson went slowly. His ears tuned out the sounds of the Company moving behind him, and his eyes began to adjust to the monochromatic wall of jungle. He focused on the relatively smooth dirt trail, but kept his mind on his peripheral vision, watching for movement. Another part of his mind monitored other things, a new ability he had developed and never questioned.

There was no conversation. The only noise from the squad was the dull step of boots and the snick of branches against helmets and rucksacks. Occasionally Grey became aware of the gurgle of water and whisky sloshing in his canteens or the gentle swish of his pants legs rubbing together. The coolness of the morning passed quickly as the sun climbed higher into the sky.

The men began to sweat. Tom watched Haynes' loaded rucksack bounce and sway ahead of him. The once olive-green nylon pack was stained a light brown-orange with the dirt and dust of Vietnam. The flat olive paint on the aluminum rucksack frame was chipped in places and worn at others to a dull metallic sheen.

An hour and a half into the march, the word came up from the Captain for a break.

Kelly motioned for silence, and the men settled down in place. Sturdy, vicious insects found the men shortly after they had stopped moving. Grey remembered a joke he overheard in a bar in Da Nang. Two mosquitos picked up a GI, and while hovering, one said, "Should we eat him here or take him back to the nest?" The second mosquito replied. "We'd better eat him here. If we take him home, the big guys will get him." He smiled at the memory.

After about 10 minutes, Kelly gave the order to saddle up, and the GIs got to their feet. The small silver Buddha medallion that Grey wore on a chain around his neck, along with his dogtags, fell out of his shirt. Hoa had given it to him. "They say it will protect you," she said. "I think maybe is bullshit." Then she shrugged and smiled, continuing, "You never know."

The steep incline broke, and they began working downhill. Tom was grateful now that the march was more straightforward. He was in no physical condition to be humping with the infantry. Already his body was beginning to protest. He kept his mind on the jungle, keeping his eyes moving and bending at the waist periodically to peer between the foliage layers.

After a second break, they left the trail and began following a small stream bed across the A Shau floor. The water was knee-deep, and there were leeches in the weeds. Grey lit a cigarette and dangled it from his lips. He did not inhale but slightly puffed it occasionally to keep the fire ready if a leech fastened onto him.

The stream dropped sharply and then came out onto the Valley floor proper. Kelly stopped the column and had a few words with Johnson. The A Shau stretched before them. The stream they had been following cut a swath of deeper green through the elephant grass as it meandered toward the ragged tree line marking the narrow river that cut through the valley centerline. Beyond the distant trees, the purple mountains of the western wall rose into Laos. The squad members slumped to the ground. A few made whispered conversation, but most relaxed against their rucksacks, making the best of the opportunity to rest. Grey could hear members of the squad that followed moving to the left and right as flank security. Bayaban leaned against the base of a tree and inspected the breach of the M-60.

Edison and the Lieutenant came up and had a conference with Kelly. The three men surveyed the broad field and a tree line about two hundred meters down and to the right, a tongue of jungle that probed the elephant grass. After a time, they agreed on the point where they would re-enter the jungle. They planned to take advantage of the extra cover before striking for the river. Johnson got to his feet in response to Kelly's nod and led the way out into the open. The rest of the squad followed slowly, spaced five or more meters apart.

Johnson was a little more than halfway across the open ground when the NVA machine gun opened up. Johnson dove for the earth. Strung out behind him, the rest of the soldiers disappeared beneath the grass, bullets snapping over their head, grass cuttings floating in the air. Johnson massaged himself into the dirt. The tell-tale movement of the grass testified to the attempts of the rest of the squad to crawl into an on-line position facing the enemy gunners, set for a fire-and-maneuver exercise.

"Haynes! Bayaban! Get that M-60 over here!" Kelly yelled.

The two men sprinted through the elephant grass, bent over as if braving a violent rainstorm. Grey rolled onto his side and snapped a quick photograph of Bayaban, his breath coming in gasps and belts of ammunition jangling behind him.

"Move, damn it!" Kelly was on his knees and motioning the men to fan out and form the line.

Bayaban hit the dirt and swung the sixty toward the enemy. M-16 fire began striking toward the line of trees. "Where do you want it?" asked the machine gunner.

Kelly was looking at the dark lump twenty meters away; Johnson. Bullets were cutting the elephant grass around him. Jones, ten meters away, had dumped his ruck and was firing around it toward the enemy. Fire from the tree line picked up, and muzzle flashes from a dozen positions became visible.

"Get some fire over between those two big trees, on that first bastard. The machine gun." Kelly ordered, his face lined with anger. Sweat from under his helmet dripped down his face.

Alvarez began thonking out grenade rounds from the M-79. The first cloud of dust it raised was a few meters short of the NVA positions. The second was well back into the trees. Soon Alvarez got the range.

"Jones!" shouted Kelly.

"Yeah!"

"Is Johnson okay?"

"He's moving around some now," Jones yelled back.

On the left, Prescott had four LAWs. He took his time and carefully fired the anti-tank rockets, observing his hit before throwing away the disposable launcher and taking up another.

The Lieutenant and Sargent Edison had maneuvered the rest of the platoon away from the stream and up along the right flank of Kelly's squad. Once in position, Grey could see the Lieutenant on the radio, his map spread before him, calling in a fire mission. He hoped the officer was good at math.

A few minutes later, artillery fire began to dance amongst the trees across the clearing, *womp! Womp! WOMP!*—branches, clods of dirt and jungle flying; high explosive and white phosphorous rounds lit small fires. Vibrations thrummed in their chests.

Grey took pictures until he'd run through the 36 exposures on the roll of film. Then he crawled a few meters forward and began firing his M-16. The light recoil felt good against his shoulder. He fired on semiautomatic. At this range, he thought he was more or less effective with single shots, so why waste ammunition? The artillery shells continued tossing dust and tree limbs into the air on the enemy position.

The ground beneath the soldiers trembled.

The rest of the platoon had moved out of the jungle far to the right and began moving obliquely toward the NVA position. The howitzer barrage lifted, and Kelly ordered his men to ceasefire. There was a smattering of gunfire as the platoon entered the woodland. It was short-lived as the troopers swept through what was left of the enemy position.

The silence seemed hollow. The ground to Bayaban s right was littered with gleaming brass cartridges and matt-black ammunition links. Sweat tricked down and stung Tom's eyes as he watched Johnson crawling back toward the rest of the squad. The soldiers held their positions. There was no conversation and no noise from the tree line. Grey collected the four magazines he'd emptied and stuffed them into the large pockets on his fatigue pants' thighs. "Waste not, want not," he thought to himself.

It was ten minutes before Edison, and his RTO came out of the jungle and up to their position. Kelly stood, and the men in the squad started moving around. "Everybody okay?" asked Kelly. Johnson got to his feet and walked over to Kelly. His left arm was bleeding slightly. Kelly examined the small neat slice in Johnson's upper arm. The sergeant tugged a canteen from

Johnson's pack, and washed the wound. He then took the compress bandage from the pouch on Johnson's rucksack shoulder strap and began to wrap Johnson's arm. "This is about the closest you can come to getting a Purple Heart for free," he said.

"Yeah," said Johnson without humor. Jones came over and put his arm around Johnson. "Man, I thought your ass was grass."

"What makes you think it wasn't?" Johnson replied sourly.

"You know what I mean."

"Yeah, I know," Johnson answered as he inspected Kelly's doctoring.

Edison and his RTO joined the small group. "Your guys alright?" he asked Kelly.

"Got a flesh wound on my point man. Nothing serious though, we won't have to evac him"

"Shit," Johnson muttered, scuffing his boot in the dirt.

Kelly pointed toward the tree line. What's the score over there?

"A couple of arms and legs is all. The main running-gear followed some blood trails." Sergeant Edison answered, shrugging his rucksack into a more comfortable position and sighing.

The RTO tapped Edison's shoulder and handed him the handset. "It's the CO," explained the radio operator.

Grey and Haynes wandered a few feet away from the group. Bayaban followed them. "How'd I do?" he asked Haynes.

"Fair," Haynes mumbled. The entire right side of Bayaban's head exploded before the sound of the shot reached them. In an instant, Haynes was on the ground. Grey stood dumbfounded and watched as Bayaban settled into a sitting position. The rest of the squad scattered and went to earth. Haynes reached up and dragged Grey to his knees by his belt.

"Get your ass down!" he screamed.

The gore on Tom's shirt front was wet and sticky, Bayaban's brains had hit him in the chest. It was warm pink stuff mixed with red, and he couldn't take his eyes off it.

"A fuckin' sniper!" Kelly yelled unnecessarily.

"Let's go! Let's Go!" shouted Edison, motioning back toward the jungle with his left arm, his right still holding his rifle pointed downrange.

The soldiers abandoned their rucksacks and began to double time for safety, zig-zagging in the hope of throwing off the sniper's aim.

"Come on," Haynes jerked on Grey's arm. "Come on you bastard!" There was a burst of fire where the enemy positions had been. Haynes released Tom and headed for the trees carrying his rifle and the M-60 machine gun and Bayaban's pistol belt with the .45 pistol.

Grey stood up again. His fascination shifted from his shirt to what was left of Bayaban's head. After a moment and without thinking, he picked up the heavy body and carried it fireman style toward the jungle.

Tom still felt disorientated when Sergeant Edison got the all-clear from the third platoon. Modeland and Schilling rolled Bayaban into a black body bag after stripping the bandoleers of ammunition for the body. Kelly led his men back into the grass to retrieve their equipment. Grey stopped, removed his shirt, and threw it aside. Behind him, Haynes, cursing under his breath, picked up the shirt and emptied Tom's pockets. Then he shook the garment viciously to free it of the remnants of Bayaban. Like it or not, it would get cold tonight, and Grey would need the shirt.

Mike was as angry as hell. Then the anger passed. He watched Grey walking ahead in only a tee-shirt. "Jesus, he's skinny," thought Haynes. He caught up and gave Grey a friendly punch to the shoulder.

"That must've shrunk your mind."

Tom nodded. He was feeling better. "Brains really are pink, not gray," he said.

Haynes laughed, "And all this time you thought biology books were just propaganda." Haynes smile drifted away as he thought, "What in hell am I laughing about?"

When they caught up with Edison at what was now the platoon CP. The Lieutenant and Edison were checking the topo map, their RTOs kneeling nearby, smoking. The other two squad leaders wandered up, one commiserated with Kelly.

Grey reloaded his camera. He switched from color slide film to black and white Tri-X and adjusted the ASA setting. While they were waiting for the resupply helicopter, he took some pictures. Johnson having his arm tended by the platoon medic. *Click*. Bayaban's body lying covered, unattended. *Click*. Edison giving instructions to his three squad leaders. *Click*. Haynes working on the M-60. *Click*.

The turbine whine and the *whomp whomp whomp* of several helicopters approaching their position caused the men to look up. A Huey B model gunship and a newer Huey Cobra circled the Landing Zone. The log bird, an extended version of the B-model, landed. Its crew chief shoved crates of ammo, large plastic containers of water, and a dozen cardboard boxes of C-rations out.

When the ship was empty, Modeland and Jones loaded Bayaban's body and equipment aboard.

The pilot cranked the bird back up, and the prop wash sent clouds of dust and debris flying. The helicopter lifted a few feet off the ground and then swung its tail gently left and right while the door gunners looked to the rear and skyward. They thumbed their talk switches and reported "clear." The chopper dipped slightly off its air cushion, rose sharply, and disappeared over the trees.

The CO came over the radio. He was in a hurry. Most of the Company had been stalled by the firefight. He was afraid if they waited around too long, they'd fall behind schedule. They were to secure the Landing Zone for the rest of the Battalion. Then the Battalion Command Post would come in, and they would move out and join the assault on Dong Ap Bia.

So, he told the Lieutenant to break for a quick lunch, and get the C-Rats, water and ammo distributed. The other two platoons would move on ahead. The Lieutenant was to fall in at the end of the column after it had passed.

Grey realized that it was nearly two in the afternoon, and he hadn't eaten all day. He broke open a can of beans and franks and ate them cold.

By the time the first platoon had passed to join the third at the river, Kelly's men had had their lunch and reloaded the magazines they had emptied at the enemy. They moved out quickly behind the rest of the platoon and hurried across what had been the battlefield. The valley floor was giving way to gently rising, undulating terrain.

The stream, where they crossed, was thigh deep. The smell of mud, fish, and some scent that reminded Grey of crawdads wafted up from the banks along with clouds of mosquitoes. By the time they had crossed, the column was reformed entirely. Prescott had ripped the crotch out of his fatigue pants. He didn't think his comrades' jokes about leeches attaching to his groin were particularly funny.

They crossed another stand of elephant grass and then plunged into the jungle along the western floor of the Valley. Grey was surprised when they broke suddenly from the bush onto the Ho Chi Minh Trail. It was a tunnel through the trees almost exactly the width of a two-ton truck. About twenty feet up, tree branches had been pulled together and lashed across the top to prevent aerial detection. The roadway was grass with two paths worn to the bare earth by the tires of the trucks going north and south. It was cool under the umbrella of trees.

The Company moved slowly throughout the rest of the afternoon. The pace was relaxed, and the trail itself was smooth and free of obstructions as they snaked around and between bomb craters. The craters were muddy and filled partially with brown water, and the landscape was lunar. It was not even particularly hot. Except for the weight of their packs and the ever-present anxiety, the men had a pleasant walk in the shade.

Small roads formed circle spurs off the main trail so that convoys going one way could get out of the way of others heading the other. There were also drive-in bunkers where a single truck with a critical cargo could hold up during one of the periodic B-52 raids.

Grey's mind began to dwell on Dong Ap Bia. His glance at Kelly's map after breakfast and the leisurely pace of the march confirmed his suspicions. They would camp tonight within easy striking range of the hill. Tomorrow the shit was going to hit the fan.

About five-thirty, the column turned off onto one of the parking loops and set up a night defensive position. Edison decided to keep Kelly's squad as his platoon reserve so the men would not have to pull perimeter duty. The loop had been used as a campground by the North Vietnamese truckers when they pulled over their convoys for the night. Small one-man bunkers the size of suitcases had been dug, and the ground was cleared in places for sleeping. Haynes and Grey found a couple of spots next to each other and dumped their rucks. Despite the ease of the day's march, Grey was exhausted. His legs felt weak, and his shoulders hurt from where the straps of his pack had rubbed the flesh. He propped his gear against a tree and unrolled his bedding on ground cleared by a Communist soldier. Haynes hung Grey's shirt from a nearby branch to dry.

Haynes began digging their fighting hole with his entrenching tool instead of taking advantage of the positions left by the North Vietnamese truck drivers.

According to the Lieutenant, the NVA positions were not set up for adequate defense. He designated the two-man positions for his platoon. While Haynes quickly excavated the foxhole next to where they planned to sleep. Grey rubbed his aching calves, wondering if joining up with the 101st on this operation was wise.

The tip of a reasonably large rock was in the center of the "bed," and Grey could see marks around it where someone had tried unsuccessfully to dig it up. He decided he could sleep around it and unfolded his olive-green poncho. Tom spread the plastic sheet out fully and folded it over like a sandwich made from a single slice of bread. The soft camouflaged patterned nylon liner was inside like peanut butter. Then he put his rucksack where his head would be and leaned it back so he could use it as both a pillow or a makeshift chair. "Easy fuckin' duty," he thought. "Boy Scout camp with guns."

Haynes, too, had made his bed and was heating Cs when Kelly came by with his chess set. Grey lit a cigarette and made a cup of coffee. The temperature was falling pleasantly, and the light was beginning to fade under the trees. Kelly and Haynes were deep in their game. Prescott was reading a novel. Jones, Johnson, and Modeland had a card game going. Crazy Eights. Wood and Alvarez wrote letters. Saunders lay on his poncho and stared blankly into the trees. Jennett had gone to visit friends in another squad.

Twilight was brief as it always was in Vietnam. Grey had given the matter some thought and decided that the band of twilight was of uniform width. Since anyone at the equator was moving at a faster surface speed as the planet rotated than those at other latitudes, they, consequently, passed through the band quicker. Grey wondered if his astronomy professor would agree.

Kelly and Haynes gave up the game as darkness settled in, and the other men shelved their activities and headed for bed. Any light might reveal their position to the enemy, so there was nothing to do at night but talk in whispers and sleep. Since the squad did not have perimeter duty, Kelly only wanted one man on guard. Haynes and Johnson worked out a schedule that would allow everyone to get a good night's sleep.

Haynes had been quiet all afternoon and evening, and Tom had the feeling he was politely ignored. Even now, as they lay next to each other on the ground, Mike did not speak.

"You pissed off? asked Tom

"No," Haynes replied after a pause.

"Come on, man, level with me."

Haynes turned on his side and propped himself up on his elbow. "You should have been dead today. It was just luck that the third platoon got to the sniper before he got to you."

"Wasn't the first time."

"You can't do shit like that, man. It shook you up. So okay. But you gotta keep your mind on staying alive. It's bad enough when a friend gets killed without him getting killed because he's a fuck-up. I don't need friends like that. "

"Okay," Grey said flatly.

Haynes laid back down. "I don't mean to come down hard," he said after a moment. "I guess I'm a little pissed at myself too. When I headed for the timber, I figured you were dead. Maybe if I'd slapped you or something, I could have brought you out of it.

"Well," Tom said, "at least he didn't get me."

"No," replied Haynes, "You're one lucky son of a bitch. If I were you, I wouldn't worry about what I did with the rest of my life, 'cause, man, it's a gift."

Grey wondered if he should tell Mike about the mountain that loomed ahead, and what MacEvy had told him about the North Vietnamese Army holed up in it. He decided that it wouldn't make any difference.

"See the tree people?" Haynes whispered.

"What?"

"You know how you can see things in the clouds. Well, you can do the same thing with the trees if there's a moon."

Grey looked up and realized that Mike was right. The roof of the jungle was broken into patterns of light and dark.

"I always see mythological things," Haynes said. "Gods and shit like that."

Grey nodded in the darkness. The patterns did resemble exaggerated human forms. "It's called pareidolia," Grey said.

"What?' Haynes said.

"It's a psychological phenomenon that causes us to see people in random patterns," Grey answered.

"How do you know this shit?" Haynes asked.

"I didn't sleep through all my classes," Grey answered wearily.

"I look up at night," continued Haynes, "and see all those immortal bastards up there, and I figure everything's all right. Stupid thing for a full-grown man to do, isn't it?" Haynes sighed.

"A full-grown man of twenty," thought Grey. "No, it isn't stupid," he said softly, looking up at the 'immortal bastards.'

It was a little after one when Mike woke Tom for guard, gave him the guard list, and told him to wake up Wood in an hour. A ground fog had settled in the area, shrouding the area like a gray blanket. Grey rolled into the foxhole while checking that his M-16 was on "safe." He looked up through the trees and saw the waning Moon as a thin crescent. He could hear the soft drip, drip, drip of water hitting the broad jungle leaves like the tap, tap, tap of a blind man's cane.

The jungle was quiet and calm. Grey got out his canteen of whiskey and smoked a cigarette, which he carefully cupped in his hand below the rim of the hole to conceal its light. He drank a little more whisky and thought about going home in just a few days. When the time came to wake Wood, Tom shook him softly and passed the list to him, then he smoked another cigarette, took a last drink from his canteen, and laid back in his poncho to sleep. The Moon had set, and the tree people had vanished.

THE MOUNTAIN OF THE CROUCHING BEAST

Grey—14 Days and a Wakeup

They did not move until noon. When the company arose, they spent the morning attending to their gear; cleaning weapons and checking ammunition loads. The day slowly faded from dawn red, through ground-haze pink until the sky cleared to Vietnam-hot blue.

In the distance the men could hear the deep throated thunder of a B-52 strike. They could feel the vibrations through the soles of their feet. The line of march left the Ho Chi Minh Trail and cut across the elephant grass back to the stream. They followed the stream north for a kilometer and then crossed and went into the elephant grass on the other side, securing a large clearing for the Battalion Landing Zone.

Once that was accomplished, the troopers saw an amazing thing. Suddenly the sky to the south east was flooded with helicopters transporting almost 1,500 men into the Valley. Clusters broke off from the massive flight and dove onto landing zone covered by Cobra gunships. The B-52s had finished, and in the distance the men could see the silver specks of the jets working the mountain.

Two Companies landed at the LZ that the squad and its Company had secured, and the two units walked toward the mountain in parallel columns. over the dark mass of the hill followed by a distant rumble. Last came in the Battalion CO and his command group. The Company prepared to move out.

Dong Ap Bia sat looming over the Valley floor. Thin, wispy clouds bannered off the top as the morning sun and high explosives began to bake the mist away.

The mountain range was a forbidding, triple canopy jungle that included dense thickets of bamboo, brush and vines that choked the tangled forest. Steaming air hung between giant trees adding to the invulnerable nature of the mountain.

As they got still nearer Grey could make out other lines of infantrymen working toward the hill like natives migrating to a sacred mountain for some exotic ceremony. There were at least six jets in the air, as well as helicopter gunships and FACs, and PsyOps planes.

Five hundred meters from the base of the mountain three companies of infantry had been established that faced the northern slope of the objective. The Company broke up into platoons as part of this line.

Elsewhere another U.S. Army battalion was preparing to assault the southern slope, augmented by two battalions of South Vietnamese Army troops. All around the base of the mountain, troops formed a giant "C" with the opening facing the Laotian border; Laos was, technically, off-limits to the Americans. The assault platoons were crossing the line and breaking into squads. The squads in turn got on line and the mountain was now almost surrounded by infantry, the northern one tightening slowly.

A hundred and fifty meters out the word went around the line to halt and get down. The jets were through and the artillery was coming in.

Kelly shouted to his squad, "*Fix bayonets!*"

Grey was on the ground between Haynes and Wood. The artillery pounding into the hill made the earth shake. Dust, pulsating from the jungle floor with each high-explosive round, began clouding the spaces between the trees. "Christ. I've never seen anything like this." Grey muttered, his heart rate climbing while he fixed his bayonet onto his rifle with the unmistakable whisper-slide of metal-on-metal, then *snic*k as it snugged onto the metal stud. His hands trembled at the simple task.

"What?" Haynes asked, the corners of his mouth white with tension, sweat streamed from under his helmet, washing rivulets in the dust on his face. He rolled onto his side getting his bayonet from his web belt and affixing it to the barrel of his rifle—*snick*.

"Nothing." Grey's stomach knotted.

The men began moving toward the hill covered by helicopter Cobra gunships. The enemy, intimidated by the heavy artillery and aerial rocket and machine gun fire, dared not open up on the approaching American infantrymen. "But, maybe," some thought, "They were using a 'whites of their eyes' tactic."

Fifty meters from the tree line the soldiers again halted. In a few minutes the artillery barrage lifted and the troopers rose to their feet and began their assault. As they entered the jungle it quickly became apparent that the terrain consisted of a series of elevated fingers divided by deep ravines. They funneled the troopers either up narrow ridges, or down deep defiles. Kelly noted that elements of his platoon were moving to his right, and troops from another platoon were climbing the ridge on his left flank. He led his squad into the tangled jungle between the two ridges.

Mist threaded between the massive triple-canopy jungle trees, rolling quietly down the defiles. Dust, raised by the artillery concussions hovered in the air, clouding areas between trees, vines and bamboo thickets. In places, trees and large branches tangled the mountainside, and the thick underbrush tugged at and snarled the American soldiers. They moved slowly, hampered by the "wait-a-minute" vines and fear. They could feel the enemy.

Before long, they began to see evidence of the North Vietnamese Army. There were increasing numbers of punji traps, storage areas, and recently abandoned spider holes and bunkers. Tension increased with each struggling step.

The first squad moved several hundred meters up the ridge when the jungle ahead erupted with the sudden fury of muzzle flashes. Ahead of the squad, Grey could see a soldier go down amidst the fusillade of small arms fire. It sounded like an electric blender grinding ice, and hurt his ears. Leaves and tree branches cascaded like confetti, and the ground quickly began to vibrate dust into the air to mix with blue gun smoke in a violent haze.

Kelly led his squad forward in support of the squad on the ridge, and into the tight ever tightening confines of the divide. From above, and to the right and left, the North Vietnamese caught the Kelly and his men in a deadly crossfire. The noise of gunfire rose and rose, dwarfing thought. The smell of cordite began to flood the jungle with a bitter taste as waves of fire belched through the trees. Bits of leaf and branch began to thicken, floating in the air, adding to mayhem. Ahead of him Grey saw Jennett go down. Tom dove for the ground, and then came up running again. He saw Haynes disappear into the jungle and followed him through the hole in the foliage. Any semblance of fire-and-maneuver vanished under the torrent of enemy fire.

Inside the jungle was dark and humid. The violent cacophony muted. Grey dove for a tree and waited, one cheek resting against the rough, damp bark. The tree vibrated with the cascading sounds of battle. He could feel his heartbeat in his temples and in his eye-teeth; rapid and strong.

As his eyes adjusted to the dreary light, he saw that Haynes was beside him and that they were at the base of a steep bank. Other members the squad were breaking through the brush. There was another squad fifteen-meters to the right on a small pie-shaped delta. They were pinned down by a heavy machine gun. On the other side of the clearing they could see Sergeant Edison, the Lieutenant and his command group, along with the rest of the platoon scrambling for cover.

Kelly was on his gut. "That's a fuckin' fifty-one," he said, listening to its slow rate-of-fire; *chunka-chunka-chunka.*

Grey stood with his back pressed against the bank. He was sweating and his heart was beating in his throat. The jungle reverberated with the sound of the big gun—*chunka-chunika-chunika chunka-chunka-chunka.*

"Wood!" Kelly yelled, "You and Modeland try going up there." Wood nodded his head slowly then slung his rifle and began climbing up to a ledge; a small cliff. His hands grasped roots and stray tree limbs. Stones and his helmet fell back on Modeland and the other men below. Angrily Wood continued to struggle up the dirt face. When he reached the top, he pulled his upper body over the lip and was preparing to swing his legs up when the RPG round hit him. It slammed into his stomach and sent him spinning into the air, arms akimbo, like he'd been hit by an invisible truck. He did not detonate.

Modeland, face white and eyes wide, looked to Kelly who motioned him back. The commotion attracted the attention of an enemy position on the other side of the ravine, and small arms fire began slicing over their heads. The distinctive blue-green tracer color of the Communist firearms could be seen under the jungle gloom.

Haynes slid around the ledge and began working forward under the crest of the hill, trying to get the M-60 in action. Prescott broke from the position and began running for a large tree at the edge of the small alluvial delta, trying to back-stop Haynes. The fifty-one-caliber heavy machine gun picked him up and rounds tore at the ground behind him. Scotty put his head down and dove for the tree with out-stretched arms. The steel-jacketed bullets from the fifty-one punched through the tree and ripped into his body.

Several blasts in rapid succession knocked Grey to his knees. Light flashes dotted his vision. He scrambled around on his hands and knees searching blindly for his rifle. He heard cries for the Medic over the din of battle. More explosions ripped the area around him. Small branches landed on his back as he slithered over the ground in desperation. Yellow smoke with the acrid smell of burnt gunpowder twisted through the brambles of the undergrowth and burned his throat. His eyes watered and his nose began running. Mucus filled his mouth and streaked his upper lip.

Someone grabbed his arm. Grey turned and saw Jones looking at him pleadingly. "You gotta help Johnson," he yelled. "Johnson's hurt real bad."

The Black GI was laying on his back beside a tree three feet to the right. His shirt glistened with dark blood. His face was taunt, his dark skin looked like it was dusted with chalk and his eyes were closed in shock. Grey jerked his knife free and cut away at Johnson's shirt, exposing his mutilated chest. Shrapnel wounds puckered purple against the bloody skin. Pieces of rib poked through in several places and the fresh crimson blood gurgled with each tortured breath.

"Oh shit," whispered Jones with tears streaking down his dusty face.

"He's had it," Grey said, cupping his hand around Jones' ear.

A grenade went off, a flash of red and brown. Shrapnel cut through the trees over their heads showering them with plant matter. Jones took Johnson's hand in his two and held it tightly. "Bill, man, come on..., *wake up*," he begged. "You gotta wake up. You got a million-dollar wound, baby. You'll be in Japan tonight. *Come on, man, you gotta wake up.*"

Johnson, his face twisting in pain, opened his eyes to slits. "You take care," he mouthed. He coughed. "I can't breathe..., God." His lips drew back over his teeth and he died, one eye closed as if giving a sly wink that said, "I know something you don't."

Grey could see Kelly on his knees throwing a grenade at the big gun emplacement. Suddenly, Kelly was tossed back as if by an invisible hand, twisting savagely and swallowed up by the smoke of battle.

Grey took Johnson's M-16 and started around the ledge into the jungle. Overhead he heard the *braap* of a Cobra's mini guns. Thorns and splintered sticks tore at this body as he crawled through the underbrush. The sounds of the battle echoed all around him. Finally, Tom laid aside his rifle and collapsed against the moist earth, exhausted, pulling his camera to his chest.

The NVA wore gray jackets, and mustard-colored pants and wore dark green pith helmets. Rice bags were slung over their shoulders and small rectangular canteens hung from their belts. They each wore three-pack magazine vests. All three of them had AK-47s with bayonets fixed, gleaming in the dim light. As soon as he saw them, he knew he had to kill them. If they kept coming, they would trip over him. Tom felt his body pumping rhythmically with the beat of his heart. His hand went carefully to his forty-five pistol. Slowly he worked it out of the shoulder holster and brought it up in front of him, his thumb slowly pulling back the hammer. Then, cupping his right hand with his left for stability, he tried to aim the heavy pistol. Sweat slipped down his forehead into his eyes. He quickly blinked the salty fluid off and took aim.

The group was no more than five meters away. His first shot caught the lead man in the center of the face. Grey moved fast and got the second one in the chest before he had time to react. The third man, confused, hit the dirt and began crawling for cover. Quickly Grey got to his feet and ran after him. The Vietnamese did not hear him over the thunderous sounds of battle. The pistol, jumping in his hand, Tom put three rounds into the enemy soldier's back from less than five feet; the body writhing under the impact of the powerful .45 caliber rounds; yellow-tinted rice erupted from the carry-sack.

Haynes had worked his way nearly under the enemy machine gun position and was trying to clear a link jammed in the receiver of the M-60 when the Communists on the other side of the draw spotted him. A round tore his helmet off his head and knocked him to the ground. In panic he ran his hand over his forehead and his hair trying to tell the difference between sweat and blood. Another round nipped at his sleeve and he rolled to the left. A third round sliced his cheek. Haynes rolled back to the right.

Several guns had found him now and bullets crashed and spanged around him. Dragging the M-60, Mike lunged ahead to a small tree. Something slammed into his left shoulder, ripping away his uniform and laying bare a red streaked canal of tissue and bone. An RPG round went off nearby, hurting his head and made his ears ring. He couldn't remember where he was, who he was with. Why did his shoulder hurt? He felt it with his right hand. "Got hit," he thought. "Not too bad. I can feel the collar bone. Seems like one piece." He struggled to his feet.

Breathing was difficult and he was tired. Where the fuck was his rucksack? Haynes couldn't move his left arm but his right arm felt good. He was aware of every nuance of texture on the cross hatched pistol grip of the machine gun. He lifted the gun to his hip and held it forward like a heavy mop. A three-foot teaser belt of ammunition dangled from the receiver. Using the tree as a support he fired a short burst and chopped the hell out of another tree five feet away. "Jesus fuck Haynes," he said aloud and laughed, "You shoot worse than the fuckin' gooks."

There was a sharp pain in his left knee. Looking down, surprised, he saw blood soaking his green fatigues. "Not so bad," he thought. "I wish I knew where my knife is. I'm gonna need it to kill those bastards over there."

Haynes felt a sharp cleaving, like an icepick, in his lower right side. Then suddenly his mind was grimly clear. He set his teeth and leaned around the tree. Edison was assaulting the position that had been firing at him, and Mike could clearly see the men through the trees. Cruz, the platoon medic, followed closely behind Sergeant Edison. Mike braced the gun against his hip and fired, walking the tracers up the hill toward the enemy; hot brass cartridges gleamed like gold as they vomited in a stream from the machine gun receiver.

The gun was empty. Haynes shook the pistol grip and worked the bolt twice before the realized what was wrong. He sat down and popped open the receiver. With his finger he carefully lifted the remaining links from the last belt out of the receiver. Then he got a new linked ammunition belt from across his chest and fitted it in. Using the sixty as a crutch he struggled to his feet, braced the machine gun between his hip and his foot and managed to chamber the first round. He closed his eyes and rested. His hand felt slick against the black plastic grip. He tried to raise the weapon, but the blood on the stock caused him to drop it. He started to bend down to pick it up but something went off near his feet. A dirty yellow cloud enveloped his legs and he felt himself rising in the air. Haynes felt hot, awfully hot.

Grey was moving up higher on the hill, squirming slowly forward just under the crest when he heard the singing over the din.

"*I got a girl in Kansas City...*"

The sounds of the battle rose and ebbed like the sea at times overwhelming other sounds. Grey moved through the underbrush toward the singing; he was feeling better now. The electric charge in his stomach and the frantic bursts of energy in his arms and legs did not paralyze him or cause him to make wild uncontrolled movements. Everything was functioning.

"*I got a girl in Kansas City, babe, babe...*"

Haynes was just below him. Grey could see a patch of uniform through the brush and he knew the voice. With Johnson's M-16 across his belly he duck-walked, sliding, down the slope. Mike was in a small clearing. His legs were shredded and his blood was seeping out into the dirt.

"*I got a girl in Kansas City, she's got gum balls...,* Grey? God damn, Grey. How are you, man?"

Tom propped Haynes up against the giant, tangled vines at the base of the tree. The body felt strange without the full weight of the legs. "You got a cigarette, Tom?" Haynes asked. The screech of war receded as Sergeant Edison's troopers neutralized the enemy machine gun position.

"Sure." Grey got Marlboro from his shirt and lit it with a snap of his Zippo lighter. Then he put it in Haynes' mouth.

"It's sure good to see you, Grey. Sure was nice to see you crawling out of those trees."

"Try not to talk." Grey said, as he settled himself against the tree next to his friend. Sweat pour from under his helmet. Grey took it off and set it next the wet vines that were as thick as his upper arms, and wiped his face on a dirty sleeve.

"It's okay, man. I'm okay." Haynes paused and tears came to his eyes. His voice was choked when he spoke. "Course I ain't got no legs. Probably ain't got no balls either." He laughed. "Other than that, I'm fine."

"Just take it easy." Grey settled down, cradling the M-16 across his lap.

"Let me rest a minute, Tom and then we'll go get them bastards. You and me Tom. We'll go kill all those bastards."

"Sure," Grey said, looking away.

"I can't walk so good. You'll have to help me walk." Haynes reached for the machine gun with his right hand and pulled it to him. "But I can shoot this mutherfucking-sixty," he said. "I can sure shoot this fuckin' gun…"

After a moment Haynes asked, "Tom?" The sounds of firing came from both flanks as troopers tried to clear paths up the ridges.

"Yeah..."

"You gotta do me a favor…, man," Haynes voice took on a pleading tone.

"Okay."

Haynes' voice was flat and now serious. "You gotta take me out."

"Don't talk crap." Grey said, looking at his friend, then away.

Haynes grabbed Grey's arm with his right hand and shook him.

"*Listen* to me, damn it," he said softly. "Listen to me you bastard." Grey was dizzy and couldn't think.

"You get off in your fuckin' head and you don't see how things are." Haynes insisted savagely. "You gotta do me up."

The blood was slowly leaking out onto the ground. The only sensible place to put a tourniquet was around Mike's neck. Grey leaned over and pulled the shredded fabric from Haynes' wound. He was a mess from his knees to his chest, his guts held into him only by a membrane. "Okay, pal." Grey whispered.

Haynes' face relaxed and he leaned his head against the tree. "I appreciate it," he said. "I could make it without legs, I really think I could. But, not without a dick. I mean, what's the fuckin' use." There were tears in his eyes, but his face was twisted into a sardonic grin. Grey slid the M-16 slightly across his lap, thumbing the selector switch.

"Good luck, Tom. I hope you have a good life."

"Sure."

"I mean, have some for me, you know. Have some of the good things for me."

◆ ◆ ◆

In the night the monsoon rains came on a cold wind. And with the rain came lightening, each putting a damper on the fighting. Sergeant Kelly hunkered down and endured the misery of the cold and wet as soldiers went by him on either side, moving up the side of the mountain searching for that moment's front line.

With the dawn came silence, broken only by helicopters laden with supplies and additional troops. American industry on display, both in quantity and efficiency. Kelly began his search for his men.

He dragged Dwight Jennett's swollen body out of the bright sun and into the shade at the jungle's edge. Jennett had been killed with one round in the center of his chest.

Kelly limped back into the mangled jungle. He was surprised that the area his squad had worked was so small. Twenty meters wide and no more than fifty deep. It consisted of tall trees, overgrown with vines, while the jungle floor was covered by a thick undergrowth of small trees, thorn bushes and large leafed ferns. There were no trails in the shallow draw which led to the cliff face which looked so high yesterday, and so small today.

The jungle was littered with brass cartridges shining red-gold in the dim morning light, hand grenade rings, GI helmets, empty M-16 magazines, torn bits of paper, occasional weapons, both American and North Vietnamese. In places, the wooden handles of the NVA grenades, brass and magazines from AK-47s, shredded tree-trunks, and lonely enemy bodies marked the ebb and flow of yesterday's fight.

At the base of the cliff he came across Wood's body. His torso had been caved in by the unexploded RPG round. He lay on his back, head down, feet pointed up the hill. His M-16 was still slung over one shoulder. Sadly he marked his map thinking this would be a job for the EOD, explosive ordinance disposal, people.

Gingerly Kelly removed a dog tag from Wood. The two tags were on separate chains. One was long and hung around Wood's neck like a necklace. The second, the size of a bracelet, was fastened onto the first. The two tags were taped together with black electricians' tape so they wouldn't rattle. Kelly had to use his bayonet to cut them apart before he could loop the smaller chain around his left wrist where it joined Jennett's.

Johnson and Jones were together. Johnson was laying at the base of a tree, partially covered by leaves and muck from the churned-up jungle floor. Nearby Jones lay, arms and legs sprawled. He had several large wounds in his face and neck, most probably from a grenade. His body was supported by his rucksack and he looked somewhat like an over-turned turtle. His helmet had skittered across the small clearing and lay open end up. The sweatband and the edges of the fabric camouflaged cover were flecked with dried blood. Both men were covered with blow flies. Johnson's chest was alive with them, a blue-black swarming, humming mass undulating like an oil slicked sea. Ants were cruising up and down his neck and in and out of his mouth and nostrils.

Jones' hands were brown with crusted blood. His M-16, the plastic foregrip shattered, was still clutched in his right hand. Kelly stood silently by the two dead men. After a time, he pulled out his plastic covered area map and marked their position along with those of Jennett and Wood. Replacing the map in one thigh-pocket, he searched under Jones' fatigue shirt for the dog tags. The flies on Jones' face and neck flared briefly into flight. The stench was almost overwhelming; metallic overlaid with putrid rot. Kelly unsnapped the smaller of the two silver chains from around Jone's neck, leaving a tag on the longer one. Then he looped the small chain and the lone dog tag over his left wrist.

When Kelly tentatively touched Johnson the mass of insects surged into flight, angrily buzzing at the disturbance. When the bugs rose, the smell swept up again engulfing Kelly. Quickly he unhooked Johnson's tag and stepped back, looping the chain over his wrist to join the others. Kelly could see a photograph of a young black woman nestled in Johnson's overturned helmet. After a moment, Kelly removed the photo and put it in Johnson's upper right shirt pocket under the name tape JOHNSON, hoping Graves & Registration would include it with Johnson's effects. Maybe the girl would find some comfort in knowing he carried her picture to his grave in far-off Vietnam.

It was relatively cool, but the air was humid, packed under the triple-canopy jungle. Sweat swept down Kelly's face and into his eyes, the salt stinging. While moving through the jungle, sweeping back and forth along the line he figured the squad had moved, he stumbled across a dead NVA soldier. Pushing the bushes aside he saw two more, all shot with a .45.

A few minutes later he came across Modeland. The insects, and even a few lizards, were working on what remained of Modeland's head. Again, he fought the bugs for the dog tags. Again, he looped it around his left wrist where it clattered dully among the others. Pausing, Kelly again, he marked the position on his map. The five aluminum dog tags made a hollow sound as he moved further into the jungle.

He stepped on Prescott's leg before he saw him. The greasy slide of skin and muscle against bone instantly identified a body. Kelly jumped quickly away, seeming to do a little two-step. Like the others, Prescott was covered with insects. Kelly kicked the corpse to shoo away the flies. Prescott was lying on his side, head nestled on one arm as if he were sleeping. A neat pair of bullet holes dotted his chest where the AK-47 rounds had penetrated.

Somehow his helmet had stayed on. It was dented slightly and the fabric cover was torn. Kelly searched the body for dog tags; checking his boots because some guys interlaced dog tags in their bootlaces. Airborne! But could not find them. He pulled Scotty's wallet from the right hip pocket and removed a military driver's license and a plastic laminated Army ID card. He carefully replaced the wallet, buttoning the pocket. Then he rolled Prescott over onto his back with his booted foot. Bending over, Kelly pried open the frozen mouth, folded the ID card into a cylinder, lengthwise, and shoved it through the reluctant teeth. Kelly felt the card unravel slightly as he released the jaw. Using the heel of one hand, Kelly struck Prescott's chin to close the mouth. He then stood, put the driver's license into his upper right shirt pocket, marked the approximate location of the body on his map.

Pushing on through the tangled and trashed undergrowth without a backward look, Kelly continued his search for the victims of the fight. The temperature was rising and Kelly's movements became more labored. His back and hip ached. He paused for a short rest, leaning against a tree. Around him the jungle was preternaturally quiet. But Kelly could hear the muffled sounds of the fight going on from up the hill. It would be several more hours before the small animals came out of hiding and the tree dwellers resumed their movements along what was left of their aboral highways.

Kelly pulled out his canteen and took a long drink before sloshing some water into his cupped left hand for a quick facial bath. Sighing, the young sergeant resumed his combing of the forest. He discovered the new guy, Alvarez. Kelly had not even had a chance to get to know this man. All he could remember was that he was small and dark. Mexican-American probably. Alvarez had been struck by four bullets. Once in the left leg, once in the right hip, once in the center of his chest, and once in the left upper arm. The force of the last bullet had ripped the arm off. Kelly did not find the arm or the M-79 grenade launcher. Giving up the search, Kelly sighed and looped the dog tag over his wrist with the others.

It took Kelly almost another half hour to find Haynes and Grey. He caught a slight motion out of the corner of his eye. Instantly he crouched, raising his M-16, and moving the selector switch off safe to automatic. Carefully he approached the small thicket from which the motion had come. Using his bayoneted rifle as a probe, he pushed aside the branches. Grey was sitting Buddha like on the ground, gently wafting aside a small cloud of hungry insects from Haynes' covered body.

Exhaling, Kelly entered the small clearing behind the thicket. Gently he placed a hand on Grey's right shoulder. Grey didn't move, but acknowledged Kelly's presence by nodding slightly and saying, "Hi."

Kelly walked around Grey, surveying the scene. In front of Grey was a body partially covered by a camouflaged poncho liner. Stooping, Kelly lifted the covering from Haynes' corpse. The earth was stained a deep brown by the pools of dried blood. In places white bone fragments poked through Haynes' torn fatigue pants. Large hunks of muscle were exposed and Kelly could see flaccid arteries and veins among the white nerves and pinkish cartilage.

Haynes' head was facing away from Grey, turned to the left, chin resting on his shoulder. It was obvious that Haynes had been hit at least once in the head by a small arms round. The right temple. His face and head were cruelly distorted from the force of the round. Kelly removed the one tag he needed, and then replaced the poncho liner. Standing erect Kelly noted the M-60 machine gun. It was lying next to the body. It was blue-black and glistening with oil and dried blood. The ground around Haynes was littered with M-60 7.62mm cartridge brass and hundreds of the small black disintegrating-belt links. A length of ammunition was draped over some bushes, flung there by the impact that had blasted Haynes.

"Time to go, Grey." he said quietly, looking at the dusty and ragged soldier. Feeling sad for his lost men, Kelly hefted the M-60 machine gun, which clattered against the dog tags on his wrist.

"Yeah, I guess so," Grey answered, taking Kelly's offered hand. As he pulled himself up, one knee-joint cracked audibly. They could hear the sounds of the battle's second day from higher up the mountain ebbing and flowing.

"Don't worry about Mike," Kelly said, "He'll be okay until we come back for him"

"Sure he will." Grey said, patting his breast pockets, searching for cigarettes.

Grey collected Johnson's M-16 and his cameras and followed Kelly through the jungle, back to where Saunders waited. He said nothing as Kelly and Grey emerged grim faced from the foliage. Saunders couldn't take his eyes from the dull silver dog tags tangled around Kelly's left wrist.

A few moments later Sergeant Edison emerged from the trees. Looking to Kelly he said, "Hoped I'd find you. This it?"

"Yeah, this's it." Kelly said in a monotone handing the cluster of dog tags out for his sergeant. He added Prescott's driver's license, almost as an afterthought.

"Want me to call it in?" Edison said, holding the receiver to the radio he carried.

"No, I'll do it." Kelly said, taking the receiver.

A couple of moments later he was connected with the Company commander. "Yessir," he spoke through the static. "Eight friendly KIAs, six confirmed NVA KIAs and three survivors, none hit." The terse conversation over the radio lasted for only a few more minutes while Kelly explained the need for an EOD crew. The C.O. said there would be a chopper in in a while to pull the bodies out. Kelly asked for some help in bringing his men out to a collection point. The C.O. said not to worry, he'd send some people over to police them up. He couldn't give Kelly a time estimate, saying, "I've got my hands full up here." Kelly could hear the chatter of a machine gun in the background over the radio.

With a "Roger that," the transmission ended.

Saunders took off his glasses and wiped them on a handkerchief. His hands were shaking slightly as was his voice when he asked, "Anybody got any smoke?"

"What?" asked Kelly.

"Some smoke grenades to mark our position for the dust-off."

"Here," Sergeant Edison said, handing three yellow-striped canisters to Saunders.

"Use these." Edison wiped his hand across his mouth once or twice then said, "Well, I gotta keep looking Not a hell of a lot left though."

"Everybody like this?" Kelly asked. They could hear the rise and fall of small arms fire from the mountain above as the Americans pressed the North Vietnamese defenders.

"Mostly just our platoon. We seemed to've stepped right in it, I'd say."

Brap brap brapppp chattered miniguns from the darting helicopters as they attacked NVA trench lines.

"I'd say," Grey said without elaboration.

"Yeah, well, I gotta go. Sorry 'bout all this." Edison looking tired and lonely, his eyes red-rimmed, face sweat and grime-streaked, disappeared back into the jungle.

The three remained there in the steaming woods, left to their own memories of the previous day's battle. Kelly lay back, resting his head against his rucksack. Saunders sat nearly upright; his arms wrapped around his knees.

Grey settled down against his rucksack and searched his pockets for his lighter and cigarettes. Finding them he lit up, leaned back and shut his eyes. He rolled the silver Zippo over and over inside his right hand. Methodically Grey finished his smoke, field stripped his Marlboro stuffing the filter into his top left shirt pocket, settled back down. He went over in his mind his next steps. He would have to get back to Camp Eagle and find someone to attest to his M-16 as a combat loss, travel back to Long Binh to file a story, or just tell someone about it, get his stuff together to be shipped back to the World, clear post and get to the airport. He dozed off.

Kelly watched what was left of his squad and wondered to himself if he could have prevented a couple of deaths had he done some things differently. He chewed on a twig, as he thought of his men.

When the soldiers from another platoon arrived along with two EOD specialists, Kelly turned over the marked map to a staff sergeant. Without comment the sergeant took the map and moved his men into the jungle. They carried plastic body bags with them. It was early evening before the men from the other platoon returned with the eight body bags sagging between the men who carried them. Others were laden with rucksacks, helmets, grenades, weapons, canteens, and a few bandoleers of ammunition. Someone had apparently found Alvarez's M-79 and it was added to the heap of equipment mounded next to the bodies stretched out in the grass. Kelly wondered if they had also found his arm, and if it was in the right body bag. Kelly thanked the sweating men for the help. Nobody responded their eyes sliding off Kelly as they followed their sergeant back the way they had come.

Kelly unzipped each bag to check the body with the a tag attached. It seemed to Kelly that this was worse than finding the men where they died. More final.

The *womp womp womp* of a helicopter's blades came nearer, Saunders stepped out into the elephant grass and popped a couple of yellow smoke grenades and guided the helicopter to a soft touchdown. The pilots kept the engine running and the blades whirling as six fresh troopers off-loaded, and Kelly, Saunders and Grey loaded the heavy sacks onto the helicopter.

After most of the equipment was stacked atop the bodies, Grey shrugged into his rucksack and slung Johnson's M-16 over his shoulder. The replacements huddled together for some psychological protection. Turning to Kelly he shouted over the rotor noise, "Well, Kelly, I guess this is where I leave you. Best of luck to you guys." He gave the thumbs-up sign.

"Roger that, Grey. Sorry 'bout Haynes." Kelly shouted in reply. The two of them stood looking into one another's eyes for a few moments. Kelly offered his hand, they shook, neither man smiled. Grey shrugged his shoulders under the weight of his rucksack, turned and strode purposefully to the helicopter and, taking the door gunner's offered hand, climbed aboard. He sat on the bench against the aft cabin bulkhead, a foot on either side of a body bag, Johnson's M-16 lay across his lap.

Kelly and Saunders stood side by side and watched the helicopter rise, dip slightly and swing away in a small, tight spiral. Kelly put his thoughts about how Haynes died out of his mind. "Six of one, half a dozen of another," he muttered to himself as he turned back to his equipment.

Kelly popped a piece of gum into his mouth and thought, "Well, that's that. I've got a war to fight." He chewed a minute and then shouted, "Saunders! Get them over here for a briefing!"

The replacement squad members walked over and bent with

Kelly over a map. "We're going back up the hill," he explained, smoothing out the wrinkled plastic covering the map, "We're going to move south along this ridgeline following the rest of the company. Saunders, you'll take point."

The men returned to their equipment. Saunders had to fight to keep from trembling as he slung several bandoleers of M-16 ammunition over his head and across his chest. He attached four grenades to the web belt around his waist and thought of the mutilated bodies lying inert in their body bags. He wondered if he would survive another day in Vietnam.

Kelly formed the small column up behind Saunders and they moved out toward the mountain, because most of the men in the squad were new, signaled by their clean fatigues, they received only a few casual nods from the soldiers stacking C-Rations and ammo crates as they passed. They stopped briefly while Staff Sergeant Kelly spoke with a Lieutenant, now his platoon leader, who was also new, and began the climb up the side of the mountain.

Helicopter gunships had laced the area with automatic weapons fire, followed by a lengthy artillery barrage. Kelly and Saunders, joined by replacements from Camp Eagle, continued in the fight, but lost no other men. As it was, Kelly still hadn't learned all of their names when the Americans had finally taken the Dong Ap Bia, Hamburger Hill. Many of the newer members returned to their previous assignments.

AND SO IT GOES

Sergeant Kelly leaned against a tree trunk in the tangled netherland between the coastal plain and the mountains of South Vietnam's northern panhandle. Even though very little sunlight filtered through the upper branches of the forest, the greenhouse effect made the air muggy and thick with humidity: it was alive with gnats and mosquitos. Despite the heat and insects, he was reasonably comfortable. The tree allowed him to take the bulk of the sixty-pound weight of the pack off his back and shoulders. In places, light shafts struck through, pale yellow and suffused with billions of tiny dust motes— contrasting with the dark green of the shadowed undergrowth. Kelly unhooked his pistol belt, further releasing the weight of the rucksack.

It had been over a month since his squad had been mauled in the A Shau Valley. Of the ten squad members who had been alive that morning— Grey excepted—only two survived. The other was Jerry Saunders, who was now the squad leader. Kelly was bumped up to platoon sergeant, replacing Edison, who had rotated out of the field, his year-long tour almost up. Kelly supposed he was back in The World by now. The platoon had yet another Lieutenant, and Company had a new commander—a Ranger Captain. Things were beginning to shake back into place.

The jungle beyond the American position seemed thicker and more complicated than that which they had passed through earlier. Its monotonous greens and blacks were woven in a pattern that jarred the eyes. The air carried the hot smell of plant rot overlaid with a strangely sweet odor. Saunders followed two places back from the man he had ordered to walk point. He watched as the young troop work as he had been taught.

Nevertheless, Saunders walked quietly and carefully and tried to use his ears. He looked for movement and inconsistencies in the thick foliage. He watched the point man who stopped, periodically, to crouch and peer between undergrowth layers.

Saunders realized that in the final analysis, the point man was primarily bait. Had it not already been there, he would have switched his M-16 to automatic. The high-speed trail was the width of an American residential sidewalk. Despite Saunders' caution, the squad moved rapidly along the ridge. Once, when he thought they were doing particularly well, Saunders heard Kelly's whispered hiss of an order, "Look with your weapon."

It was an essential lesson. It was one of the first things Saunders learned back in advanced infantry training at the miserable Fort Polk in Louisiana. "Keep the rifle aimed where you're looking. If you move your eyes, move the weapon." To have forgotten, it made Saunders feel stupid. In AIT, they had preached, "There are two kinds of soldiers. Good ones and dead ones. If you don't want to die, don't make mistakes. If you get killed, it's your own damn fault." Saunders didn't really believe that after the fight for Hamburger Hill. Sweat ran down from under Saunders' helmet, blurring his glasses where they touched his eyebrows. He wiped his forehead with his left sleeve.

Kelly stopped him with a brief pat on the shoulder. "You're doing fine. Relax."

Kelly had Saunders turn down a narrow trail to the right. Following the steep path down into the coastal plain was much more difficult than following the near-freeway that ran along the ridge. Saunders held his loaded and safety-free M-16 in his right hand while grasping at branches with his left. The pistol grip of the Colt felt surprisingly good in his hand, like an old friend. Saunders moved further down the slope, feeling more confident with each step.

The steep terrain of the mountains gave way suddenly to that of the coastal plain. The jungle vegetation stopped and was replaced by a narrow strip of rice paddies; sun-glittered reflections bounced off the paddy water. A small group of Vietnamese huts dotted an area beyond the paddies, emanating a rank odor. Saunders did not notice these details. His attention was riveted on three young men in black pajamas carrying rifles and walking casually along the trail next to the paddies. They were the enemy, and they were no more than forty, fifty meters away.

Saunders paused his squad at the edge. His body was transfixed. He watched abstractly as one of the enemy soldiers suddenly turned his way, raised the weapon, and drew a bead on his chest. He would have died then if Sergeant Kelly's M-16 had not riddled the man. The other two Viet Cong turned and ran. The spell clouding Saunders was broken by a stiff punch.

The two veterans gave chase, and Saunders soon outran his platoon sergeant. They splashed through ankle-deep water and mud in a paddy, running on a diagonal line trying to head off the fleeing VC before they could reach the village. Saunders leaped atop a dike wall and saw the two Viet Cong attempting to escape across a small dry field.

Chest heaving, Saunders felt a unique kind of joy. He switched his weapon to semi-automatic and calmly put a bullet in the back of one of the two men running for their lives. He did not think it strange as he watched the lifeless body fall to the ground in a small puff of dust. The rifle bounced from barrel to butt before falling to the dirt.

A strange feeling of power swept over Saunders at the kill. Sergeant Kelly mounted the dike seconds later and they greeted each other with broad, youthful smiles. They were joined shortly by Kelly's RTO and medic, and the rest of Saunders' squad. The balance of the platoon pulled up at the edge of the jungle behind them.

Neither Kelly nor Saunders saw for sure where the third man went. They did see him run toward the village and disappear behind a small faded blue-painted stucco well-house on the edge of the hamlet. Saunders and Kelly ran to it and surrounded it as best they could. They heard movements within.

"Surrender!" Kelly shouted in English, "Come out!" He repeated the orders in Vietnamese, saying, "*Dau Hang! Chieu Hoi!*" When there was no reply, he motioned towards the grenades on Saunders' belt and held up three fingers.

Suddenly, a Chinese Communist grenade was tossed out the door, hissing like a Komodo Dragon. With remarkable speed, Saunders kicked the ChiCom grenade back into the hootch. Both Americans fell to the ground as it exploded, raising a dust mat several inches from the concussion.

Kelly was inside first, his weapon firing in brief bursts. Saunders followed closely. The M-16 jumped in his hands as he expended a full magazine into the gloom, firing from the hip.

FINIS

EPILOG

Los Angeles, California

1980

Tom Grey stood in the billiard room of a mid-century mansion in Los Angeles. It was the home of a successful movie executive a friend of a friend sort of knew. It was a late afternoon Southern California day, as perfect as the one before had been, and as the next one would be.

Through the floor-to-ceiling window, Grey could see a beautiful girl in a pale-yellow sundress on the patio. She was holding a champaign flute down by her side, her long red hair tumbled down her back, and was haloed by the sun. She was facing away from him, toward the expanse of the City below the hillside. He could not see her face, but he knew she was beautiful. She was graceful and beautiful in a town of beautiful women. He could see her shape, backlit, as the sun was setting in front of her. She appeared to be alone.

He was leaning on the table, billiard cue in one hand, cigarette in the other, while he regarded her slim form. She would move from time-to-time, shifting her weight from one foot to the other, one hip rising and the other falling. Her slim arms and legs entranced Grey. He excused himself from the conversation he had been having with a paralegal who couldn't find her date, and placed the cue in the rack, and stubbed his cigarette out in the brass ashtray on a small game table. He threaded his way through the crowd to the door on the far side of the room. It led into a hallway jammed with young executives and their dates. He pushed his way toward the door that led to the outside.

He pulled the glass door open, and stepped onto the patio. She was gone.

Grey knew that he was never going to find her, nor was he ever going to forget her. He would write of her if he ever wrote the novel that all writers for the *Hollywood Reporter, Variety, Photoplay*, or any of the hundreds of new industry publications that sprouted like mushrooms in the damp LA mornings, spored writers and ideas during the afternoon, and were plucked, scrubbed and added to the frenetic Los Angeles gravy by dinner time. If not a novel, then maybe, he thought, a screenplay.

Sighing, Grey returned to the house looking for the colleague who gave him the invitation to the hillside affair. He found him in the kitchen, pouring single malt Scotch whisky into a large crystal tumbler.

"Ah, Tom," the chubby colleague said, with a wave of the bottle. The ceiling neon lights reflected across his glasses. "Here, have another, old man," he continued in a fake British accent.

Grey regarded the man for a few moments before pulling the Marlboro pack from his blue blazer pocket. He shook a cigarette from the pack and took it with his lips. Replacing the pack, he pulled his worn, scratched and dented Zippo lighter from his pocket. *Snick, click, snick*, he lit his cigarette, and answered, "No thanks."

Grey looked around the kitchen that was larger than his apartment. He half-heard his friend saying something, but he did not know what it had been. "What? I'm sorry, I missed that."

The short, overweight man that was his age stirred his drink with one finger, pushing the ice around. He was wearing a pair of bright grapefruit-colored slacks, a light blue shirt, a white linen jacket, and white shoes. No tie. Ties were out in Los Angeles that season. He said, "You're a Vietnam Veteran, aren't you?"

Grey couldn't tell if it was a question or a statement. The man in the white jacket swayed slightly, his eyes beginning to blear behind the lenses of his glasses. Grey thought he was probably drunk, or maybe high. Cocaine had become as fashionable that year as ties had not. So, perhaps he'd been dipping into the drug in ample and ostentatious display in the living room. "You can't get addicted to this stuff," his friends claimed.

Cautiously, Grey answered with a "Yes."

"You know, I was in college during the draft. I often thought of dropping out and joining up for Vietnam," the man said. "But I had to change majors, which added a year, and prep for grad school." Grey realized that being a Vietnam Veteran was suddenly fashionable, like cocaine. "But I never did," he continued."

Grey looked at him steadily, wondering where this was going.

Sipping the expensive whisky, the friend continued. Waving the crystal glass for emphasis, he said, "I envy you, Grey. I really envy you your Vietnam experience."

Grey turned and left, muttering, "Fuckin' asshole."

AUTHOR'S NOTE

An Unusual Request

This book began its life in about 1974 or '75 I was working for an aerospace firm in Los Angeles, and Dana Welch was working in Illinois. I wrote to him, sending a draft opening, asking if he wanted to join me in writing a book of the Vietnam War. We had initially planned on a slapstick story filled with irony, but the story quickly morphed into this work, which reflected more closely the feelings of Vietnam Veterans at that time.

Dana and I first met at Fort Leonard Wood in 1967. He was an information specialist and later editor-in-chief of the post newspaper, and I was the illustrator. We also sat on the same plane to Vietnam, which is where we parted ways; he to the 101st Airborne Division (Airmobile), and me to the Command Information section of the Information Office of Army Headquarters as its combat artist.

Twice I managed to spring him from his duties at a brigade information office; one time, we went to Hue, an off-limits town in those days. Like the protagonist in this story, I had travel orders that restricted me to the territory and waters of the Republic of Vietnam. Within those borders, I could go pretty much anywhere I want to go.

At one point, Dana moved to Los Angeles, where he worked as a technical writer by day, and we struggled as novelists at night. After a few months, the story began to flounder, and then, gasping, it lay down in a battered stationery box for about 45 years. Dana moved back to Peoria. I moved that box from my house to an apartment during a divorce, to two other rented places in the California beach towns of Hermosa and Manhattan, to a new marriage that caused even more movement to two houses in Los Angeles, two in Minnesota, two in New Jersey, one in Maryland near Washington, DC, to the Texas Hill Country, and finally to Baltimore.

Once in Baltimore, and now retired from my position at the Army Historical Foundation—fundraiser for the National Museum of the U.S. Army, I scanned the ancient writings into my computer and began a rewrite. I have tried to stay as close to the attitudes expressed in what Dana and I had written all those years ago.

Over the years, Dana and I lost track of each other. When I began the rewrite, I tried to find him and traced him to the Twin Cities area of Minnesota. That was a close as I got. The trail went cold.

So, here is the unusual request. If any who happened to read this and know the whereabouts of Dana C. Welch, please let both of us know of the other. My email address is dslewis46@gmail.com.

Printed in Great Britain
by Amazon